FIGHTING LINCOLN'S WAR

RETURN TO GETTYSBURG

LOUIS SALTZMAN

BALBOA.
PRESS

A DIVISION OF HAY HOUSE

Balboa Press books may be ordered through booksellers or by contacting:

Balboa Press
A Division of Hay House
1663 Liberty Drive
Bloomington, IN 47403
www.balboapress.com
1 (877) 407-4847

Because of the dynamic nature of the Internet, any web addresses or links contained in this book may have changed since publication and may no longer be valid. The views expressed in this work are solely those of the author and do not necessarily reflect the views of the publisher, and the publisher hereby disclaims any responsibility for them.

The author of this book does not dispense medical advice or prescribe the use of any technique as a form of treatment for physical, emotional, or medical problems without the advice of a physician, either directly or indirectly. The intent of the author is only to offer information of a general nature to help you in your quest for emotional and spiritual well-being. In the event you use any of the information in this book for yourself, which is your constitutional right, the author and the publisher assume no responsibility for your actions.

Any people depicted in stock imagery provided by Getty Images are models, and such images are being used for illustrative purposes only.
Certain stock imagery © Getty Images.

Print information available on the last page.

ISBN: 978-1-9822-2250-5 (sc)
ISBN: 978-1-9822-2249-9 (hc)
ISBN: 978-1-9822-2251-2 (e)

Library of Congress Control Number: 2019902123

Balboa Press rev. date: 03/22/2019

To my sons and their families—Joshua, Amy, and Sadie Saltzman and Daniel, Suzy, Brody, and Piper Saltzman—my parents, Bertha and Paul Saltzman; my sister and cover artist, Alisha Diamond Saltzman; my aunt, Clara Mahler; my cousins, Norma and Richard Mahler, Jeannette and Alfred Mahler, Tina Mahler, Stan Jacobson, and Martin Saltzman; and my friends, Susan and Barry Berger, Gene Braunstein, Steve Butler, Jay Leno, Gerry and Steve Visco, and a special thanks to Pauline and John Sarjoo.

These are just names on a page. But each one gave me support with a word here and there that gave me the confidence to follow a dream, and I thank them so much.

AUTHOR'S NOTE

As a young boy growing up in a housing project in the Bronx, New York, I had many friends from families who had moved into the new neighborhood that was built in 1950. It was a melting pot of races and religions. I played punchball, basketball, marbles, and baseball.

Something happened when I was about seven years old. I began to read. My parents bought me books, The Hardy Boys, Chip Hilton, and Tom Swift. I could not get enough and read every night under the covers with a flashlight. Lastly, they gave me three Landmark biographies of different presidents. The first two were on George Washington and Thomas Jefferson, and I loved reading about them. But something special happened when I read the third. It was a biography of Abraham Lincoln, and it touched something in me that I could not understand. It would take many years before it would make sense. All I knew was that this man's life fascinated me. I had no concept until years later of what the Civil War really was and the horror of over 600,000 deaths. At the time, all I cared about was learning about this strange-looking tall man who saw things that others could not. I identified with his statements, among them, "A house divided against itself cannot stand." He said also, "If slavery is not wrong, then nothing is." He was a spiritual, if not a religious, man. Both the North and the South claimed God was on their side. Yet Lincoln wrote a note that was discovered after his death that said, "God cannot be both for and against the same thing."

I spent more than seven years writing my first book, *Zefram's Journey*. It was most personal, and I struggled, as I had never written before. Being in my early sixties did not help matters, as I was frustrated when it came to putting it in a proper framework. Yet I was finally able to finish and publish it. Many people said nice things about it, for which I am most grateful.

I believed I was capable of writing something else and spent weeks thinking about different ideas but was not satisfied. Having a love for history I "visited" many different centuries and narratives. But in the end, I always returned to the nineteenth century and the tall man with his scraggly beard who suffered from depression and grew as a president more than any other who occupied his office before or since. His story captivated me.

I realized that I had neither the means nor the knowledge or time to write anything based upon reality that could add to the legacy of Abraham Lincoln. Finally, I began to "see" an idea. Lincoln was not perfect and had to do a great deal of learning on the job. Since the Ric Burns documentary series, *The Civil War*" was released in 1990, interest in the war and Lincoln began to dramatically increase. That increased interest led to many new books and films, and the genre of fantasy fiction became popular. Most alternative history books about the Civil War had to do with the South winning the war. My own "what if" could not duplicate what had been done before. That held no interest. What did excite me was the alternative of the North winning the Civil War earlier with the aid of the future Government of the United States.

By early June 1863, Robert E. Lee and the Army of Northern Virginia had won stunning and devastating victories—at Fredericksburg in winter 1862 and at Chancellorsville at the end of May 1863. There was serious concern in the states of the Union that the South could win. The numbers of casualties continued to shock the public, and the newspapers filled page after page of the names of dead Union soldiers. The president signed the Emancipation Proclamation on New Year's Day 1863, and the focus of the war shifted to freeing the slaves, in addition to the president's earlier stated goal of preserving the Union.

While this story is fiction, two things became very important as I wrote it. Firstly, I wanted to have the people who were central to the story be where they were in 1863. Secondly, I wanted to do my best to present the president as the man he was. All I can say is that I hope I came close to finding him.

Most political pundits of the period underestimated his political abilities. He was frustrated with the quality of his generals, and it took time to find men who agreed that the way to win the war was to defeat Robert E. Lee. Lincoln knew the North had more men and supplies, and that was how they would finally win. This story depicts a way it could have happened sooner.

I hope you enjoy reading and learn a few things along the way. Most importantly, I wish to thank all those who supported my work these past years. I will always be grateful to them for it.

A special thanks to Rosie Lenoci for putting in so many hours editing my drafts. I confess I did not make her job easier.

I hope you enjoy reading the story as much as I enjoyed telling it.

Thank you.

Louis Saltzman
November 2018

While the rest are grinding their little private organs for their own glorification the old man is working with the strength of a giant and the purity of an angel to do this great work.
—John Hay on Abraham Lincoln

He always worked with things as they were, while never relinquishing the desire to make them better.
—John Hay in John Taliaferro's *All The Great Prizes: The Life Of John Hay, from Lincoln to Roosevelt*

Better to remain silent and be thought a fool than to speak out and remove all doubt.
—Abraham Lincoln

Judge not and be kind
Me

CAST OF CHARACTERS

Washington, DC, 2022

Paul Diamond, Time Travel Team Leader
Captain Jackson Barlow, Team Member
Captain Steven Butler, Team Member
Captain Gene Shanahan, Team Member
James Conklin, Mission Director

Army of Northern Virginia, 1863

Robert E. Lee, Commander
James Longstreet, Commander Corps I
A. P. Hill, Commander Corps II
Richard Ewell, Commander Corps III
Jeb Stuart, Commander Cavalry Corps
George Pickett, Brigade Commander, Longstreet
Walter Taylor, Chief of Staff, Lee
Charles Marshall, Aide-de-Camp, Secretary, Lee
Sam Hood, Brigade Commander, Longstreet
Lafayette McLaws, Brigade Commander, Longstreet
Johnson Pettigrew, Brigade Commander, Hill
Porter Alexander, Artillery Commander, Longstreet

Washington City, 1863

Abraham Lincoln, President of the United States
William H. Seward, Secretary of State
Edwin Stanton, Secretary of War
Gideon Welles, Secretary of the Navy
Salmon Chase, Secretary of the Treasury
John Nicolay, First Secretary to the President
John Hay, Second Secretary to the President
Francis P. Blair
Frank Blair, Congressman (R), Missouri
Martin Duffy, Servant, Francis P. Blair
Fernando Wood, Congressman (D), New York
Thaddeus Stevens, Congressman (R), Pennsylvania
Charles Sumner, Senator (R), Massachusetts
Herman Haupt, Manager, US Railroad System
Montgomery Meigs, Quartermaster, US Armies

Gettysburg, Pennsylvania, July 1863

Harry Heth, Brigade Commander (CSA)
John Buford, Cavalry Commander (US), Corps 1
John Reynolds, Commander (US), Corps II
Daniel Sickles, Commander (US), Corps III
Winfield Scott Hancock (US), Corps II
Alexander Webb, Brigade Commander (US), Corps II
A. P. Hill, Commander (CSA), Corps III
Richard Ewell, Commander (CSA), Corps II

CONTENTS

PART THREE

PROLOGUE

On June 15, 2022, Dr. Paul Diamond sat in a wooden chair in a NASA laboratory at the Goddard Space Flight Center just outside of Washington, DC. He wore a wide-brimmed brown hat, a long brown lightweight coat, and brown leather boots that were scuffed to make them appear worn. On his lap was a saddlebag that held the clothes and papers he would need for his trip. He was surrounded by five six-foot-high machines with spotlights pointed at the wooden chair. They would generate enough electrical power to send him on his trip back through time. Paul had no clue how they worked and what they did. His specialty was American History and he had a Doctorate in 19th Century American Studies. All he knew was that the machines would generate enough power and he hoped he would reopen his eyes when he was transported to his destination.

The machines began to hum for thirty seconds and a voice began a countdown beginning with ten. At five, the hum got louder, and Paul closed his eyes and tightened his grip on his bag. Through his eyelids, he was able to see bolts of electrical energy and a bluish-colored orb that was created by the electricity that encircled him. Paul felt the now familiar jolt that threw him back into the chair. And then he vanished.

PART
ONE

CHAPTER 1

Washington City, June 15, 1863

The trip was a bit bumpy. In the end, though, he arrived somewhat dizzy but otherwise no worse for wear. Paul attributed this to the number of times he'd made the journey, and he already he knew this would be his final one. There were only so many one's body could take. If this one were not so important and personal, he would still be back in his office with reference material in piles all around his desk. Every trip he survived was a blessing.

The landing spot was a wooden chair in a narrow alley behind the Willard Hotel in Washington City. His head was still spinning, so he tried to focus on what had led him there. All the jumps had taken their toll on his mind, and the last had put him out of commission for six months.

Goddard Space Flight Center, Greenbelt, Maryland, May 28, 2022

Paul Diamond had been back at work for almost a year when the phone had rung and his assistant had told him Dr. Conklin was on his way to see him.

Paul worked in a secret division of NASA at the Goddard Space

Flight Center fifteen minutes outside of Washington, DC. Technically his department was in the Astronomical Investigation Unit where he researched black holes and spatial phenomenon having to do with the possibilities of string theory. There was no mention of parallel universes and alternate time lines that had been proven to exist twelve years earlier or the ability to travel back and forth in time.

A small group of nations had begun to work together fifteen years earlier, and they were managed by the highest levels of each government. While the United States ran the program, Switzerland, England, and France provided scientific and financial support.

The transport was done via the "time jumper" sitting in a chair and his or her body being bombarded with electrical charges while surrounded by a circular blue orb that would propel the person to a prearranged time and place. A handful of scientists could make it work, maintain the machinery, and reverse the trip.

Theoreticians designed an implanted electric device that could send simple Morse code messages from the past to the present to advise of the status of the time jumpers. The inside joke was the old expression "You never saw me, and I was never here."

The true purpose of the department was developing a means of transporting individuals through time to critical hot spots in history to avoid potential disasters. Besides the potential damaging outcome if it did not work, there was a concern about the effect on the health of the travelers themselves and the impact on the time line by mistakes that could be made, as well as their connections to people they would meet. It was imperative to avoid any instance of affecting anything other than what their actual mission was.

It was virtually impossible to eliminate all possible contingencies for contact, but the travelers were trained to limit interactions with people who were not involved in the mission on the ground. There was a careful selection process for team members, with a premium placed on individuals with scientific and military backgrounds; and they needed to have historical knowledge of the times they were sent to, as any mistake could have serious repercussions.

Paul was a different case. His area of expertise was American history, with a specialty in the nineteenth century. At forty-seven years old, he was also older than all the other team members. Paul's last jump had been physically difficult and had not been successful, but events had proved to be beyond his control.

Andrew Jackson had finished his second term as president and was succeeded by his vice president, Martin Van Buren. President Jackson had succeeded in his quest to break the Bank of the United States. He pulled out all federal funds and then transferred them to several politically cooperative state banks, shutting the national bank down. Combined with the bursting of the bubble of land speculations in the western lands, the young nation found itself in its most severe depression. Van Buren and his administration were doomed. He was defeated in his bid for reelection.

Diamond was sent, not to save President Van Buren, but to try and stem the financial collapse. Shortly after his arrival, he realized he brought too little and had arrived too late. No jump could last more than twenty-one days before the physical effects of time travel literally ate up the cells of the body. There was not enough time to do anything, and his return to 2022 had been a rough one. Paul had suffered a brain aneurysm. He'd been told by the NASA medical staff that, without undergoing an untested new procedure, he would be grounded. Even if the procedure was done successfully, there was no guarantee he could survive another round trip.

Unable to return to the time when history was being made and so many events were taking place had been extremely difficult for him to accept. He'd decided to have the surgery and had been told it was successful, but the surgeons gave him enough caveats about returning to active status that he felt his hair was going to catch fire.

So, he'd returned to his first love—historical research of the nineteenth century. He had come to accept his new status. After all, he was helping the jumpers train and learn about what they were doing and what they would find when they arrived at their destinations.

Management was very cautious about approving trips, and a great deal of research was done before any were approved. When he was told that the director was coming for a visit, he found it unusual and a bit surprising. Normally, he would have been asked to make the trip downstairs.

CHAPTER 2

There was a knock on the door, and Dr. James Conklin rushed in to Paul's office. "I see all the books are right where they were the last time I was here," he said with a smile.

Paul answered, "You know me well enough by now, Jim. Now what brings you rushing up here?"

"Paul, it's important, and the subject is right in your wheelhouse. I don't know if I should even be telling you about it."

Paul stared at his friend and quietly said, "What is it?"

The director whispered, "How are you feeling?"

Paul immediately answered, "You get my monthly exam reports. I feel fine."

Jim turned to look at a painting hanging on a wall. It was of Pickett's Charge at the Battle of Gettysburg in the Civil War. Then he quietly said, "You may want to sit down."

Paul sat down in his chair and stared at his friend.

Conklin continued. "Today is May 28. At this moment in 1863, General Joseph Hooker is preparing his newly trained and refitted Army of the Potomac for an attack on Robert E. Lee's Army of Northern Virginia."

Paul Diamond sat in his chair and said quietly, "Chancellorsville."

"Yes," answered his friend, "but that is not our objective. We found some information that our friends on the other side made a move that we were not prepared for but did not work, but you know all this."

A few years ago, an unknown group of ultraconservative industrialists hacked the NASA computers and stole programs that allowed them to try to duplicate time travel.

Dr. Conklin went on to explain that their adversaries had tried to send back a modified version of an Uzi handgun to Antietam in 1862 that had failed to operate. "It was found," he said, "A photograph was in a file of General Sedgwick Corp. It was forgotten for decades. A junior research assistant named Jacob Hansen found it by chance."

"Someone is doing a book on General Sedgwick, and we always provide help when we can to make sure nothing is revealed that should not be. This led us to begin asking questions and put together a basic plan that we think can work. And it ties in to another related issue."

"What?" Paul asked.

"It would involve someone going back with a supply of automatic rifles that could theoretically be used at Gettysburg and Vicksburg."

He turned away from the painting and stared at Paul. "That person would have to see President Lincoln."

All Paul could say was, "Oh my God."

Jim Conklin knew there was no other historical figure Paul Diamond thought more of than Abraham Lincoln.

Conklin went on to explain that, if used properly, thirty of these automatic rifles could stop Lee from escaping the Union Army by cutting him off after the Federal victory at Gettysburg. Knowing how Lee was going to try to get away and cross the Potomac to Virginia was invaluable information for the Union Army to have. The rebels could be sealed in from both sides, and their soldiers could be cut down like wheat from a thresher. The other guns would go to Vicksburg.

"Paul, it could end the war right there. Is it possible?"

Paul placed two fingers of his right hand on his forehead and thought for a moment. Then he said, "Theoretically, it could. But there are problems with transporting the guns and training men to use them. I seem to remember Secretary of War Stanton having a group of men he used for special projects. But there is such an enormous risk for collateral damage by the number of people involved and all the moving parts in a project of this size. You know how I feel about messing with the time line, Jim."

Jim Conklin continued, "There is another matter, and it involves Robert Lincoln. You know he lives a long and successful life. There is one exception."

Paul held up his hand to interrupt his friend. "The death of his son."

"Wasn't he named for the president?" asked Conklin.

Paul answered, "Yes, you know everyone called him Jack. It was a lot to expect for a young man to take on being named for the assassinated president who led his country to victory in the Civil War. Robert accepts an appointment to serve as ambassador to Great Britain, where his only son dies. It must have been devastating."

Jim finished by saying, "We would like to avoid that taking place. I can say no more at this moment, but it could be very important."

Paul stood and put one hand on a book and stared at his friend. "There is so little time to prepare," he said. "Are you giving me the assignment?"

"Paul, we have to help the president. The answer is yes, Paul. But you must pass another physical exam. And don't even suggest not taking it!"

Paul had to go through three days of medical examinations before he was approved to lead the team. He could not remember feeling so excited and fulfilled.

CHAPTER 3

Once medically approved, Paul could begin planning the mission. He'd been fully aware that, had he not passed the battery of medical tests, there would not be a qualified team leader with his level of expertise. In addition, he would have to sit in with Jim on a Steering Committee meeting led by Dr. Hans Zimmer of Switzerland, a specialist in string theory, who would give the ultimate decision on whether the mission would proceed.

Paul met with Jackson Barlow, his colleague's mission name, to talk about the other two potential team members. Barlow asked who he wanted to take.

Paul replied, "Our regular group, why?"

Jackson paused and then asked, "Gene is great. But what about Steven?"

Paul smiled and said, "What about him?"

You don't see it as a problem that he is black?" asked Barlow.

"Not one bit. But I will tell him everything and let him make his own decision. Frankly, I can see him being with us as an advantage."

Jackson quietly said, "He is waiting for you outside."

Paul laughed and said, "You three are like sons to me. Get him in here."

Jackson smiled and stood to open the door and waved Steven Butler inside.

He was so wide and big he had to come in sideways. Steve was six foot two and weighed 235 pounds of pure muscle. It was as if his body was carved from marble.

He saluted Paul, who said, "Stop that."

Butler said, "Yes, sir."

Paul began the conversation by saying he hoped Steven knew how highly he thought of him and the reason they were talking was because of that. He explained how important this mission was, and then told him all he could. "I want you with me because I need you and know you will give me all you can, just like Jackson and Gene. You will be coming as a free man and will work very closely with me. That does not change the fact that you are black and going to what is, in effect, a Southern city in the middle of a revolution."

All the while Paul spoke, Steven sat erect and stared directly at his superior—with one exception. He could not stop his hands from clasping each other and continuously twisting his fingers.

"What is wrong, Steven?" Paul asked.

"Sir, you know how I feel about you, Jackson, and Gene. But I don't know if … when we get back there, the first time someone calls me 'boy' or 'nigger,' if I will be able to control myself."

"Steven, do you trust me?"

"Absolutely, sir."

"Then we agree, because I am not going without you. Besides, there is a chance you will meet Abraham Lincoln, and you can tell him yourself how you feel."

Steven took his right hand and rubbed his eye looked back at Paul and said as firmly as possible, "Thank you, sir."

Paul said to Steven, "I have a Steering Committee meeting at 9:00 a.m. tomorrow to present the plans of the mission and request approval." He told Steven he wanted the three of his men to go with him to the National Archives that afternoon and help him do a search for further odd weapons in General Sedgwick's corps files from the battle at Antietam. They requisitioned a NASA car and raced to DC to the archives.

What they found astounded Paul. Gene Shanahan found evidence of four additional Uzis further back in the same file where Hansen had found the first. Diamond asked for copies of the pictures, and he and his team brought them back to their offices at Goddard. He had a file of notes prepared and inserted these new pictures in with the other. He sent his team home, and he kept working until after 7:00 p.m. and then left for the night. He slept fitfully but was awake by six.

On his drive to Goddard the next morning, he was stuck behind two accidents and did not arrive at the complex until 8:45. He parked, rushed inside, took his very important cup of coffee, grabbed his file, and rushed to the conference room where this all-important meeting would take place. At precisely 9:02, Paul rushed into the meeting room.

Dr. Zimmer turned and said, "Thank you for joining us, Dr. Diamond. You are our final participant to arrive."

"Forgive me, Dr. Zimmer, but I discovered additional information that may have a bearing on your deliberations."

Zimmer replied, "That is interesting. At the appropriate time, I will call upon you to present it to us. Everyone, please take your seats."

The chairman explained to the group—a mix of physicists, politicians, mathematicians, and historians—the purpose of their meeting and asked Jim Conklin to begin the presentation. The members of the committee were from the four different countries involved in the program and were acknowledged experts in their fields. They were not housed in Washington, but all attended meetings of the committee to advise and consent to missions. They also contributed recommendations regarding the science and protocols.

Conklin was about to begin his presentation, but Paul motioned to him. Jim excused himself for a moment and went over to Paul, who whispered to him, "We found four more guns from Antietam."

Conklin smiled and went back to the head of the table.

"Ladies and Gentlemen, allow me to explain the basics of our proposed mission. In a moment I will turn the meeting over to Dr. Diamond, who, as you will hear, had a most valid reason for being two minutes late."

That generated smiles from the specialists sitting around the table.

Conklin began by setting the parameters of the mission that included the year 1863 and the problems facing the Federal armies, especially after the devastating defeat at Fredericksburg and the most recent one at

Chancellorsville. The significant problems President Lincoln was facing with the woeful performance of his generals added to the concerns. He then introduced the picture taken at Antietam that showed an Uzi handgun next to a dead Confederate officer. That generated whispers around the table, as the members of the committee knew exactly what it meant.

Dr. Conklin interrupted the group by saying, "I believe Dr. Diamond has some new information, and I will ask him to reveal that now. Dr. Diamond, if you please?"

Paul grabbed his file of pictures and walked to stand next to his friend Jim. "Ladies and Gentlemen, forgive me for being late, but I was stuck in traffic and needed to make sure I picked up this file. Our young Mr. Hansen made an incredible find, and I went back to the archives with my team to dig further. After a few hours, one of my men, Captain Shanahan, found these four additional photographs that were taken at Antietam."

He opened the file and showed pictures of thee additional Uzis next to dead Confederate soldiers. It was difficult to know for certain, but the guns did not appear to have been fired, and there did appear to have been some melting of the weapon. This generated animated conversation around the table.

Paul finished by saying that this information provided more evidence of the attempt by "our adversaries" to influence the conflict on behalf of the Confederacy. Conklin explained that the genesis of the plan had come about when the picture of the first gun had been found in the archives by Mr. Hansen. The discovery of the second set of pictures now reinforced the validity of that plan. There was no evidence that their competitors had done anything but "sent" the guns to the battlefield. He noted that the Confederate success at Chancellorsville over the next few days in 1863 would only strengthen their resolve and push General Lee to request Jefferson Davis to agree that he make another foray into Pennsylvania. The dreadful decisions made by General Hooker of the Army of the Potomac would beat down the morale of his forces and increase that of the Army of Northern Virginia. Conklin stressed that the current plan would be to aid the North to change commanders and provide advanced weaponry that would arrive in time to help defeat the Confederates at Gettysburg and Vicksburg and force Lee to surrender. This would save thousands of lives that would be lost if the war continued for another two years. Those lives would be forever lost along with those of their children that would be now unborn. Finally, Conklin admitted that this mission would not be able to prevent the assassination of President Lincoln. Given the twenty-one-day limitation on mission length, the hope would be that the new time line created on its own could prevent the assassination in April 1865.

Conklin paused and looked at the men and women around the table and continued, "There is another facet to this mission I am proposing for your consideration. I alluded to this in my initial conversation with Dr. Diamond. President Lincoln's elder son, Robert, will be in Washington City during this period. He will live a long and productive life. He will have his own son, Abraham Lincoln II. The son will be known as Jack. And when his father is appointed ambassador to Great Britain, he will die during his father's service in London.

"Based upon our mathematical algorithms and projections, if he is to live, he will become a lawyer and, ultimately, choose to run for the United States Senate from Illinois. Because of the change in the political climate, he will become a member of the Democratic Party, develop a close friendship with Franklin Roosevelt and work closely with Roosevelt during his run for the presidency. They will develop a strong working relationship. His primary policy concern will be to help the millions of people who will be devastated financially by the Depression. He will drive the legislative agenda of President Roosevelt in the Senate and help millions of people. He will follow in his grandfather's footsteps in that regard.

"By our contact with Robert in 1863, we can plant the seed in his mind that he should decline the future appointment in England and reinforce it years later via a brief mission with someone he would remember from 1863. Because of the differences in the time line, whoever should return will appear to have only slightly aged.

"This secondary objective, I believe, only reinforces the purpose of this proposed mission. I am, and Dr. Diamond is as well, available to answer any of your questions during your discussion and deliberations."

Conklin went back to his seat, and Dr. Zimmer said, "Thank you, Dr. Conklin and Dr. Diamond. This is an interesting proposal. We will now meet privately to review it. On behalf of the committee, I thank you. There are many things for us to review."

Conklin led Diamond to his office to wait to be summoned for any more questions.

Forty-five minutes later, his assistant Margaret answered her phone and said, "Yes, sir. Right away." She came in to her boss's office to tell him, "They want you both back in there."

Conklin and Diamond "power walked" their way back to the conference room door.

Paul raised his hand and said, "One second." He took a deep breath, smiled, and then simply said, "Okay, let's go."

Conklin smiled and opened the door.

The committee members were huddled in groups. Dr. Zimmer welcomed them back. "Some of our members have a few questions if you don't mind," he said. "It should take only a few minutes."

He called on Dr. Auschlander, the director of medicine for the program.

The doctor opened a file, looked at Paul, and began to speak in a calm businesslike manner. "Dr. Diamond, I have reviewed the results of your recent tests, and everything seems to be in order." And then he paused. "But I am concerned about how your body will react to being thrown back in time almost 160 years and then return. So I must ask how do you feel? And do you think you are physically up to this mission?"

Dr. Diamond thought for a moment and gathered his thoughts before he answered, "Dr. Auschlander, we have known each other for a number of years, and I have great respect for your opinion. But since the surgery after my last mission, I have taken great pains to take care of my health. And honestly, I have not felt this good in a long time. To answer your question directly, I have no doubts about my physical status and my ability to get through this mission and a safe return."

"Thank you for your candor, Paul," Dr. Auschlander said with a smile.

Dr. Zimmer then called on Senator Joan Murray.

She took off her glasses and spoke to Paul. "Doctor, it seems that one of the most important parts of your mission will be to gain entry to the White House and see President Lincoln. How do you propose to do that?"

This time Paul did not hesitate. "I have thought of almost nothing else since Jim came to my office the other day. I will have to find the right person, someone whom the president trusts and is not looking for anything in return. The cabinet is a den of vipers and is constantly in turmoil and split in different factions. To try and use one of the cabinet members could cause all kinds of problems. I have a few outside parties from outside the government in mind."

Senator Murray asked, "And who might they be Dr. Diamond?"

"I would prefer not to reveal that Senator Murray. We are flirting with changing the time line now," Paul answered.

Dr. Zimmer said, "I agree with Dr. Diamond on that question. We must trust his judgment."

He turned his head and nodded at General Paul Banner, who spoke bluntly. "I have concerns about the weapons and your team's ability to interact with soldiers from that time and to train them properly."

Paul looked over at Jim Conklin and nodded his head. Paul looked at the general and answered. "I have worked with this team on three missions. I am a historian and do not have experience in weaponry and training. But I can tell you that they are all captains in their respective services and are smart, experienced, and have never had a problem dealing with the locals from the past. They follow my orders to the letter, and I have full confidence in their abilities and experience. I will defer to Jim on the weapons aspect and training."

Jim turned to the general and picked up where Paul had left off. "Sir, I have already spoken with my counterparts at the FBI, Army, and Marines. They suggested using the Browning automatic rifle with a carousel and mortar attachments. One box with two rifles will be initially transferred to the Naval Yard in Washington. We will have the layout for the building later today. The first shipment will be used for demonstration purposes. Once the team has received approval to proceed, two additional shipments will be sent to Vicksburg and Gettysburg. Secretary of War Stanton has a group of men at his disposal—men he calls 'the best of the best'—who he uses for special missions and intelligence. They have experience in weapons and are also used to test new firearms and explosives. We believe they will have the capacity to learn and practice with the BARs once trained by our team. It is important that you understand we now have the capability to transfer these weapons to specific points within fifty feet of their target. I hope that answers your question, General."

The general nodded his head and said, "Yes thank you. Well done."

Dr. Zimmer looked around the room to see if any of the members of the committee had any other questions. None did. He said, "Gentlemen, I thank you for your help. We will continue our deliberation and let you know of our decision as soon as we have one."

Jim thanked the group and led Paul out the door. They took three steps down the hallway, and Jim said, "Paul, my friend, I think we are in business! To save some time, if I were you, I would get to work. I am going to talk to our supply people about clothing and the like. You did very well, Dr. Diamond." Jim patted him on his back.

Paul was smiling, but something clicked in his mind. He suddenly stopped and looked at Jim with a look of concern.

Conklin said, "Paul, what's wrong?"

"Jim, they never pressed us on the changes in the time line."

CHAPTER 4

Jim and Paul again went back to Conklin's office to wait for word. It was three in the afternoon, but Jim counseled patience.

At precisely 4:30, there was a knock on the door and Margaret entered, a Navy ensign following with an envelope in his right hand.

He handed the envelope to Jim Conklin and said, "Sir, I have been instructed to deliver this to you personally."

Jim answered, "Thank you, Ensign."

The ensign smartly turned and left.

"Margaret, please close the door."

She understood and left.

"Well, here we go, Paul."

He opened the envelope and began to read the contents out loud:

> Gentlemen:
> It is the opinion of this committee that you receive a green
> light for your mission.
> However, we have several caveats and concerns.
>
> 1. This trip would be the most extensive that has ever been
>   attempted. Given that our primary concern in every case

is that the time line not be disturbed, it is of paramount importance any potential changes be limited to as few as possible. In this case, the goal is to change the time line as to ending the Civil War two years earlier and doing what is possible to prevent the death of Abraham Lincoln II.

2. I have reviewed the projections and equations as to Mr. Lincoln, and I agree, reluctantly, that they are logical and make the risk worth the potential reward.

3. The team will be in a city that has Southern leanings. I cannot stress strongly enough that a single sentence uttered by your men overheard by a Confederate sympathizer could jeopardize the entire plan.

4. Your mission parameters do not include doing anything to prevent the assassination of President Lincoln. If, because of your actions, it does not happen, I do not think we would be disappointed.

5. A final comment. Our most important concern, I must reemphasize, is about creating a new time line. As we have discussed many times, "time" does not react positively to changes in the past. It always seems to push back at us. The intensity of the push back seems to be directly related to the level of the changes in the past. We have no way of knowing when and what the reaction will be. In this case, we will be forced to wait and see what "time" has in store for us.

Please file your status reports through the normal channels.

You have all our best wishes for your successful efforts and safe return.

Hans Zimmer
Chairman-Steering Committee

"He is not wrong Jim," said Paul.

Jim answered, "No, he is not, but now it is up to us."

Washington City, June 15, 1863

Paul's eyes began to clear, and the fogginess he had felt was passing. It was supposed to be early afternoon on June 15, 1863. He placed his hands on the arm of the wooden chair and tried to stand. A rush in his head reminded him to go slowly. He brushed his long brown coat, which was especially designed to withstand the heat of Washington. Conklin and his staff had warned Paul how hot it was going to be, even though he was aware of the temperatures in Washington City in June and July, and had technicians work on designing and stitching appropriate clothing that would help make it more bearable. The entire team's boots were made of paper-thin leather and made to look worn and beat-up to the average eye.

The one thing he'd demanded was a soft brown hat with a wide brim. Paul had found on prior missions that it was a good idea to be able to be as inconspicuous as possible. The problem he had was his height of six feet five inches. Lincoln was considered a freak, and he was an inch shorter. Paul stopped and shook his head. If all went as planned, he would be meeting his hero the next day. The sound of a horse neighing outside the alley made Paul decide to get moving, and he hoped his room would be waiting for him.

He had not come alone. His three handpicked operatives should have arrived the day before to prepare the way for him. He had previously worked very well with them, and that was extremely important. They were all well-schooled and experienced military men. One was a Navy SEAL, and the other two were Army and Marine Special Forces veterans. The only difficulty was they had different names for each mission.

To make it easier on Paul, they kept the same names they'd used on their last trip. They were Gene Shanahan, Steven Butler, and Jackson Barlow. In fact, Paul never knew their real names. There could be no evidence whatsoever of their existence in this time line. But they all had backstories that had been put together by experienced members of the department. Paul had reviewed and approved every bit of it.

He had two big issues with which to contend. The decision to use the Browning Automatic Rifle had already been made by Jim Conklin and his military contacts.

The second was solely his responsibility. That was getting into the

White House and seeing President Lincoln. Diamond would need to approach someone close to the president who had full access. He initially thought of William Seward and Edwin Stanton, but he knew there was so much infighting in the cabinet, it would raise too many questions if he chose one over another.

Seward was the heavy favorite to win the Republican nomination for president in 1860. After Lincoln won the nomination and then the election, he offered the plum position of secretary of state to Seward, who had a low opinion of Lincoln's potential. After considering his options, he accepted, believing he could control the new president and, in effect, run the government through the State Department.

Before Lincoln was inaugurated and in the early days of the new administration, the first group of Southern states seceded, and the crisis at Fort Sumter exploded with the Confederacy beginning their attack on April 12, 1861, less than a month after President Lincoln's inauguration. Seward was very unhappy with the president's response and wrote him a letter suggesting that Seward take more of an active role in determining the response of the Federal government. Lincoln was upset by it and made his feelings clear in an answer that said whatever decisions would be made would come from the White House. Seward had badly misjudged Lincoln's abilities and resolve and, in time, would become Lincoln's most trusted advisor.

Stanton was an entirely different story. He was appointed to be secretary of war in January 1862, to succeed Simon Cameron amid reports of rampant corruption in the War Department under Cameron's stewardship. There were rumors that Lincoln operatives at the Republican convention in Chicago had made promises of a cabinet position in exchange for Cameron's throwing Pennsylvania's votes to Lincoln.

The candidate had sent a telegram to his people at the convention in Chicago, instructing them not to make promises to anyone for a position in his administration in exchange for their support. But they went ahead and did it anyway.

By any benchmark, Cameron was not a productive member of the cabinet. Stanton secretly campaigned to succeed Cameron at the War Department, and many people were not in favor of Stanton, a Democrat, joining the cabinet in such a key role. His reputation as a brilliant lawyer notwithstanding, many people in Washington accused him of being arrogant, manipulative, demanding, and of working to steer Lincoln to focus on his own agenda.

The fact remains the Union Armies went through a series of commanders who failed to bring victories until 1862 at Antietam, and that declaration of victory was debatable.

It went without saying that Stanton and Seward were enemies within the cabinet. And if Paul Diamond chose one or the other to contact the president, it could come back to haunt him.

His choice would have to be someone of stature outside of the administration—someone who Lincoln respected and did not owe favors to. After a few days of consideration and research, he came upon someone who would fit the requirement. Francis Preston Blair was the natural choice. Blair was a strong Democrat during the 1820s and became a member of Andrew Jackson's infamous "kitchen cabinet." He was brought to Washington to be the editor of the *Washington Globe*, which was the administration-sponsored newspaper. Diamond had walked past him on the street during his last unsuccessful trip to Washington City.

Blair was instrumental in melding together different political factions when the Republican Party was formed and nominated John C. Fremont to run—and lose to James Buchanan in 1856. Blair was a member of the conservative wing of the Republican Party and watched Lincoln win the nomination in Chicago in 1860.

Blair saw what was coming, and he believed completely in the Union but was nowhere close to be an abolitionist. But Lincoln trusted his bluntness and political experience. Blair was powerful and had two sons in politics, from whom Lincoln needed support. He put one Blair son, Montgomery, in his cabinet as postmaster general, and he did a very good job before the president was forced to ask him to resign in 1864 in order to keep Seward for political reasons who was under attack from the enemies of the Secretary of State. With the introduction of a new time line it remained to be seen if the removal of Montgomery Blair would be necessary.

Paul's man, Jackson Barlow, would be the one who would deliver a letter to Blair requesting an interview for the next morning, at which time

Paul would make full disclosure to the man who could make or break the mission. He saw no other way.

Paul stood and looked down at the wooden chair that he would see again in three weeks' time and then walked slowly toward the end of the alley and a busy Pennsylvania Avenue. The main entrance of the Willard Hotel was halfway down the block, and he slowly made his way through the many people who were going in and out of the hotel. There were at least ten horse-drawn buggies that acted as taxicabs in this time, as well as another fifteen horses tied and awaiting their riders. Many men in various Union uniforms stood on the sidewalk smoking thin cigars and posing for the women who walked by.

Paul smiled as he remembered a line from one of his favorite fictional books of the period, written by Michael Shaara. "Follow the cigar smoke and find the fat man."

Paul had his saddlebag slung over his shoulder and walked up the steps of the entrance while holding on to the shiny bronze railing for support. A doorman held the door open for him while he stared up at Paul's height. He smiled back and walked in to the very crowded, noisy, and smoky lobby.

Paul had to blink a few times to get used to such a large room that had no electric lights and so much smoke. The furnishings matched what he had seen in the pictures and re-creations. There was enough red crushed velvet on the chairs to fill twenty plus homes, and the smell of gas lamps was everywhere. He could not help but smile at what he was seeing.

As Paul became less disoriented, he saw the long front desk that was manned by at least six people appropriately dressed in uniforms. All were helping guests. He noticed a spot open and walked over to the marble countertop.

The man behind the counter turned to look at Paul and said, "May I help ... Oh my, you are tall! You are taller than the president!"

Paul smiled and tipped his hat and said, "I believe someone has made a reservation for me. The name is Diamond, Paul Diamond."

The deskman answered, "One moment, please. We are just so busy. Let me check, sir."

While the desk clerk was checking, Paul looked down at that day's newspaper, and he confirmed the date—June 15. Paul had forgotten to ask what day it was.

The clerk went over to a huge, wide, and long book and began turning pages. He ran his finger down one and said, "Oh, yes, here you are, Mr. Diamond! And I have an envelope waiting for you as well. It has this strange adhesive on it."

Paul took the envelope. "Thank you," he said. "It's something my company has been working on for the army."

"Do you need someone to help you with any bags, sir?"

"No, I'm fine. Just my room key, please."

The man handed him the key. "You are in room 206, just up the stairway and to your right."

Paul tipped his hat, thanked him for his help, and gave him a dollar coin. He picked up his saddlebag and put it over his left shoulder, holding the envelope and key in his right hand. He was returning to full consciousness but still held onto the railing as he walked up the steps to the second floor.

Without looking back, he knew the man behind the desk was watching him. He should have reminded Jackson not to use tape from their time. That was exactly the kind of mistake that was to be avoided. He found his room at the end of the floor and opened the door easily and then went inside and carefully locked the door behind him. He dropped his saddlebag on the bed, put the key on a night table and hung his coat on a hook behind the door with his hat over it. Before he opened the envelope, he took a moment and rubbed his forehead with two fingers of his right hand. The first thing he had to do was send a coded Morse message home. He found the implant that had been inserted in his thigh and slowly tapped, "Arrived safely in hotel."

He felt fine, but he could not believe where he was sitting and what could happen in the next twenty-four hours. Paul took a slow deep breath, tore open the envelope, and read the one page that was written in pencil.

CHAPTER 5

Boss,

I assume you are in your hotel room if you are reading this. Our friend from Maine, Gene S, made the reservation, and I believe the package was delivered last night. I dropped off your note this morning. He came out to say hello and asked a few questions, none of which I answered except to say you would arrive today.

He said he would send his man and carriage and asked that you be in front of the hotel at ten tomorrow morning. He did say sending someone with the name Jackson was a nice touch. I will be in the hotel lobby after 1 tomorrow, and we can all have lunch or separately if you think necessary.

The manservant had an odd air about him. Keep a clear eye. Steven will be waiting for you outside the main entrance at 9:45 a.m.

J

Paul put the letter next to him on the bed, rubbed his eyes, and whispered, "Yes!" He opened his saddlebag and took out a copy of the letter Jackson had taken to Francis Blair. He reread it:

Dear Sir:

My name is Paul Diamond, and my employee, Jackson Barlow, has delivered this to you. I am en route to Washington City and hope to arrive sometime later today. My purpose in writing is to introduce myself and request an interview, if possible, sometime tomorrow, at your convenience. It is regarding a matter of urgency regarding the war.

You have my word that you will not be disappointed with what I will tell you. I assure you that the information will help our armies end this bloody conflict.

I have instructed Jackson to wait for your response. Please note that the coincidence of his name was not lost on me. Thank you for your attention.

I remain your most humble servant,

Paul Diamond

Paul had been so worried about the letter that it had taken him two days to write it. But it looked as if it worked. Jackson was well trained and had a sharp eye after his years of interrogating prisoners as a Navy SEAL. This servant he'd mentioned would bear watching. Paul had no appetite. He took out his replica pocket watch and saw it was after 7 and decided to unpack his bag and get ready for what should be a very interesting next day.

Paul carefully removed an envelope from one side of the saddlebag that contained material he was going to share with Francis Blair. It was all important, but one item that could be the most important was the color print of the automatic rifle with the mortar attachment. He slowly went through the other material and then went down the hall to use the privy and get into bed by nine o'clock. The trip always tired him, and he fell asleep within minutes. The watch he had made had a silent alarm built in it. If it was within three feet of him, it would vibrate at a certain time. He set it for seven thirty but was sure the anticipation would have him awake before, and it did.

At seven the next morning, Paul had used the privy, washed and tried using the straight-edged razor he'd brought but clipped a piece of the goatee he had grown and had to try and patch that up. That set him back a few minutes, but he was still fine on time. He got dressed and took out a muslin collarless shirt that buttoned at his neck and still gave him enough room to move. There was a black vest picked out for him by the design team that he grumbled about wearing, but now he realized they were right. He put on his coat and hat and slung his saddlebag over his shoulder and slowly turned around to look at his room to make sure he was not forgetting anything.

He looked at himself in the mirror and thought, *Not bad for a graying forty-seven-year-old in 1863*. He smiled but still never forgot how important this day would be for himself and his country.

CHAPTER 6

Down in the lobby, Paul walked to the restaurant to have some breakfast. He asked for a corner table, where he could watch the other diners and see if he could recognize anyone. The waiter brought over a menu of totally unappetizing food for his time, and Paul settled on coffee and a hard-boiled egg.

As he waited, Secretary of State William Seward came in, already smoking a cigar, and was led to what seemed to be his regular table in the center of the room, where he could be approached by those currying favor from the man closest to the president. Paul remembered that Lincoln rarely left the White House to eat and what he did eat was very light.

The waiter brought over his egg and coffee, for which Paul said thank you. He kept on eye on Seward, who was continuously approached by various people, some of whom he rudely waved away—until Gideon Welles, the secretary of the Navy, came in to sit with him. The waiter brought Seward eggs and bacon, and coffee for Welles. The naval secretary had a thick white beard and a wig that occasionally moved around his head when he began to animatedly speak, which he was doing now.

Paul could not help but overhear. Welles was talking about the campaign to free Vicksburg and reopen the Mississippi River to Union ships from one end to the other. It was extremely important, and General Grant was having trouble breaking through the defenses at Vicksburg.

Little did he know, all that could soon change because of Paul Diamond and his men. It also occurred to Paul that all these officials, senators, congressmen, and newspaper reporters could be transported to his time and be having similar conversations, with two important exceptions— there were no women or people of color. Paul could clearly see how many citizens were either ignored or overlooked.

Women were beginning to find their voices, led notably by the two Grimke sisters, who left their Southern plantation home for the North to fight for abolition. And Frederick Douglas, a giant voice, was beginning to energize his own people, as well as many whites. for the cause of abolition. One of the most well-known white abolitionists was newspaper publisher William Lloyd Garrison, who wrote of his stance, "I am in earnest-I will not equivocate-I will not excuse-I will not retreat a single inch-and I will be heard."

The real problem was the depth and horror of racism that existed in the country. Some twenty years prior, John Quincy Adams had spoken of slavery as "a great and foul stain on the American Union." But, as Paul knew and these people could not, it would take 160 years in his time for relations between the races to be close to what it should be. Hopefully, his mission could help make things go faster.

Paul thought of Steven, who should be in front of the hotel, and decided to go and wait for him. Steven had a room in a "coloreds" only boarding house, while Jackson and Gene were in rooms in another house a few blocks away. He walked through the already smoke-filled lobby toward the front door and down the steps to the street where Steven stood waiting. They were both a few minutes early for the carriage.

Paul put his hand on Steven's shoulder and whispered what Jackson had written about Francis Blair's man.

Steven nodded his head and said. "I can feel the hatred all around me."

Paul answered by squeezing his shoulder and saying, "If anyone says anything, leave it to me."

At precisely 9:55, a large well-appointed carriage with the letter B in blue script on both sides of the carriage pulled in to an open spot directly in front of the Willard. A well-dressed driver tied the reins to the brake and stepped off and then walked directly to Paul Diamond and said, "Mr. Diamond, I presume?

"I was directed to look for a very tall man. I will be bringing you to meet Mr. Blair. He looked at Steven with a look of disdain and said, "Mr. Blair did not say anything about anyone else."

Paul could feel Steven's body stiffen just from the tone of this man's voice. Paul responded by saying, "Forgive me, I did not hear your name."

"It is Martin, sir."

Paul said with a good deal of firmness, "Good. Martin, first I would like you to open the door so Steven and I can get inside, and then I will explain something to you. Can you do that for me, Martin?"

"Yes, sir."

"Excellent," he replied as Martin walked over to the side door and opened it, giving Steven a wide berth. Paul said quietly to Steven, "I am going in first because I want to be directly behind Martin, so he may clearly hear what I have to tell him."

"Yes, sir," Steven answered. He knew exactly what was about to happen. He was still furious with this Martin but controlled himself and waited for Paul to get in and followed, sitting next to him.

When he was settled, Paul put his hand on Steven's arm and squeezed as he moved forward to Martin and began to speak quietly. "Martin, can you hear me?"

He nodded yes.

Paul continued. "Good, because I am going to say this once, and it is important you understand. Steven and I have worked together for more than five years. He performs very important duties and I trust him with my life. And more importantly, he is a free man. I have seen him react very physically to people who have insulted him less than you just did. Where I go, so does he. And nothing is going to change that. Do you understand what I am saying, Martin?"

He nodded again.

Paul said, "Finally, I would prefer you say, 'I understand.'"

Martin quietly replied, "I understand."

"Very good. Now, Martin, please drive us to Mr. Blair."

As familiar with this time in American History as he had been, Paul was still not prepared for the blatant racism he'd just experienced face-to-face. It was one thing to read and understand and quite another to face it in person.

The Blair House, as it was known in this time (and still was in Paul's time) was less than two minutes away from the White House. They could have easily walked, but due to the heat and protocol, this was how things were done in 1863.

Martin pulled the carriage directly in front and stepped down to open the door on Steven's side first. Steven said, "Thank you very much."

Paul slid over and got out after him.

Martin closed the side door and said, "Gentlemen, please follow me."

CHAPTER 7

The Blair House, Washington City, June 16, 1863

Paul replied with a "thank you," and Martin brought he and Steven to the front door and knocked.

A female servant opened the door and said, "This way, please." She could not help but stare at Paul's height and Steven's color. Paul took pleasure in it for both reasons.

They followed the woman through a few rooms to a parlor with wide open windows and four chairs surrounding a wooden varnished table. Paul was impressed with the home and furnishings. As they walked in the room, an older well-dressed man stood to greet them. "Mr. Diamond, I presume. Welcome." The man was short, balding, and impeccably dressed.

Paul had forgotten to remove his hat and coat, and as he did take them off, someone appeared behind him to help and take them away.

Paul said to Blair, "Sir, may I present my associate Steven Butler, who happens to be a free man, a fact I seem to have to say continuously in this part of the country."

Blair shook Steven's hand and said, "A pleasure."

Steven simply said, "Thank you, sir," and seemed taken aback that someone of Blair's stature would say such a thing.

Mr. Blair pointed to the empty chairs for Paul and Steven to sit and called Martha to see what they wanted to drink. They both asked for coffee, and she brought a plate of hot biscuits as well.

After the coffee and biscuits were served, Mr. Blair opened the conversation by saying to Paul with a smile, "Your man Jackson was very mysterious yesterday when I spoke with him about your note."

"He is a fine employee and does his job well. He has learned when to answer and when not to. I would not have requested this meeting to waste your time, sir. If you do not mind, I would like to show you a few things because what I am going to tell you, with all due respect, will most assuredly be something you have never heard or seen before."

Blair smiled and said, "You would be surprised at how many times I have been told that."

Paul just smiled in response.

Paul began talking about the status of the war and then decided to be more specific about what had recently happened and what was ahead for the Northern armies. "We know that General Hooker had a plan he was very confident would badly hurt General Lee. His army had superior numbers to those of the Rebels, but he never took into consideration the audaciousness of Lee and Stonewall Jackson. He explained that Hooker's indecision and inability to stop Lee would result in a debacle for the Union Army. The Battle of Chancellorsville was over, and it was a disaster for the Northern Army. Lee shockingly split his army in two—sending Jackson and his corps on a night march around the Union forces to an open flank on the Union right and, thus, rolling up the Union forces and inflicting 18,000 casualties, a devastating blow.

Paul went on to explain that the state of Virginia had been stripped bare of its natural and food resources and General Lee had been looking for an opportunity to go north and take the fight to Pennsylvania. He wanted the population there to experience what the people of Virginia had to endure for the past two years. Lee also knew that he did not have an inexhaustible number of men and supplies that the Federal Army had access to. By mid-1863, the manufacturing power of the North was in full force and pumping out weapons, supplies, and foodstuffs to fill their needs.

There were real problems however. They needed commanders

that would challenge Lee and Longstreet. Losing Stonewall Jackson at Chancellorsville was a terrible blow for General Lee. But Lincoln was watching his own generals for signs of potential replacements. Lee knew he could not survive a war of attrition and petitioned President Davis and his cabinet to release him from protecting Richmond and attack Pennsylvania. Many of his men were starving and shoeless. After weeks of pleading and allaying their fears of Richmond being exposed, the Confederate cabinet relented, and President Davis issued the order for the Army of Northern Virginia to move north.

Blair did not know a good amount of what Paul told him, and he was concerned about what else there was he did not know and Diamond seemed to know. But Blair did not think Diamond was prepared to tell him, at least not yet.

"Mr. Blair, some of what I have told you the president does not know. He will when I see him. Disclosing this information to anyone outside of the federal government could be considered an act of treason.

For your information as of yesterday, General Lee had one corps under Ewell in Pennsylvania and another on the way."

Blair's head snapped up. "How can you possibly know this?" he said. "There are not more than five or six people inside the administration who are aware of it, unless that idiot Halleck has opened his mouth."

Paul smiled and said, "I can assure you it was not General Halleck. And I promise that, when we leave you this morning, all your questions will be answered. One thing, if I may, Mr. Blair. The door to the living room is open. Could it be closed?"

"I did ask my son Frank to sit in. Is that all right with you?"

Paul said, "If you can vouch for his ability to maintain secrecy. You will see why in a few minutes."

Blair called for Martin, who happened to be standing behind that open door.

"Yes, sir?"

Blair said, "Find Frank and ask him to join us. And keep the door closed please."

Frank Blair quickly came in, and his father introduced him to Paul and Steven. He was a congressman from Missouri and a colonel in that state's militia, as well as the family's hope to succeed President Lincoln after a second term. There were rumblings about that, unless the fortunes of the war shifted.

The Confederacy, despite having a smaller fighting force and fewer supplies, was more than holding its own in the fight. Most Northerners had initially believed the war would last no more than a few months, let alone the two years it already had.

Paul and Steven were obviously aware that the Battle of Chancellorsville was a complete disaster for the North, and General Hooker's bravado was false. But they were the only ones in the room who knew that. The senior Blair explained what Paul had just told him and about Steven.

Regardless of the fight being about preserving the Union, the Emancipation Proclamation issued and signed by President Lincoln on New Year's Day 1863 had brought the abolition of slavery out from the shadows and in the forefront where it belonged. It gave the South the opportunity to claim Lincoln was an evil apostate black Republican, stating he was a lover of the colored race and proclaiming that is what he was really fighting for.

The timing of Steven's appearance in Washington could not have been worse, insofar as the underlying suspicion of so many people. For many, any black Americans were just "niggers," and any free black men were fakes unless they were under the protection of people of importance.

After the conviction and death of John Brown in 1859, even Frederick Douglas had to leave the country for England, in fear for his life. He was a runaway slave and could be captured and brought back to the South. Before the jump back to 1863, Paul had made sure Steven had an authentic-appearing document stating he was a free man. Even with that, black men were taken and sold as slaves.

Blair Sr. motioned to Frank to make sure the door was closed so they could be assured of privacy. His daughter Elizabeth lived with them and was extremely bright. Blair relied on her advice. But he felt having her in the meeting would not be appropriate. Depending on what he was told, there would be time enough to tell Elizabeth everything.

Paul said to the father and son, "Gentlemen, allow me to show you two pictures." The first was a black and white taken by a photographer in General Sedgwick's Corps. The photograph was not clear, but the gun it featured was clearly not a weapon of that time.

Frank exclaimed, "What the hell is that?"

Paul looked at Steven to answer.

"If I may, sir." He took the picture and pointed to the barrel and the bullet feeder, which slid into the barrel. "This is called a machine pistol, which simply means that it can shoot many rounds at a very high rate of speed. It will not be invented for almost eighty years, Mr. Blair."

Simultaneously, both Blairs said, "What?"

Steven continued, "Fortunately, it did not work. I will let Paul tell you the rest."

"Before I answer your obvious questions, I must show you another picture and one other item." He removed the color photograph of the automatic rifle and placed it on the table in front of the Blairs.

Frank stared at it and said, "This picture has colors!"

Blair Sr. said, "It is a weapon. Where did you get this?"

Without saying another word, Paul took one other item out of his saddlebag and placed it on the table next to the picture of the Browning automatic rifle. Then he said, "Gentlemen, this is yesterday's edition of *The Washington Post*. Please note the date. I purchased it yesterday morning from a newspaper stand in the year 2022 before I traveled here. I'll give you both a minute to let that sink in, and then I will answer your questions, because there is a little more to tell."

Frances Blair Sr. and his son sat in stunned silence.

There was a knock on the door, and Martha stuck her head in to ask if they needed anything.

All Sr. could do was wave her away. But Paul said. "Could we have a few more biscuits? They were delicious."

She curtsied and was back in a few minutes with the biscuits.

In the interim, the Blairs asked if Paul minded if they stepped away for a few minutes.

Paul said, "Please do."

Father and son walked to a veranda outside. Frank was pointing back inside to the table, and Paul asked Steven, "What do you think?"

He laughed quietly and said, "Boss, they are so freaked out."

Paul answered, "Can you blame them? We just turned their world upside down and inside out at the same time."

The Blairs had been talking for fifteen minutes, and Paul was not sure how it was going. The father and son returned to the room, and Sr. said, "Thank you for allowing us to do that. If you meet my daughter, Elizabeth, you will see that we are a close-knit family, along with my older son Montgomery."

"Yes. I am aware of his position in the cabinet."

"Regardless of whether I think you two gentlemen are insane or telling me the truth, what is it you want of me?" he asked.

Paul said, "I mentioned there was a little more to tell. I have been authorized by the government of the United States to offer your government at least thirty of those guns to use in two very important upcoming battles that will take place in the next month. What I did not tell you is that the shells fire at the rate of one hundred rounds per minute. Imagine five or six of these automatic rifles strategically placed on a battlefield. It would be like a thresher cutting down fields of wheat." While referring to the thresher and wheat, Paul thought of Jim Conklin's use of the same expression a few weeks before.

"Where are these weapons now?" asked Frank Blair.

Steven answered, "Two are already here, in a safe place. We expect the president would want to see it fire and then approve or disapprove of your using it. If the answer is yes, the rest will appear outside of a small Pennsylvania town, as well as in the Vicksburg area in Mississippi, within twenty-four hours. We have two other members of our team already here that would train a group of selected soldiers in how to use them. We are aware of soldiers attached to the War Department who could be available to work on this mission."

Sr. turned to Paul and said, "How is this possible? And why are you doing this now?"

"There is more that I cannot tell you than I can, Mr. Blair. We are in our own fight, so to speak. The people who sent that gun to this time, and thank God it did not work, desperately want the Confederacy to win this war. We have evidence of at least four other weapons of the same kind that were found at Antietam. There is an expression that is used in our time: Follow the money. That group would make untold billions of dollars from perpetuating slavery and controlling the trade in cotton for all time. Or so they think." He took a deep breath and went on, "Gentlemen, I wish we were crazy. But I assure you; this is quite real. These weapons offered to you will give you the opportunity to end this war within two months.

"Unfortunately, there is only one person I can have that conversation with, but I will tell you one last personal item. Since I learned to read, I have always returned to American history, and the one man I have admired more than any other is sitting in his office less than two miles away. The idea that I could meet and help President Lincoln is overwhelming to me. So I assure you; this is all quite real." Then he put his right hand on his forehead and stroked it for a few moments.

Steven reached over and squeezed Paul's knee.

Mr. Blair looked at Paul and said, "I make no promises. Go back to the Willard and wait in your room. If I can do anything, I will send a message to you there. But before you leave, I want to write a note to the president. This information is too important to keep to ourselves."

He went to his desk and began to write. It did not take long. When he was finished, he called for Martin and instructed him to take Diamond and Butler back to the Willard and then go right to the White House and deliver the sealed note that was addressed, "Urgent. For the president's eyes only." He added, "Give this to either John Nicolay or John Hay only and tell them you were told by me to wait for the response of President Lincoln. Do you understand, Martin?"

"Yes, Mr. Blair. I understand," Martin replied.

Blair said to Paul and Steven, "I am not sure what to say to you. This conversation has been unlike anything I have ever experienced. I hope to see you again soon."

With that, Mr. Blair walked them to the carriage, and Martin began the trip back to the Willard.

When the carriage arrived at the hotel, Paul told Martin not to bother to open the door and go right across to the White House. By this time, it was 12:30.

Paul took Steven in with him to look for Jackson and Gene.

The two were sitting on a couch in the lobby. Paul tipped his hat and continued to walk to the restaurant. The two got up to follow. They were greeted by a maître d', and Paul asked for a table for four.

The host stared at Steven. Paul put his hand on Steven's arm again to calm him as he said, "This man is my employee and is a free man."

"Of course, sir. Please follow me," the maître d' answered as he led the four to a quiet table in the rear of the dining room.

Gene said as they sat down, "I would like to have about two minutes alone with a guy like that."

Jackson chimed in, "Count me in on that one. But for some reason, I think we are going to have a chance sooner or later."

Paul held up his hand. "Easy, boys. We must be patient." But he did feel continued surprise at the depth of the racism that permeated this city.

He then proceeded very quietly to tell Jackson and Gene about the meeting and Blair writing the president. The reaction of the father and son came out funnier in the retelling. Paul confirmed Jackson's concern about Martin and said he would bear watching. Paul decided they should stay together for the next few hours because he had a feeling there would be a response from the White House sooner rather than later. It all depended upon whether the president received the note from Blair.

After Paul paid for the meal, the four went to Paul's room to wait. There were more stares at Steven Butler on the way up, and Paul took his arm for support.

The room was a little small for four people. Paul said, "Find a spot to sit boys. I have to get these boots off and close my eyes for a few minutes."

CHAPTER 8

The White House

Thirty minutes earlier, Martin Duffy was squeezing through the crowds congregating outside the main entrance to the White House and the two soldiers trying to keep people out. He had to scream at one to tell him he had an urgent message for the president from Mr. Blair. That worked, and he made it into the lobby. But there was another throng of soldiers and officers and a mob of office seekers who seemed to follow the president wherever he was at any given moment.

All these people had no idea what was about to happen in Pennsylvania. Many of them did not care; all they wanted was a promotion or a job.

Martin made his way to the staircase to fight his way up to where he hoped he would find either John Nicolay or John Hay. The hallway was full of people waiting to try and speak to President Lincoln. Lincoln's penchant for understanding was already well known. Many of those people were there to take advantage of that and try and get permission for their soldier sons to come home and help with the family farms or to get a pass to see their wounded sons in the South.

Martin finally saw Nicolay talking to three people at once and waved at him. They had met, and Nicolay knew who Martin worked for. He waved again and waved the envelope, and Nicolay slowly extricated himself from the three people and came over to Martin. He passed the envelope to the presidential secretary, who looked at the envelope addressed to the president and labeled *urgent*!

"He is in with Welles and Stanton about the Mississippi River problem. I will go in and show this to him," Nicolay said.

He squeezed his way through the ten to fifteen people waiting in the narrow hallway and ignored the questions people asked as he went to the door to the president's office and knocked twice. That was the code that it was either him or John Hay, and it was important.

The first secretary to the president opened the door and quietly walked in.

Secretary Welles said, "Hello, Nicolay. How are you?"

"I am well, sir. Thank you for asking."

As per usual, the secretary of war ignored him and kept staring at the map and his notes while muttering to himself.

The president had his back to him and waved Nicolay to come over. Without lifting his head, Lincoln said, "What is it, son?"

Keeping his voice down, Nicolay said, "Mr. President, I have a message from Mr. Blair marked urgent and for your eyes only."

The president lifted his head and stared at Nicolay and the envelope in his hand. Nicolay went on, "He instructed his man to wait for a response, sir."

The president stood up straight and put his hand out for Nicolay to hand him the envelope. Staring at it, the president said, "It is unlike Blair to do this. I should read it now. Gentlemen, I am just going to sit down and read this note from my friend Blair. Keep working on our problem."

***

Thirty minutes later, an envelope from Francis Blair was slipped under the door of Room 206 at the Willard Hotel. The note read:

Dear Mr. Diamond,

Please be outside the hotel at 3:00 this afternoon. Martin Duffy will be there to ride you over to the White House for a meeting with the president. I will meet you there.

Francis P. Blair

Gene yelled out a quiet yahoo, and Jackson fist-bumped Steven. All Paul said was, "Mr. Butler, get ready to meet Abraham Lincoln."

Paul would comment later that the Lincoln White House reminded him of a Marx Brothers movie.

***

The president slowly walked to his favorite comfortable chair, the one Mrs. Lincoln had bought for him and said, "Now let's see what is so important to Mr. Blair." He told Nicolay to wait while he read the note.

Dear Mr. President,

I believe you know me well enough to understand that I do not overreact to information I receive that I do not think is important. I do not like to bother you with minor issues. It is important that I see you as soon as possible regarding a matter of utmost urgency. I just concluded a meeting with a gentleman named Paul Diamond who has come a long way to deliver information that can be invaluable to the success of our armies in the field. I would like him and his associate to join Frank and myself when we see you. There is much to tell you, but that will keep until we meet.

I eagerly await your response, and I am available at any time you can see us. I have instructed my man Martin to wait for your response.

I remain, your most humble servant,
Francis P. Blair

Lincoln took off his reading glasses, brought his legs down from the chair and closed his eyes for a moment. "Mr. Nicolay, what time is it?"

"It is almost one o'clock, sir."

"What business do we have next?"

"You wanted to go with Secretary Stanton to the telegraph office to check on messages from Generals Grant and Sherman."

"I do not want to miss that. Tell Blair's man to have them here in my office at 3:30 this afternoon, and we can see what is so important. He rarely sends me an urgent message. Go, John."

"Now Stanton, I think we should see what our generals have to say from Mississippi. I think Admiral Porter will be sending a report too. We must find a way to break through down there and get to Vicksburg and open that darn river. I feel like having a little something to eat, and then we can walk over to the telegraph office."

Stanton, of course, had no interest in waiting an extra minute and stormed out, telling the president he would meet him there. The president smiled benevolently at Stanton, while Secretary Welles waited for the president to eat his hard-boiled egg and apple. Then they walked over together, accompanied by Ward Lamon, the president's perpetual companion and self-styled bodyguard.

The president never saw the need for that kind of protection. He may have been the only person in Washington who did not think he needed it.

It was a short walk over to the telegraph office, and when he and Welles arrived, Stanton was already reviewing the reports from Grant, Sherman, and Porter. These three worked very well together, and Grant was the one who Sherman truly respected more than any other army commander. He and Grant led the armies of the west, and they were a different breed than the Army of the Potomac. They were rougher and looked down on their eastern counterparts.

CHAPTER 9

"So, Stanton, what is the news of the day?" Lincoln asked.

The secretary grumbled, "No real change. Grant's idea is not going to work. He is going to have to circle around Vicksburg and come at the city from the west. Sherman is still locked up by Pemberton's men shooting down at him from the heights. The Rebels have dug caves in the hill, and Sherman had a bloody mess there the other day. I have tried to explain this, but they just don't listen."

The president smiled and said, "Do you think it has anything to do with how you say it to them? That reminds me of a story about two farmers who were always arguing about this fence—"

"No more of your damn stories," Stanton said loudly. "I have work to do here. Welles, what about Porter?"

Nemo, as the president liked to call him, said, "The same. He is stuck about eight miles north of Vicksburg. He can't dislodge these big guns Pemberton has pointed straight down on his ships. Everything is tied together. We need a lucky break for all this."

It was now half past two, and the president wanted to review some things with John Hay on suggested executions of deserters and soldiers who fell asleep on guard duty. Most of them were young boys who were just too dang tired to stay awake. He pardoned as many as he could get away with.

"Ward, let's go back to the White House, I have to sit with Hay. Boys, I will see you later. Stanton, I may need you. Something has come up." Lincoln relied on his intuition, and there was something in his head about this Blair meeting. But he pushed it away with a wave of his hand, as he was prone to do. "Ward," he said, "let's head back."

They started walking. As always, there were well-wishers who said hello, and he always tipped his hat in response. The office seekers he ignored. Those he had learned to spot two blocks away. They made their way past the guards at the front door, who saluted. He tipped his hat because he always felt strange saluting back. These were men who were ready to give their lives for their country while all he did was sit in his office and deal with Congress. On the other hand, he thought, that alone should allow him to salute. He thought, *Dang.* He forgot that Sumner and Stevens might come by after joint meetings at the Capital. He would have to see them for a little while.

The White House

The president began to walk up the steps past the public, apologizing as he took the steps two at a time. Waiting for him were two of his "favorite" Radical Republicans, Senator Charles Sumner and Congressman Thaddeus Stevens. In the first six months of his administration, Lincoln quickly came to strongly believe that the key was maintaining the loyalty of the border states. If Kentucky, Maryland, Delaware, and Missouri seceded, the "water was out of the tub," as he was fond of saying. Sumner, Stevens, and the core group of radicals did not have that concern. Their interests were solely about abolishing slavery, the conduct of the war, and Mrs. Lincoln's spending; and that was an entire story on its own.

CHAPTER 10

The Willard Hotel

Paul took a black vest and pants, along with a white shirt that buttoned at the collar. It was too hot to wear his coat, but he did take his hat. Steven was so nervous that Gene had to help him button his pants and shirt. Gene grabbed him by the shoulders, looked him in the eye, and said, "You are going to meet Abraham Lincoln. Be the good man we know you are, brother."

Steven whispered a thank you to both of his friends.

Diamond said, "You two better wait up here. There is no cause for anyone seeing you in and out of the room. And now we better move, Steven."

They slipped out of the room and headed down the stairway slowly. Suddenly, Paul felt a wave of anxiety mixed with excitement. He could not believe what was about to happen. He wondered what Jim Conklin was thinking at that very moment.

***

Sumner and Stevens had similar traits but were different in certain important areas. Sumner was a great orator and that had gotten him in trouble, and almost killed. In 1856, he gave a speech on the Senate floor that he called "The Crime against Kansas." Those in Congress spoke differently then. Very often, speeches by both parties were vindictive, rude, nasty, and cruel. One of the most popular adjectives used against someone was to call the person "an evil apostate." In that speech, Senator Sumner had called Senator Andrew Butler of South Carolina a "pimp for slavery." Butler's cousin, Congressman Francis Brooks of South Carolina, was told what Sumner said and immediately marched to the floor of the Senate and proceeded to beat Sumner over the head with his cane, turning the Massachusetts Senator into a bloody mess and rendering him unconscious. Several Republican members rushed to Sumner's aid but were prevented from reaching him by Southern Democratic members. Sumner was in the hospital for weeks but was still reelected by Massachusetts, even though he was not well enough to return to the Senate for another year. The attack caused an uproar on both sides of the aisle and, if anything, increased the acerbic level of the rhetoric between the sections.

Sumner was a tall man, slightly taller than the President and presented himself very well. He was very educated and studied in Europe but never changed his political views and was constantly in the president's ear about slavery.

If anything, Thaddeus Stevens was even more vitriolic than his friend Sumner. If it were up to him, every Southern plantation would be burned to the ground and the land given to slaves to farm and the government of each of the seceded states driven from the Union. They would be made to pay for their crimes against man. He was unyielding and was sure he had the moral high ground.

Neither Sumner nor Stevens had to worry about the sensitive political questions. They both were in favor of the Emancipation Proclamation the president signed on New Year's Day in 1863 but still criticized him for not going far enough. The President issued it under the War Powers clause of the Constitution and was never convinced it would not be struck down by the Supreme Court. But the President had to have been aware of the speech made by John Quincy Adams in May 1836. In it, he proclaimed that, in the event of a civil war, the Constitution allowed for the emancipation of slaves as a military necessity.

Lincoln stopped short of abolishing slavery completely because he believed that could only be accomplished by an amendment to the Constitution. The Radicals believed that the states that left the Union were no longer under the authority of the Constitution, while others believed that the Union was "unbreakable," and regardless of what those states believed and declared, they would be under the nation's laws.

"Hello, my friends. I am sorry to keep you waiting. I was at the telegraph office waiting for some news."

Stevens interrupted the President, which he had no difficulty doing. "Is there anything new from Vicksburg?"

"Not really," answered the president with a note of sadness in his voice. He thought better of saying anything about the meeting with Blair, but he knew Sumner and Stevens were not Blair supporters. Blair was much too conservative for their tastes. Lincoln knew Blair was due in a few minutes. He had to cut this conversation short, so he improvised. "Congressman, I think I will have something to tell you in a few days. But don't ask me anything about it. I promise to tell you two first."

Stevens said, "Don't fool with me, Lincoln. I will hold you to it."

Sumner smiled and said, "Thank you, Mr. President."

They finally left, and the President laughed and took a deep breath in front of John Hay, who said, "Robert just got in and wants to say hello."

"Oh, of course, send him in before Blair arrives."

John opened the door and pulled Robert Lincoln in.

His father shook his hand and said, "Bob, it is so good to see you."

"Thank you, Father."

"I see you have added a little growth on your upper lip."

Bob answered, "I am trying anyway."

The president said to Robert, "I received a note from Mr. Blair asking to see me about a very serious secret matter. He is due here any minute. Can we talk more afterward?"

"I should have remembered. After all, you are the President of the United States. I will go find Mother."

"Thank you, Bob. And I am sorry."

As the president finished talking to his son, there was a double knock on the door and Nicolay peeked in and said the Blair party was there.

"How many are there?" the president asked.

"Four, sir."

"All right, bring them in. And, Johnnie"—he called Hay Johnnie to separate him from Nicolay. "Please bring those chairs over from the back."

Nicolay kept the door open as Mr. Blair walked in, followed by his son Frank and then Paul Diamond, who took his hat off. Steven Butler followed.

"Blair, my friend, it is good to see you. And you, Congressman. Who do we have here? I can see there is a tall man." He smiled. He walked over to shake Paul's hand and then put both hands on Steven's as Blair made the introductions.

Steven had a smile on his face as wide as the Potomac, and Diamond looked stunned that he was in the presence of the man he thought higher of than any other.

The elder Blair began to speak, but the president interrupted him and said, "We have to have a measurement first. Mr. Diamond, come over and turn around, and Frank can do the measuring."

Paul turned around to put his back to the president, who he did the same, while Congressman Blair put his hand on Paul's head and held his fingers about an inch apart.

"Dang," said the president, "I lost," and laughed. "Now you all pull up a chair and tell me what this mystery is all about and why it is so important."

Blair looked at Diamond, who nodded at him to start the conversation. As was his custom, the president slung one of his legs over the arm of the chair, exposing half of his lower leg because his pants were so short.

"Mr. President, yesterday, a man who works for Mr. Diamond delivered a note requesting an interview for this morning. I was intrigued, so I agreed. This morning at ten o'clock he appeared with his associate, Mr. Butler, who is a free man, by the way."

Lincoln kept his eyes on Blair but nodded his head when heard the words "free man."

As Blair continued Paul's mind began to wander to his own history. He grew up in the Bronx, a borough of New York City. His family lived in a middle-income housing project, and it was customary for many families to take short summer trips in the oppressive heat in August. Families rented bungalows or cabins; they visited state parks or motels with swimming pools, anything to get away from the summer heat of the city.

This one summer, Paul's family went to Pennsylvania and visited Gettysburg. They spent the day on the battlefield and ended up in the center of town and visited the Wills House, where the president slept the night before he gave his address to commemorate the dedication of the cemetery. That day, in Paul's time, was forty years ago. He'd been walking around the ground floor and had turned a corner to find a single brown wooden chair that had a sign over it that said: "Abraham Lincoln sat in this chair during his visit in October 1863."

The young Paul had frozen. His mother was right behind him and said, "Why don't you sit in the chair?"

Paul said, "I shouldn't. He sat in it."

His mom smiled and answered, "I don't think he would mind."

So he had. After all these years had passed, he could still feel his hands gripping the arms and his bottom on the wooden seat. Here Paul was, sitting three feet away from the man he had grown up idolizing— the man he'd studied for almost thirty years. It was unfathomable and overwhelming. He knew what he was going to say. Paul just had to hold himself together.

Blair reviewed what Diamond had said about the potential importance of the information and mentioned the pictures that Diamond had just taken out of his saddlebag.

Paul said, "Mr. President, forgive me if I appear nervous—the reasons for which will become clear in a few minutes. This first picture was taken at Antietam, after the battle, by General Sedgwick's field photographer."

He passed the photograph to the president, who stared at it for a good thirty seconds and then said, "This is some sort of weapon!"

"Yes, sir," Paul answered. "But it was not invented until the late 1940s."

"What are you saying, Mr. Diamond? That a gun invented eighty-five years from today ended up on a battlefield in our civil war?"

"That is not all, Mr. President. We have recently found photographic evidence of four additional weapons of the same kind. The pictures were in long-forgotten files of General Sedgwick's corps. This weapon was found next to the body of a Rebel officer. It appears not to have been fired. For that, we should all be grateful.

"There is more I must show and tell you. With all due respect, I must ask that the Blair's give us some privacy." Diamond also asked that Mr. Hay join the meeting. "It would not be fair for Mr. Nicolay to hear this alone."

The president stood to shake hands with Frank and Francis Blair and spoke quietly to the elder Blair. "Is this real?"

"Mr. President, I have seen and done a lot in my life; you know this. But what you are about to hear I believe without hesitation."

CHAPTER 11

The Blairs stepped out, and John Hay came in with a quizzical look on his face. Lincoln made introductions and showed him the Sedgwick photograph and told him that the weapon was sent from the future.

"How is this possible?" Hay exclaimed, looking at his comrade Nicolay, who was in a state of shock.

Now Paul brought out the color photo. Lincoln, Nicolay, and Hay huddled around the picture and murmured. "This is in color." "When was it taken?" "Where is it from?" "There are no color pictures!"

"Gentlemen," Paul said, "this picture was taken last week in the 21st century in Washington, DC. The weapon is called a Browning automatic rifle. It has an attachment that will allow it to shoot mortar shells. One of these guns is already here, in a very safe place, so we may show the president how it works and what it would do to Rebel soldiers."

With a tone of incredulity, John Nicolay said, "This weapon is here now?"

Paul said, "Please allow me to tell you my story. I was born on June 28, 1975, and was raised in the Bronx, New York. I studied American history and received my master's degree and doctorate in that subject. My doctoral dissertation was on the period of 1856 to 1861 just past the surrender of Fort Sumter."

"Ouch," interrupted the president.

"I taught for a few years and was recruited by the Smithsonian Institute, where I stayed for seven years. Then I received a visit from a good friend, who was chosen to start a new program at a government facility that involved the exploration of outer space but was really a secret program that was working on the science of the possibility of time travel. All of this is top secret and, forgive me, is way beyond the understanding of this time. But we partnered with four different nations for financial and research reasons. The costs were enormous and the risks indescribable. In the last eleven years, I have made four jumps back in time. This one will be my last, due to my age and several health problems I suffered on my last trip.

"By the way, during my last jump, I walked past a much younger Mr. Blair on Pennsylvania Avenue while he was walking to the White House.

"I have been in conversations with many learned people in my time and the question periodically comes up as to who we would want to talk with on our trips back in time. For me there is only one person, and I am sitting three feet away from him right now. When I was given this opportunity, I was checked, tested, prodded, examined and tested by a staff of twenty-first-century doctors. I would have done anything to make this trip. If for any reason, I do not survive the return, then it will still be worth it."

The president reached over and patted him on the knee and said, "You are a good man, Paul, and I believe you."

"Sir," Paul continued, "there is one more piece of evidence to show you." He took out *The Washington Post* and showed him the front page, which showed the day and date. "You really should not read any of this, but I wanted to bring it along to ease any concerns about our story." He went on to talk about Steven's role in all this as a black man and one of the three men who'd accompanied Paul. "They have all worked together before and are officers in different services. Each has served with distinction. But Steven has his own reasons for joining this mission and has already been exposed to the racist views of this time.

"We work for the government of the United States of America and are prepared to have thirty of these weapons transmitted to places where there will be two major battles in the next month. It is obviously too late to help at Chancellorsville. But it can help at Vicksburg and at a small town in Pennsylvania called Gettysburg. My three men will help train a select group of your soldiers in learning how to shoot and clean these weapons. I have used this analogy before. The results will be like wheat cut down by a thresher. Since we have an idea as to what will happen at Gettysburg, we can deploy the weapons at both ends of General Lee's movement after the battle and put him in a box, forcing surrender or loss of untold thousands of his men.

"One last thing that is most important. To repeat what I have just told you would be considered an act of treason."

The president stood and walked to his desk with his hands behind his back. He looked out the window and then dropped his head to his chest. Nicolay and Hay were simply struck dumb with this information.

"You say that one of these weapons is in Washington City now?" asked the president.

"Yes, sir," answered Steven.

The president asked how long it would take to get ready for him to see it tested.

Steven answered, "I have to get Jackson and Gene. And we have to have clearance at the Naval Yard and a very private area there to set it up."

Lincoln told Hay to go over to the Navy Yard and to talk to Commander Montgomery and have him be ready in thirty minutes.

"How is that, Paul?" he said with a smile, adding that he was having a hard time understanding all this, but the stakes were so high and so many boys had been killed in this nightmare that he would do anything he could to save some. He then asked what Paul's government knew about their adversaries.

"I can only tell you certain things. But their roots started with your Clement Vallandigham and the Knights of the Golden Circle. They went underground, and every so often, we find a few hints that they are still around. More than that, I should not tell you."

The president understood. He knew it would not help him to know too much. He called out for Ward Lamon, and they went down the stairs to get the president's carriage for the ride to the naval yard.

A second carriage driving Barlow and Shanahan followed.

"Thank you, James," said the president as an orderly opened the carriage door.

"You're welcome, Mr. President," James replied.

Lincoln had to twist his long angular body into the back seat.

After Paul had squeezed in next to him, Lincoln said, "Good afternoon, Mr. Wilson. How are you today?"

The driver laughed and said, "I still be above ground, Mr. President."

Mr. Lincoln laughed in response and patted the driver on his back.

Paul was touched that the president always had a kind word for everyone who worked for him and seemed to genuinely care about each of them.

The carriage slowly pulled away from the White House and headed toward the naval yard. The ride would take ten minutes, and in between intermittent waves to people in the streets, the president had time to ask Paul some of his own questions. As he stared out at the people, they passed he said to Paul, "You have really sent my mind into a tumble, Mr. Diamond. It is hard for me to think of all this as real. It is real, isn't it?"

"Yes, sir. I am sorry to say it is very real. I am still getting used to the idea that I am talking to you." He smiled.

"Am I what you expected?" the president asked with a laugh.

Paul answered, "I am a historian, so I look at things and people almost like a doctor looks at a patient. But so far as you are concerned, I am glad to say, you are very much what I expected."

"You have come at an opportune time. After the disaster at Chancellorsville, the country is in an uproar—18,000 more casualties." The president just shook his head. He went on to say that, if Hooker had not announced that his plan would destroy the Rebel army, it might not be so bad. He muttered, "But now I must replace him after all the others. He is just not fit to be commander of the Army of the Potomac."

"What do you think of General Hooker, Mr. President?"

Lincoln thought for a moment and said, "He proclaimed he had a grand plan to defeat Lee and end the war. He is arrogant. I had no one else to put there, so I was stuck in a corner with someone who should have kept his mouth shut and given us victories without telling the country about it before it happens. I gave McClellan enough rope to hang himself, and he did. General Lee is like a cunning wizard, working magic with his limited army and moving around like a ghost. I find that my own actions are guided by events I cannot control. Like McClellan, Hooker is a good organizer, but something seems to happen to him in the face of the enemy. He missed one thing at Chancellorsville, and it nearly ruined us. His staff said he hit his head, and it almost knocked him out. But that does not excuse leaving one end of our line unprotected.

"McClellan is getting ready to run against me, and Chase plots against me from inside my own cabinet. I may be a country boy from the sticks, but my ears still work."

Paul answered, "Mr. President, what you are about to see might ease your concerns."

They pulled past the guards of the navy yard as the president waved. When the carriage stopped, a young soldier ran over to open the side door.

The president got out and said, "Thank you, son."

Paul opened his own door and squeezed out.

The height of the two men walking together was quite a sight. Jackson Barlow and Gene Shanahan left the second carriage, and Paul introduced them to the president. They shook hands with him and were obviously affected.

Steven had been in the carriage with them and his training had taken over. He'd continually watched the streets during the ride over. Only once the president and Paul were safely inside the door did Steven leave the carriage and shake Mr. Wilson's hand.

President Lincoln said to Jackson and Gene, "I want to thank you both for coming and trying to give us some help. Lord knows we can use some. I hope we can have the chance to talk sometime while you are here."

Gene said, "It is our honor, Mr. President. Let me show you the way to the room we have set up for the demonstration."

They followed Commander Montgomery through a maze of rooms filled with muskets and mortar shells to one in the rear of the one-story building. The door was padlocked, and the commander opened the door.

Inside were mattresses were hastily nailed to the four walls and ceiling, and just inside the doorway were the pieces of the weapon to be assembled.

Suddenly, they heard a furious knocking at the door, and they heard Secretary Stanton yelling to be let in. "What is going on in here?"

He had been told by a messenger to meet the president at the naval yard but not what the meeting was about. It was not unusual for Lincoln to have Stanton observe trials of new weapons, most of which never worked or were not practical. So, he had no idea what he was there for.

The first thing he shouted was, "Who are these people? They do not belong here!"

The president interrupted him. "Now, Stanton, calm down. They are with me and are going to demonstrate something they say can help us win the war. I hope they are right. And I will explain everything to you when we are alone."

CHAPTER 12

P aul nodded at Steven and Gene, who in less than a minute, assembled the automatic rifle and placed the barrel on the tripod. Steven lay down on the ground and winked at Gene, who fitted the clip with forty rounds and connected it to the barrel. Steven flicked up the sight piece and nodded at Paul.

Jackson cautioned the group of observers, "Gentlemen, I would strongly suggest that you move behind Steven." He placed himself directly in front of the president, just in case an errant shell bounced off any of the mattresses. The far wall was a good fifty feet away.

Steven said, "This may be a little loud. Here we go."

Jackson stood in front of the president and Secretary Stanton, and Gene knelt beside Steven. Steven pointed the rifle at the far wall and pressed the trigger.

The sound of the firing had everyone covering their ears before they realized it was over. Steven had aimed to create an outline of a square on the mattress on the far wall.

Paul turned to Gene and asked, "How many bullets?"

"Forty, sir."

Then he turned to Jackson and asked, "How long?"

"Twelve seconds, sir."

Paul responded, "I am not very good at mathematics, but you can figure it out."

People who knew Stanton for years would never recall him unable to speak.

The president took Paul's hand in his, shook it, and simply said, "Thank you, Mr. Diamond."

He did say to all in the room, "What you have seen is a state secret. Anyone discussing it is subject to being charged with an act of treason. Now I would like to be alone with Secretary Stanton."

CHAPTER 13

Ten minutes later, a white-faced Stanton came out of the room and shook hands with the visitors, got in his carriage, and went to find Secretary of State Seward and bring him to the White House, along with Gideon Welles and General Halleck. There were plans to make, and quickly.

As the viewers of the demonstration went riding around Washington in their carriages, General Robert E Lee was preparing to move his Rebel army of 70,000 troops toward Pennsylvania from Maryland, and Hooker was frantically trying to cut him off and stay between Lee and Washington City.

After their victory at Chancellorsville, Lee realized it had come at a terrible cost. Although the Union Army had lost 18,000 men, Lee had lost over 17,000; he could ill afford to maintain that ratio indefinitely. The North had a substantial advantage in men and supplies, one that would only get bigger as the war continued at this pace.

There were two other equally important points. The great Rebel General Stonewall Jackson was dead. An infection from his amputated right arm had quickly spread and taken his life. Lee was crushed by his loss. He still had Longstreet, but Jackson would throw caution to the wind and attack against insurmountable odds if there was a chance to throw the

Union Army back. A supremely religious man, he believed that God was on the side of the South and would have no compunction against ordering his troops to kill any Federal soldier standing. That was a contradiction, but Jackson believed that anything done in the name of God was excusable. Now, he was forever gone. Longstreet was a clever aggressive leader but only when he had the tactical advantage; he preferred to counterattack from a defensive position. He was loyal and acted as a counterweight to Lee when his "blood was up." Their differences in philosophy of warfare and as men would be seen soon enough.

Lee had important decisions to make, with so many of the important battles being fought in Virginia the state had become a wasteland. Stripped of foodstuffs, supplies, and men, he saw no way to successfully continue the war, other than to take the battle to the North. The state of Pennsylvania was filled with farms and food that the South desperately needed.

Lee's first foray into the North had been unsuccessful due to tactical mistakes and a lost copy of orders that was recovered by two Northern soldiers, who did not fully appreciate what they had found at Antietam. They turned their find into their superiors, and the papers slowly went up the chain of command to General McClellan, who in his infinite wisdom, decided to wait overnight rather than attack immediately. This ill-fated decision gave Lee the time to send for General A.P. Hill's Corp, who really did arrive in the nick of time.

If this new invasion was handled properly, Lee would get the food and supplies he needed. And, he hoped, by making a successful attack in the North, he would bring the war to these people, who would feel the horror of what the South had felt in the last two years. Lee was a soldier. He hated the idea of senseless death but would do his duty regardless of the cost. That was another reason he and Jackson were so well suited to each other.

The commander needed the approval of President Davis, Secretary of War Seddons, and the rest of the Confederate Cabinet, as well as the detachment of North Carolinians, to be released from the defense of Richmond. They were in conditions not that different from the North and Washington City. General Hooker wanted to take his army and get behind Lee and race to Richmond.

President Lincoln was beginning to fully understand that, if his army took Richmond without beating Lee, it was senseless. To defeat the

Confederacy, Lincoln knew, Lee had to be beaten. He also knew Hooker was not happy and did not realize how close he was to being replaced. Hooker had been told by the president, in no uncertain terms, to keep his army between Lee and Washington and forget about making a mad dash to Richmond.

In his carriage with Paul Diamond and Steven Butler, the president was energized and happy with what he had just witnessed. He was amazed at the power and accuracy of the weapon and began to ask Butler questions as to how long it would fire for and the distance it would shoot.

Then he turned to Diamond and said, "Do you know Hooker sent me a letter and said we needed a dictator?"

Diamond finished the story for him, "And you said, you worry about the victories, and I will worry about the dictatorship!"

Lincoln whooped out a laugh and slapped his knee and said, "You know what I am going to say before I say it!"

Both the president and Paul laughed, but Paul's smile vanished as he said, "There are some other things we should discuss. A few I purposely did not mention."

Lincoln's mood quickly changed, and he exclaimed, "What is wrong?"

CHAPTER 14

"It is not a matter of anything being wrong. One is a practical matter."
Paul quickly explained the problem of having topographical maps that were accurate. Both sides had troubles with having access to information on a specific basis that showed back roads where troops could move without detection. He then revealed to the President that he'd brought with him exactly the kinds of maps the northern armies would need to make plans for the two key upcoming battles. They would also help for placing the weapons that would be coming to Vicksburg and Gettysburg in the next week.

"Mr. President, this time line has changed by our being here and your seeing the weapon perform. But once we look at these maps, the balance of power will change. You will have an unprecedented advantage. Everything from this point changes, both good and bad."

"Paul, is there something that you are not telling me that you want to tell me?"

"Yes," Paul said, "but I should not, as much as I want to. It is very personal, and my affection for you may cloud my judgment. We will be active in helping you plan, and I will give you some suggestions as to personnel and movements. But right now, I will tell you that everything will turn at Vicksburg and Gettysburg. If I were you, I would send for Meade, Sherman, and Grant."

The president asked, "Why Meade?"

Diamond responded, "Because by now, you may have already spoken with General Reynolds, and possibly others, about replacing Hooker."

The President sadly nodded his head yes.

"Meade will be defending his home state of Pennsylvania and will be a fine leader of the Army of the Potomac if he has an aggressive general directing him. That will be Grant. Grant will still be able to help Sherman in Vicksburg. And he is a far more stable leader than he was two years ago. You will learn in time that is true. If you place Grant slightly above Meade and allow him the discretion, Meade will be fine leading the army with Grant looking over his shoulder and with John Rawlins as his chief of staff watching his friend Grant. The drinking problem should not be an issue, Mr. President, and this conversation never took place."

Lincoln said to the driver of the carriage, "Mr. Wilson, would you mind pulling off to the side? I want to send a messenger to Secretary Stanton."

He scribbled a note on a piece of paper with the pencil he always carried and called for one of his messengers, who was always nearby. He said quietly, "Find Secretary Stanton and give him this. It is most important."

The messenger folded the message three times and immediately rode off as fast as he could toward the War Department office.

"That will save us a little time," said the president. Then called for another messenger, to whom he said, "Find General Halleck and have him report to me in my office. Halleck has been a disappointment to me, but he does have an eye for logistics and strategy. We must tell him about all this immediately."

By the time they returned to the White House, certain things had been done. Stanton had found Seward, Secretary of the Navy Gideon Welles, General Halleck, Treasury Secretary, Salmon P Chase, and Attorney General Edward Bates. Lincoln did not trust Chase, and this was not in the treasury secretary's purview. But he wanted Chase where he could see him whenever he could, and this would be as important a meeting as the administration had ever had. In addition, if Chase were there, he could not deny being told about either the new weapon or anything else that came up in this meeting.

When the carriage pulled up in front of the White House there were the customary group of office seekers and people wanting things from the president. Shanahan and Barlow were already there. They tried to keep some of the people away from the president.

Thomas Wilson opened the carriage door for the president.

"Thank you, Thomas," the president said. My, we are busy today."

Wilson smiled and said, "Yes, sir."

The president could not help his nature and greeted as many people as possible. He was grateful for Butler joining his two friends in clearing a path to make it easier for him to get to the steps that led to the front door, where Mr. Wilson moved ahead and was waiting to open the door with a smile.

"Thank you, sir," the president responded.

Paul Diamond had been behind him the entire way, gently guiding him inside.

Lincoln whispered to Shanahan, "Get me to my office."

Gene responded, "Yes, sir. Let's clear the road, boys."

They almost carried him through the people waiting for him on the narrow staircase. Nicolay and Hay were waiting and then led him into his office and closed the door behind him. Waiting inside were Seward, Stanton, Bates, Welles, Chase, Halleck, and Quartermaster General Montgomery Meigs, who would prove invaluable to the Army of the Potomac in the next month. They all stood when the president and Paul walked in.

Paul walked to the back of the room and stood by an empty chair.

The President took off his long overcoat, sat down in his chair and began to brief the group. "Gentlemen, thank you for coming so quickly. There have been developments over the last day that require our immediate attention."

He was about to say something when Secretary Chase interrupted, "Excuse me, Mr. President, but who is this man?" Chase was looking at Paul. The team members waited outside the President's office.

The president, not surprised that it was Chase who interrupted him answered, "I was about to introduce Mr. Paul Diamond, who happens to be the reason for this meeting. What I am about to tell you is a state secret. If any of you repeat what I am about to say, I will consider it an act of treason, and you will be fully punished to the fullest extent of the law. Revealing this information would most certainly adversely affect our armies in the field. So we understand each other, I would like each of you to say, 'I understand.' And you will each sign a statement confirming your understanding. Mr. Nicolay and Mr. Hay will distribute the statements in the next few minutes."

After each man in the room said he understood the president's request, he directed Nicolay to bring in Francis and Frank Blair.

The President began to explain their presence by saying he had received an urgent note from Francis Blair after he had met with Paul Diamond and Steven Butler, one of Paul's associates. He asked the Senior Blair to summarize that meeting. Frank chimed in with his own thoughts, which jived with those of his father.

Now the bombshell came. The president went on to explain that Paul Diamond claimed he was from the future and, along with three comrades, had traveled back in time with a weapon they were willing to give the Union, along with thirty others—weapons that could help the Union Army defeat the rebels in as little as two months.

President Lincoln grinned at the dead silence in the room and commented that he'd had the same initial reaction that the cabinet members who had no idea of any of this were now having.

"Did they bring Jesus with them too?" Secretary of State Seward asked.

Paul could not help but laugh, along with others in the room.

Lincoln excused the Blairs from the meeting. After they left, he explained they had just come from a demonstration of the ferocity and accuracy of the weapon. He proceeded to say that the future United States government was willing to send the other weapons within twenty-four hours. It seemed there was a way for Paul to communicate by some sort of magnetic energy to the future. The communication was very basic but enough to tell those on the other end to go ahead and send the weapons to the Naval Yard or to a certain place they had worked out before Diamond's arrival.

Secretary Chase, of course, asked how the president knew this was all true.

Lincoln stood and turned to the bay window behind his desk, his hands behind his back. He looked to be thinking. He slowly turned around and stared at Chase, saying in a very cold voice, "Because, my dear Mr. Chase, we have just lost 18,000 men and boys at Chancellorsville, partly because of the inferior performance of our generals. And I am prepared to do almost anything to stop this madness."

"In addition, we have reason to believe that the Rebels received a weapon." He explained that a photographer attached to General Sedgwick had taken a picture of an odd-looking handgun lying next to a dead Confederate officer the year before at the Antietam battlefield. It had been missed and was sitting in the files of General John Sedgewick's corps. The photograph had been found in the future and had set off all kinds of alarms in Washington. "Diamond is a specialist in Civil War history and was asked to lead this mission," he explained, adding. "And it will be his last. It would seem time travel has a cumulative negative impact on the human body, and without certain medication he brought with him, he would not survive the trip back."

Continuing to stare at Secretary Chase, he asked, "Is that satisfactory Mr. Secretary?"

Chase, almost meekly, said, "Yes, sir."

Almost every official in the room knew that, if any information leaked from this meeting, it would come from Chase. The president's idea of a signed statement was a brilliant idea.

Lincoln moved to the large square table in the center of his office that was filled with maps. He had Halleck pull out the map showing Maryland and Pennsylvania and then said, "We know that Lee is on the move to Maryland. Then he will go to Pennsylvania, if he is not there already. The fact that we do not know exactly where he is is most disturbing and does not speak well of our cavalry." He went on to explain that some of the maps might be inaccurate.

To that, Halleck said, "Mr. President, I have been told that our maps are very precise."

The president asked Paul to come to the table with the maps he had brought with him and lay them on the table next to Halleck's.

There were significant differences as to certain towns and roads in both Maryland and Pennsylvania.

Secretary Stanton immediately said, "How can this be Mr. Diamond?"

"Because, with all due respect, Mr. Secretary, in my time we have far more sophisticated equipment that allows the creating of maps to be a science, rather than, in many cases, guesswork."

Lee had already split his two corps into three and was sending them on different paths to Pennsylvania. The one "mistake" he made was to focus his attention on the state capital of Harrisburg, Pennsylvania. The Federals were moving toward Lee from the opposite direction. The Army of the Potomac had concealed the movement and had crossed the river. The troops were reaching Frederick, Maryland, and they were about to cross to Pennsylvania.

General Lee would belatedly recall Ewell and Jubal Early to head back toward Gettysburg. The Confederate Cavalry Commander Jeb Stuart had left his Army of Northern Virginia to find supplies and was no longer in contact with General Lee, leaving him with no way of knowing where the Federal main body was.

President Lincoln then said, "I have sent telegrams in the last hour asking for Generals Grant, Sherman, and Meade to come for new orders, as well as to be advised of these recent developments."

"What orders are you referring to, Mr. President?" asked Gideon Welles.

"An excellent question, Mr. Welles," the president responded. "But before I answer it, I would like to ask my friend Diamond to speak to us and explain, in words we can understand, the implications our actions may bring upon us or to events in the future."

CHAPTER 15

Paul stepped toward the map table and stopped so everyone in the room could clearly see him.

He began to speak. "Gentlemen, approximately forty-eight hours ago, I was in my bed in my apartment in Washington, DC, in the year 2022. I work for a department in the government of the United States. My specialty is nineteenth-century American history. Because of my background, I provide aid and assistance to, as well as actively participating in, a top secret program that studies time travel and has sent a number of teams of men back in time to certain 'hot spots' where we could, hopefully, be of assistance. We are now here in the year 1863.

"By 1900, there will be unthinkable advances in science, technology, and manufacturing. In fact, this period will be known as the Industrial Revolution. The advances of the hundred years after will dwarf what will take place in the next forty. But there is one thing that will continue to mystify all of you and all of those who follow—in one simple word, *time*.

"Yesterday is now the past, today is the present, and tomorrow is the future. But what I just said is now in the past, and tomorrow will become the present. For more than two thousand years, scientists and philosophers have tried to make sense of what time is. It has been uncontrollable and will continue to be for another 140 years. We have learned to measure time but not control it.

"Two months ago, in my time, a junior civil war historian was reviewing Civil War files and made a remarkable discovery. In one file of General Sedgwick's corps, he found a grainy picture of a dead Confederate officer. Next to the body was what looked to be a weapon. There is a copy of that photograph on the map table. Please examine it closely before I continue."

Paul stepped away from the group examining the picture and stood next to the president and John Nicolay.

Nicolay whispered to the President, "What do you think they will say?"

Lincoln smiled and said, "They will not care what might happen in another one hundred years, Nicolay. They want the war to be done and the soldiers from both sides to go back to their farms. Then they can pound their chests and say, 'Look what I did!'"

Diamond turned to Lincoln and asked, "What do you really think?"

The president stared at the group surrounding the map table and said quietly, "Paul, I fear for the implications of my actions and what they will lead to. But I have an enormous responsibility to the men who have died, on both sides, and their families. I have an even bigger responsibility to those who will die if the war continues. Seneca wrote something about this question. If I go ahead and approve the use of your weapons, we can save an unknown amount of lives. But what if that decision changes history and causes even more loss later? I am locked in a room without a door to get out of. To answer your question directly, I am sworn to do whatever is necessary to stop this river of blood and death."

Paul thought for a moment and then said, "I could not have said it better myself."

He returned to the table and took the picture from the hands of Salmon Chase. "Gentlemen," he said, "may I have your attention please? My government is prepared to supply you with several weapons from my time." He then took the color picture of the BAR rifle from his bag and gave that to Chase and the others who were not at the naval yard earlier.

Halleck was dumbstruck, and Chase said, "Oh my God, this is in color."

Chase went on to say, "How is this possible?"

The president was about to answer, but Paul put up a hand and said,

"Excuse me, Mr. President, allow me. Mr. Secretary, would you admit that you see me standing in front of you and I shook your hand a few minutes ago?"

Chase looked confused and turned around the room before answering, "Yes of course."

Paul responded by saying, "If this is true, then my presence here and what I am offering to the Union Army has already changed your history. If you had not signed the confidentially statement, you could leave this room and tell the next person you see that you met a man in the president's office who offered you weapons so far advanced you could win the war in two or three months. Don't you see? My being here has changed your time. And ultimately, it's changed your history! Would you agree with that, Mr. Secretary?"

"Yes, I suppose," Chase answered.

Diamond felt he could not relent and came back at Chase. "You are a strong abolitionist, Mr. Chase?"

"Very much so," he answered.

Diamond replied, "What if my being here with my weapons would allow all Negroes to be free within six months rather than going through two more years of fighting the Rebels and losing countless more good men? You see, everything is already changed. That is what I am asking that you understand and accept."

Mr. Stanton asked, "How will the weapons arrive?"

Paul went and sat in a chair across from Stanton and answered, "Half will be transported to a certain spot near the Union lines in Vicksburg. The other half will be delivered to the other battle field in Pennsylvania."

Chase interjected, "I apologize if I gave you a hard time, Mr. Diamond. All this is very difficult for me to understand, sir."

Diamond took a deep breath and answered, "I do not blame you. Others in your position would have responded the same way."

The president asked everyone other than Halleck, Seward, Meigs, and Stanton to leave the room and reminded them of the oath they had taken.

One by one, they all said, "Yes, Mr. President," and quietly left without another word.

Lincoln smiled and said, "Paul, you handled the Treasury Secretary very well."

Paul replied, "Mr. President, you must remember, I have been a serious student of this time in history." He laughed.

Seward was Lincoln's closest ally in the cabinet and had said very little in the meeting. Now he said, "This is the most outlandish story I have ever heard, but I believe it."

Stanton and Seward were not close and, in fact, were on different sides of many important issues. The Secretary of War said, "Seward, we have disagreed on many things, but I saw something at the Naval Yard this morning that was unbelievable. If these weapons can do what Mr. Diamond claims, we can see the end of this horrific war."

William Seward stared at his frequent opponent and silently nodded. Although he had not witnessed the demonstration, he'd heard enough from the ones who had to believe this could be the answer.

Before Meigs left the room, Lincoln took his arm and told him it would be extremely important for their men to be adequately supplied in both food and arms before the coming battles.

Meigs, who had lost his own son in the war, took one of the president's hands in his and squeezed it as he whispered, "You have my word, sir."

CHAPTER 16

T he guests left the room, leaving the President, Paul Diamond, John Nicolay, and John Hay alone. The president sat behind his desk and asked what everyone thought about the meeting.

Nicolay looked at Paul, who nodded. "They all certainly seemed in shock," Nicolay said. "But Chase remains as dangerous to the President as ever, or even more so with this information."

Hay agreed and commented that, once the cat got out of the bag, it would be hard to get it back in.

Paul stood silently until the president called on him next. "I am in an awkward position, sir. I know enough to make your hair catch fire, but I am prevented from telling you many things. I have already come close to telling you too much. I think these men don't really believe everything they were told. All they care about is doing whatever it takes to win the war, and I can't blame them for that. Even though some of them saw the demonstration of the gun, they saw what they wanted to see. They will agree to use it and will not care what the ultimate price may be sometime in the future."

The president turned and asked Diamond, "Do you know for a fact that there will be some sort of reaction in time to what changes we make?"

Paul tried to explain that he wished he could but there was so little data from prior events. The scientists he had met with in his time believed that the reaction of time to changes in the past might be related to the size and scope of the changes. He said there had been deviations, but they were not considered to be major. None compared to the level of change they were considering here. Paul added that he would not know until he returned to his time, or even after.

President Lincoln stood, clasped his hands behind his back, and stared out the window behind his desk.

He asked, "How long have you been studying my life, Paul?"

"More than twenty-five years, sir."

"Then you know about the good and the bad, including my bouts with the hypo."

Paul, knowing that *hypo* was the word of this time period that translated to depression in his, answered quietly, "Yes, Mr. President."

Lincoln quietly went on to explain the losses of his birth mother, Nancy Hanks Lincoln, when he was six years old, and his sister Sarah, with whom he was very close, when he was sixteen. He briefly mentioned a young woman named Ann, whom he'd cared for deeply but who was engaged to another man, who had left town. Lincoln explained that, because of his isolation growing up and his concentration on making a "name for himself," he found it difficult and uncomfortable to talk to women. He told Paul that he realized that, because of his height and appearance, there were many other young men who were far more attractive to the fairer sex. They also had more to offer. Ann died when he was about twenty-four, and he had no idea what could have happened between them if she had lived and been released from her engagement. Her death was a crushing blow. Combined with the deaths in his family earlier, the "hypo" came and took control of his mind and heart. Friends were so worried about him that they removed sharp objects from the house where he lived, for fear Lincoln would do something to hurt himself during an attack.

"Paul, the only person who knows all this is my old law partner in Springfield, Herndon, and not even he knows the whole story. My two young friends Nicolay and Hay are aware of much of this and they treat me with respect, and they do what they can to help. Even now as we sit and talk about my problem, they are here working but will never say a word about what I have told you."

While the president talked, Paul flashed back to his own father, who had suffered from depression before he died. Paul had tried to understand and help. But since he had escaped the malady, all he could do was offer comfort and his love.

Lincoln looked down at his desk and said, "I think I am telling you this because you know me so well—although it is hard for me to grasp why someone in the future would have studied my life in so much detail—and you will be leaving us soon enough." He smiled, with a hint of sadness on his face.

He understood that he was different than most men—from the way he looked and thought to how he made his decisions. He rarely talked about the sadness that would pass through him like the wind on the prairie and tried to shield those around him from it.

Even though one or both of his secretaries were always nearby, Lincoln knew Nicolay and Hay saw his episodes they never discussed the attacks of the hypo he suffered. Their devotion to the President would keep them from intruding on his thoughts of sadness and grief over the past. Nicolay and Hay never repeated anything they witnessed. They would only ask if he wanted company when they saw and felt the hypo taking hold of the president.

The president finally mentioned the loss of Eddie, his newborn, and the devastating death of his son Willie. His wife had taken Willie's passing very hard, and President Lincoln had thought of moving her to a mental sanitarium if she could not control her grief.

Added to all he felt was the weight he carried of the war. His orders sent hundreds of thousands of young boys and men to their deaths. He told John Hay that it all hurt his heart in ways he could not explain.

He quieted for a moment and then continued. "But, Paul, this weight I carry allows me, in ways I do not understand, to see people differently. And I have learned how to somehow deal with it."

Lincoln would spend time alone until the "hypo" passed or dig out his batch of funny stories when others were around. In fact, Hay asked him once about how he could tell his stories during the war amid all the horror the rebellion brought. The president simply responded that, if he thought too much about it all, it would tear him apart.

Lincoln admitted, "It affects my thoughts and every decision I make.

I am more sensitive to the soldiers and their needs because of it and less patient with my generals who have sent so many of them to their end because of their lack of feeling for their welfare. It is also why I make it a point to see wounded Rebel soldiers to pay them respect."

The president clasped his hands and looked down at them. He seemed lost in his thoughts. After a moment, he looked up at Paul and began to talk again. "I think I have always been an outsider to a certain extent, especially since I assumed this office. My cabinet is made up of experienced politicians. I see things in a different way than they do. There are times when I find it frustrating. Sometimes it angers me. I see things, and I cannot understand their reaction to it, Paul."

Lincoln asked, "Based upon your study of me, what do you imagine I am feeling now?"

Paul was stunned by all that the president had revealed to him. He was very touched that he felt comfortable enough to tell him about what was, obviously, a very personal subject. It was Paul's turn to stand and stare at the president. "It would have to be an educated guess, sir," he said. "But I think that, although you have real concern about the impact on the future, you feel you almost have no choice but to go ahead with using the weapons and try to end this war now."

The president slightly smiled and said, "You have learned well, Diamond, and I am glad you are here. There are very few people I can talk to like this, except for Seward and the boys. But there are limits with Nicolay and Hay." The two secretaries then quietly excused themselves and left the President and Paul alone.

Paul smiled and said, "With all due respect, sir, I think I have read all your jokes too."

That brought a broad smile to Lincoln's face. He laughed and slapped his knee.

A few minutes later, there were two knocks on the office door. "Speaking of the boys, that is one of them right now. Come in," he called out.

It was John Hay, who said, "General Meade has arrived in Washington, sir."

"Where is he now, John?"

"He is on his way to the White House from the cars."

The president thought for a moment and said, "When he gets here, have the kitchen put some lunch together for him and then send him here. I have a few decisions to make before I talk with him."

Hay replied, "Yes, sir," and excused himself.

Lincoln clasped his hands together and was lost in thought for about thirty seconds. He then spoke. "Paul, I wanted you to know what I told you about the hypo—"

Paul interrupted him, "Sir, that is between you and me. I will never speak to anyone about it."

The president wanly smiled and said, "No, it is all right. I cannot imagine what the future is like in your time. You are a historian and seem to be a darn good one. If you feel that it will be of help to write something—without including how you got this information—and it can help other people understand who I was, all I ask is that you do it with gentleness and compassion."

All Paul could respond was, "Thank you, Mr. President."

"Besides," Lincoln answered, "I will not be there to know what you will do." He laughed.

The president and Paul Diamond spent the next twenty minutes talking about the decisions open to him, the use of the weapons, and where best to use them. They also discussed the proposed new hierarchy of the command of the Army of the Potomac and the western armies currently under Grant's command. Every indication was that Lee was on his way to invade the North again. With Hooker still in command, he drew up very specific orders for Hooker to stay between Lee and Washington. After the debacle at Chancellorsville, President Lincoln had lost whatever remaining faith he'd had in General Hooker. He would be replaced; the question was, By whom?

Lincoln had gone through a series of commanders. All were disappointing. The Rebel armies had a clear advantage in their command structure, but some were beginning to fall. If Lincoln could structure new and better leadership, it could close the gap between them.

An ongoing problem was battle plans and command orders. This was especially noticeable at Chancellorsville. Corps and division commanders were running around like chickens with their heads cut off.

Lincoln believed General Meade would have added incentive in defending Pennsylvania, his home state. It should not make any difference what state it was, but the president was grasping at straws. Meade had a reputation for being grouchy and showing a lack of patience with the generals under his command. He also looked like a turtle, but Lincoln couldn't care less.

Lincoln had two other pieces of his plan. He would bring Grant in as lieutenant general as commander of all the Northern Armies to supersede and advise Meade, who would act as commander of the Army of the Potomac. There had not been a lieutenant general of the United States military forces since George Washington.

Then, he would appoint General Sherman as commander of the Western Armies. The Union Armies were close to strangling Vicksburg, whose inhabitants were running out of food, and their soldiers were running out of bullets. General Pemberton, the commander of the Confederates defending Vicksburg had been begging for reinforcements. But General Joe Johnson, the commander of the nearest Southern army, saw no way he could get there in time to help. Sherman was accused of having emotional problems in the early days of the war because he kept proclaiming the war would go on for years. To him, that was a fact that was indisputable. He could be erratic and emotional, but his instincts and military skills were genuine and sound.

He turned out to be right, though. And he climbed back into command through his friendship with Grant and his brother John Sherman, the Republican senator from the state of Ohio. John spent hours with his brother getting him to understand how important it was to keep his mouth shut.

General Sherman proved his worth. Lincoln had faith in his ability. And at this point, Vicksburg looked close to falling and could spare Grant to come north and work with Meade. Lincoln had no idea how Meade would react.

Suddenly, Lincoln stood and went to gaze out the window behind his desk. He clasped his hands behind him and lowered his head to his chest. The president turned and looked sadly at Diamond. Paul could sense the hypo take hold of the president, who said, "Paul, I misjudged the impact of the Emancipation Proclamation. I said once that I have been guided by events and people, rather than guiding these events myself. In this case, I did not really appreciate the impact it would have on the Negroes themselves. I had hoped it would spur them to take independent action against their owners. Some of that has happened. But the plantation owners have come down against their slaves even harder, and I am called a 'nigger-loving black Republican' by the South. You should read the threats that we receive every day. Nicolay and Hay try to intercept them daily.

"The abolitionists, like Stevens, Sumner, and their friends, welcomed the proclamation but criticize it for not going far enough. They do not understand that, if I went further, we would lose the border states, who could leave us and switch their allegiance to the Rebels.

"I could only have issued the proclamation as a necessity for military purposes during a war. That is John Quincy Adams wrote. The Founders did not erase slavery because they could not lose the support of the Southern states and the plantation owners. There would be no Constitution without them. The only way I could do what I did was this way. Why do they not understand this?

"Now finally, the generals, armies, and people of the North are only beginning to understand that the Negroes have a right to the same freedoms white people do, and they are not here to threaten us. They are entitled to the same rights every white person is entitled to. The colored troops have begun to show they can fight just as well as their white comrades, if not better. They have more purpose. They will not turn from the Confederate soldiers, who will kill them if they are captured. They fight for their freedom and liberty. I am sure you know that, when our armies pass through the South, many Negroes grab whatever they can carry and follow our soldiers. Commanders try and get them to leave and go back to their owners, but they refuse. They must be fed and taken care of, but they do not care. All they want is to be free.

"I am sorry, Paul. I seem to have gone off on a story whose ending you know." He smiled sadly.

Within ten minutes, there was a double knock on the door, and John Hay announced General Meade.

Lincoln warmly said, "Welcome, General. Thank you for coming on such short notice."

Meade had taken off his hat and gloves and shook the president's hand. One must remember that Meade was a follower of the deposed commander George McClellan who had not gotten along well with the president and, among other things, called him among other things a "baboon." There had been some complaints about Meade, but they were confined to impatient treatment of underlings and unhappiness when his orders were not followed. He was also criticized for not being aggressive enough at certain times.

The followers of the deposed General "Little Mac" were called "Mclellanites." Surprisingly, there were many generals in command who still were followers of McClellan. Meade himself was one, along with Ambrose Burnside, John Reynolds, and Winfield Scott Hancock. The problem was simply the ranks of capable replacements were thin indeed.

Hooker was not a follower of McClellan but had proved his lack of mettle at Chancellorsville. Lincoln was convinced Grant would provide the push Meade needed.

Lincoln explained that Hooker was to be replaced and he was convinced that, with Grant as general of the armies and Meade as commander of the Army of the Potomac, they could fit well together. Meade expressed reservation about Grant and his alleged drinking problem. But the president believed Grant's chief of staff and friend, John Rawlins, and the importance of the position would provide the proper deterrent, and Meade would also be of help. Lincoln quietly said that he appreciated the general's position. He stated that, nevertheless, they were entering a critical phase of the war. He believed this triumvirate of generals gave them the best chance of success. He added that they had something special to discuss when Grant and Sherman arrived the next day.

Meade said, "I am at your service, sir."

Lincoln said, "One more thing, General. What we discussed is totally confidential."

Meade answered, "I understand, Mr. President."

CHAPTER 17

While Lincoln was meeting with Meade, Paul Diamond was doing the same with Butler, Shanahan, and Barlow. They had much to discuss. They had to arrange the transfer of the weapons, as well as the training of Stanton's men, along with the placement of the weapons at Gettysburg and Vicksburg. Diamond impressed upon them the importance of secrecy. One word from any of Stanton's troops would be disastrous. That included the transfer to both Gettysburg and Vicksburg; the timing of the attacks was of paramount importance. They could not interfere with the Gettysburg battle until after Pickett's Charge on the third day of the action. They would have to wait to dig their gun placements for the Browning rifles until Pickett's men retreated and before Lee ordered the retreat to begin to the Potomac. They must be prepared for Southern skirmishers, and they could not be detected. They must be concerned with making the transfer of the weapons and ammunition without being seen.

Paul said he would speak to Stanton's men as soon as all the plans were ready, that would take at least two days. He was going to meet with Stanton in the morning and begin to review all the details, including the discussion of how many men he could contribute. He hoped that the importance of the entire action would be understood.

Paul instructed Butler to send a message home to bring Conklin and the others up to date on their status and to alert them to be ready to transfer the weapons soon. He wanted them to know that Lincoln agreed with their plans.

Each of his men brought up good points on the logistics of the proposed plan. But there was one potential problem. There were only three of them and they would need at least eight groups of two team members. How many men did Stanton have at his disposal? And what if there weren't enough? Where would the others come from?

Barlow pointed out they may have to draft sharpshooters from Vicksburg and Gettysburg. But the draftees would not have any practice with the new guns.

Butler said, "We can use them as backup or ammunition feeders." Gene jumped in and said, "First we have to see what kind of men Stanton has."

Paul said, "You are right. We have a lot of balls to juggle. Let's take one thing at a time. Gene, send another message home: Everything okay. Need at least one more day for transport. Will advise location and date."

"Yes, sir."

The four had dinner together in the hotel. One thing never changed regardless of where they were. Wherever they went together, people stared at Butler. Paul made sure he walked next to him wherever they went. He could feel Steven's large body tense when they were outside of the hotel room. Paul saw people stop and stare. It made him furious.

Finally, Diamond could take no more of it. Although he knew he should not do anything to call attention to himself, he could no longer control his reactions to what he deemed was nasty behavior to his friend. A very well-dressed man and woman walked directly toward them in the lobby of the Willard and stopped dead in their tracks as soon as they saw Steven walking and talking with Paul. The woman's face displayed a look of disgust. Paul reacted. Steven put his hand on Paul's arm to hold him back. Paul whispered, "Enough is enough. We must always keep in mind that Washington City is a predominantly Southern city, and just across the Potomac was Alexandria, Virginia, the site of the first Northern casualty of the war."

With Steven behind him, Paul slipped his arm from his underling's grasp. He faced the man and woman and said, "Good afternoon. And pardon my intrusion, but I could not help but notice the look of disdain on your face as you looked at my employee and friend, and a freeman, Steven. Was there a particular reason?"

Without answering, the man, presumably the husband, stepped in front of the woman, faced Paul, and sternly said, "I do not think it is any of your business, sir."

Steven stepped next to Paul, and his eyes darkened as he looked squarely at the man opposite Paul.

Now Paul put his arm on Steven's and said to the man, "I found that look rude and disrespectful and want you to know that, one day, you will pay the price for it. He is a man just like you and is entitled to the same respect as you. Soon enough colored people will have the same rights we have." Paul leaned over, lowered his voice, and said, "With one word, I could unleash him upon you. At the very least, you'd find yourself lying on the floor with broken bones. But what I am going to do is say something appropriate in front of your wife that will allow you to retain your dignity."

Paul took two steps back from his adversary and said, "Thank you for your understanding. Good day to you, sir."

Paul knew what he'd said would not eliminate the man's racism. But he felt better, at the very least.

Butler could not help but smile as he and Paul walked to meet Jackson and Gene. At that moment, he had never been prouder to serve under Paul Diamond. He would do anything for that man, and time would prove that true.

CHAPTER 18

Stanton's carriage was waiting for Paul and Steven when they came outside. They were in front of Edwin Stanton in less than ten minutes.

Without saying hello, the secretary of war said, "Is it necessary for both of you to be in this meeting?"

Paul answered simply, "Yes, Mr. Secretary."

Stanton answered, "Very well, but I have many questions that I must have answers to."

"That is why we are here, sir," answered Paul.

Stanton quickly asked, "How many of my men will you need?"

Paul responded," I will let Steven answer. That is his area of expertise."

Steven quickly answered, "We will need two men per team, and we'll need at least six teams in each location. I, Gene and Jackson will lead three, so we would need five team leaders and twelve others. Those numbers might change when we are on the ground, but I am close in my estimate."

Stanton sat silent while he stroked his beard and then began talking. "Only the president knows what I am about to tell you. I have at my disposal somewhere around fifty men who have been taken from different corps because they possess unique talents in different areas, from weapons to explosives to undercover work. These are the men I would transfer to your command under my supervision.

"Despite what some people in Congress think, I am not a megalomaniac; all I care about is winning this war as fast as possible. Our command structure and communication to the troops has been abominable, and I have been trying to correct that every day. The major problem is the time it takes for the orders to filter down in the field. I have no way of knowing how long orders sit before they are passed down to the next level and finally to the brigade Commander.

"But I am convinced the men I just told you about will not have that problem. You will give them an order once, and it will be carried out without delay or question.

"Anticipating your wishes, I have called for a group meeting with twenty-five of my best men at 2:30 this afternoon. I thought we would use the naval yard for privacy purposes. The only problem is getting you there without anyone seeing you."

Neither Paul nor his team members knew, but someone would be watching the naval yard and tracking their movements.

Stanton said sternly, "You can be sure of this. If any of these men say one word about this operation, they will be hung, and I will be the one who pulls the lever."

The three then reviewed the positioning of the delivery of the weapons. Stanton thought it would be safest to have the Vicksburg delivery go outside Sherman's tents, where they would be relatively hidden. He would tell Grant and Sherman when they arrived at the White House. Steven pointed out they had requested additional weapons be sent. There would be a mortar attachment for each gun and a carousel with 100 bullets to be attached to the barrel, along with a mortar attachment that would clip to the end of the barrel. When one was finished, the shooter could pop the empty one loose and insert the next carousel with a fresh 100 rounds. Time would be saved, and the element of surprise would be crucial. Another weapon the three men requested was a claymore. The best way to describe it would be a pipe bomb inserted in the ground that was filled with bullets. Stanton just stared.

The weapons for Gettysburg would be sent directly to the field in a quiet spot near Meade and Grant's tents. They would have to do the demonstration again later for Stanton's men. Paul suggested they talk first and see if there were any men who were either not paying attention or not clear as to the need for secrecy. They would be removed immediately. Stanton agreed.

He said, "The man who runs the unit is Lieutenant O'Malley. I have complete faith in his ability and discretion. I will have him there fifteen minutes earlier so you can talk to him."

Paul asked that it be thirty and Stanton agreed. "I will send word to the Willard on your transportation to our meeting," he said.

Paul nodded, and they shook hands. By the time Paul and Steven were leaving the secretary's office, he was already calling loudly for one of his aides.

CHAPTER 19

In the two weeks before Diamond's arrival in Washington City, there was activity in the field. On June 3, Lee began his movement by deploying his three corps to Culpeper, Virginia. While there, his troops held a "Grand Review" for their beloved general before heading north into the Shenandoah Valley. Before that movement began, Lee ordered his cavalry under the command of the flamboyant General Jeb Stuart to launch a diversionary attack on the Union forces in the area. But Union cavalry General Pleasanton anticipated the raid and attacked Stuart at Brandy Station on the morning of June 9. It evolved into a wild melee that was the largest cavalry battle in US history, and Stuart barely came out the winner. The fight proved that the Union horsemen had made inroads to the Southern cavalry in their fighting skills.

Based on the amount of men from both armies, there had been a disproportionately low number of fatalities. Stuart took a lot of criticism in the Richmond and other Southern newspapers for being unprepared for the attack. Pleasanton took too much credit for the action, but it wasn't the complete defeat that the Union was accustomed to in cavalry fighting.

Hooker continued to plead to be allowed to go around Lee and take Richmond. When Halleck refused, Hooker went to the president, who refused to hear him and sent him back to Halleck. The situation was toxic, and Hooker finally accepted his neck was on the chopping block. Little did he know that Lincoln already had contact with John Reynolds and Darius Couch, who had resigned his commission as general of the Second Corps after Chancellorsville. Both had declined the offer.

Halleck assigned Couch to handle the defense of Pennsylvania, as the rumors were flying that Lee and the Confederate Army were headed for Harrisburg and then Philadelphia. Lee's problem was that he had no idea where the Union Army was. With Jeb Stuart on a raid and out of touch with Lee, the army was blind as to where its foe was. But the Confederates were about to get news from an unexpected source.

A rider showed up at Longstreet's picket line and could have been shot but asked to speak to General Longstreet because he had some important information for him. The guards warned him that, if the general didn't know him, he would be hung. They brought him to the general's tent. The man, whose name was Harrison, had done some spying for the army. Longstreet remembered because he'd paid him some time ago. Harrison, an unemployed actor by trade, had now come back with the position of the entire Federal Army and the news that Meade was likely to replace Hooker.

By this time, it was June 27, and Grant and Sherman had arrived in Washington City to meet with the president along with Meade. Stanton, along with Diamond and his men were meeting Stanton's troops at the naval yard. Time was becoming very precious.

A carriage delivered Generals Grant and Sherman to the White House. Meade was already meeting with President Lincoln. Meade had a day's head start on the planning, but Lincoln did not tell him about their guests from the future or about the weapons that would be on the way in the next day.

John Hay ushered in the two generals. The president greeted them warmly, and they both shook hands with Meade. They took off their coats and gloves and immediately took out cigars.

The president asked Hay to please bring over ashtrays to the table. "Better make it two," he said. He added, "Thank you for coming so quickly at this critical point in your campaign. I know you will find the trip worth it when you hear what I am going to tell you. We will be joined by other guests as soon as another meeting with Secretary Stanton is finished. Allow me to begin."

The cigars were lit as the president recounted the events of the past two weeks and explained, in detail, what Paul Diamond had presented.

General Sherman snapped his head up and exclaimed, "What did you say?"

As Lincoln talking about the weapon and the demonstration, he noticed Sherman stared at Grant, who continued to puff away at his cigar and took out his whittling knife and a stick to work on. He asked the president, "Do you mind, sir?"

The president smiled and said no.

While the generals smoked and Grant whittled, President Lincoln explained his plan of transferring Grant to work with Meade and sliding Sherman to command the Army of the Tennessee to finish the siege and gain the surrender of Vicksburg with the aid of the new weaponry. It was important that Meade "buy in" to the new alignment, and he did not hesitate. He would be in command of the Army of the Potomac but would be under the guidance of General Grant, who Lincoln announced would be submitted to Congress as the first lieutenant general of the United States since George Washington.

Grant stopped his whittling and stared at the president, while Meade smiled and Sherman whooped in delight. All Grant was able to say was, "Thank you, Mr. President. I will do my best."

There was a knock on the door, and Nicolay announced that Paul Diamond had arrived with his men.

Lincoln said, "Show them right in. Gentlemen, you are about to meet our guests from the future."

CHAPTER 20

Lincoln stood to greet his guests, followed by Grant, Sherman, and Meade. The tall Diamond introduced himself, shook hands with the three generals and introduced his men individually. Sherman was most surprised to see a black man and even more surprised to hear he was a captain in his own time. There were no Negro officers in the Union Army, especially one with a grip like Butler's. Diamond made it a point to emphasize that each of his men were officers and had made several jumps through time with him before.

They finally all sat, and the president turned the meeting over to Diamond, who began to explain the proposed plan in detail. He began with the weapons and their transport. They would be sent to Vicksburg and Gettysburg directly. They would go behind the forward lines, and they would arrive in two days. General Sherman would have to notify his staff that several crates would appear behind his tent during the night and twelve of Stanton's men would arrive with him by train and accompanied by Gene Shanahan. Barlow and Butler were assigned to Gettysburg.

Lincoln interrupted Diamond to tell Nicolay that he needed to find General Herman Haupt, who was in charge of the railway system, and have him come to the White House with Stanton. They were going to need help cutting down travel time to both Vicksburg and Gettysburg. There was no one better at organizing the trains and squeezing every possible minute from the schedules than Henry Haupt.

Grant would leave with Meade for Pennsylvania, and Sherman would go directly to Vicksburg. On the trip, each would be told the specifics as to the placement and timing of the attacks.

The president recognized the importance that railroads had on the war. The North had a clear advantage on the South in the amount of rail mileage available to its armies for transportation of supplies for its soldiers. Recognizing the need to lay as many rails as possible, as well as run them efficiently, Stanton appointed a civil engineer, Herman Haupt, to manage and administer the nation's railroad system.

Haupt created a communication network via telegraph to make sure that trains ran smoothly and there were no bottlenecks when it became necessary to move troops and supplies as quickly as possible. In the next two days, General Haupt would be charged with delivering fifteen men thousands of miles to Vicksburg without interference and with as much speed as possible. Under normal circumstances, it would take more than thirty plus hours to reach Vicksburg from Washington City by rail.

Through changing schedules and tracks, the two-car train carrying General Sherman, Gene Shanahan, Lieutenant O'Malley, and twelve of his men arrived in Vicksburg in twenty-two hours. They left Washington in the early morning of June 28 and arrived in Vicksburg midday of the twenty-ninth.

Sherman's horse was waiting. He yelled out to Shanahan, "I hope you can keep up with me son."

Shanahan laughed and answered, "I will give it a go, General."

Sherman was surprised at how well Shanahan did, not knowing how much experience he had in his training in the twenty-first century. They arrived at his camp in twenty-five minutes, and Sherman immediately called for a meeting of his general staff and division commanders for one hour later. It would be a busy day. Sherman then went behind his tent with Shanahan and found eight wooden crates where there had been empty space when he'd left with Grant for Washington.

He lit a cigar and whispered, "Well I'll be damned."

Shanahan appeared and asked with a smile, "Do you believe us now?"

Sherman puffed on his cigar and smiled at Shanahan, "I have to tell you, son, this business sounded like the craziest thing I have ever heard in my life," he said. "If what is in those crates will help us end this horror, I will be the first man to apologize for thinking otherwise. In the meanwhile, let us go meet my staff and see what General Pemberton is doing to keep us out of Vicksburg."

PART TWO

CHAPTER 21

Washington City, June 28, 1863

In Washington on the morning of June 28, General Haupt had a different logistical problem as it pertained to Generals Meade and Grant. There was no railroad station in Gettysburg, and the Rebels were covering ground from Harrisburg to York. So if the train passed Gettysburg and doubled back with carriages and escort, they would land in the middle of Rebel troops. That left Maryland, which seemed to be clear of Southern soldiers, as they had all moved across the border to Pennsylvania. Halleck ordered a cavalry brigade to Frederick to check if it was clear and it appeared to be.

Haupt had a two-car train ready to go for the relatively short ride there, and a cavalry brigade would be used as an escort to accompany the generals, Diamond, Barlow, Butler, and Stanton's men to Gettysburg. A colonel rode with them, carrying the official orders to relieve Hooker and replace him with Meade as commander of the Army of the Potomac.

They arrived at the Federal camp in late morning of the twenty-ninth. Hooker handled his removal with a certain amount of grace and brought Meade to the tent that held the maps showing the position of the Army of the Potomac. Meade had spoken to Grant about making a stand at Pipe

Creek near Taneytown, Maryland. But the diminutive Grant preferred to wait until they were on the ground before offering his opinion. It depended, to a large degree, on where the Rebels were.

Hooker showed them that Ewell and Early were leaving Harrisburg and York, and the departure seemed to have happened suddenly. Depending on their direction, Pipe Creek might not be appropriate. What few Union men were in Harrisburg and York were just relieved to see the Confederates leave their positions and let them be.

The Rebels corps seemed to be moving east. A. P. Hill and Longstreet's two corps seem to be moving the same way, with Hill in the lead. There were unfounded rumors about a stash of shoes in the town of Gettysburg, and with so many Confederates walking barefoot, General Harry Heth was losing control of his Brigade. He'd gone to Hill, who had given approval for him to go into Gettysburg via the Chambersburg Pike in search of the shoes. Many thought this would be a leisurely march without opposition.

Gettysburg, Pennsylvania

It was the first of July, and General Heth had no idea where the Union Army was or who was in front of him.

What was there was Colonel John Buford, along with his cavalry. They had arrived the night before and set up their position in front of the Lutheran Seminary just outside of Gettysburg. Buford notified his commander of the First Corps, John Reynolds, to get up as soon as he could because the rest of Hill's corps was following Heth's brigade. Buford could see that what was in front of him was more than that. He saw the necessity of getting Reynolds men up as soon as he could. Buford climbed to the top of the cupola of the seminary to get a better view of the Rebel brigade. Hopefully, Reynolds's corps was coming from the other direction.

Reynolds was still not in sight, so Heth began to move against Buford's few thousand dismounted cavalry. The Union troops had to hold off Heth and what was behind him for possibly a few hours until Reynolds' men had a chance to fill in on the field. Buford could look up the hill of the Chambersburg Pike and see thousands of Confederate soldiers coming up behind the brigade already on the field. The Confederate general was totally unprepared to see Buford's dismounted cavalry in front of him. The

Federal cavalry could not hold indefinitely, and it appeared that Heth's men would not have the chance to look for those shoes.

As the minutes passed, more Confederate infantry began to put more and more pressure on Buford. As good a job as his men were doing, they could not withstand an onslaught. They had the higher ground, but even that fact could not deter the thousands attacking Buford's 2,500-strong cavalry. He was constantly looking for General Reynolds and his First Corps.

Then suddenly, a group of horsemen rode up, escorting General Reynolds. Buford was ecstatic. He spoke to Reynolds to give him a report on what had happened and was happening. Reynolds immediately began sending on the field as many men as he could.

Reynolds followed his men, urging them forward. He was very popular with his troops, and they followed his instructions to the letter—until disaster struck.

A Confederate sniper hiding behind trees on the Federal right shot and hit Reynolds, killing him instantly. The news spread through the corps, and panic ensued, allowing the Confederates to storm the Union line and send the troops rushing to the rear. There was confusion as to who would assume command, and that directly affected the reaction of the men on the field.

Because of Reynolds's death and the confusion of the commanders, the Union forces were finally pushed back into Gettysburg in the afternoon in a state of disarray. But many made it up the hills surrounding the town and Cemetery Hill. It was late in the afternoon by this time, and Confederate General Ewell's Second Corps had made it to the battle and was in pursuit. General Lee had given Ewell orders that said, "If at all practical, pursue the Federals up Cemetery Hill." But Ewell delayed and finally made the decision not to do so.

Jubal Early, a hardnosed brigade commander, was furious and filed a complaint with Lee.

By nightfall the Confederates could hear the Union troops cutting down trees and building fortifications to defend against what was sure to be another Rebel attack in the morning. But now the Federals had the high ground and, more importantly, more men. Winfield Scott Hancock and his Second Corps were on the way to help. And for his efforts, on the second and third day of the battle, he would be forever known as "Hancock the Superb." Thus ended the first day.

CHAPTER 22

That evening, meetings and planning were taking place on both sides. For time immemorial, the results of major battles have rested on the mistakes of a very few. Gettysburg was no different. As John Buford did all he could to keep the Rebels outside of Gettysburg until Reynolds came up with his First Corps, with the news of Reynolds death, everything changed. There was confusion between Generals Howard and Doubleday as to who would take control. The Union soldiers kept being pushed back through Gettysburg until they were in front of Cemetery Hill, a key vantage point that held the high ground. But it was getting later, and General Ewell decided against making a charge up the hill. A key moment in the battle passed. An hour earlier would have given him and Jubal Early the chance to secure this all-important hill.

That night, Robert E. Lee decided on his battle plans for the next day. He was happy with the results of the battle for the first day, and all that all happened, considering he had no knowledge where the Union Armies were and how many of them were there. But they had still prevailed, and since he didn't think George Meade was likely to leave the field, neither would he. General Longstreet reminded him of their agreement to fight a defensive battle, but Lee said he could not withdraw and had never left his opponent in control of a battlefield. Lee believed this was an opportunity to sweep the Union Army from the field based upon the results of the first day. He would do whatever was needed to continue the battle, as Meade was still finding his way with his army and commanders. The one disappointment was the failure of Ewell to take Cemetery Hill. That decision would prove to be a fatal mistake.

From the time humans began to walk the earth, there have been conflicts between different groups of people. Among other things, they fought over land, money, and God. At the time of the Crusades, a priest, who would later become a saint, called for a holy war against the Muslim empire to take back the holy city of Jerusalem because "God wills it." And yet, in every one of these conflicts for more than a thousand years, battles were won and lost due to mistakes in judgment, as well as the good fortune and luck of one side or the other. Throughout recorded time, historians and philosophers point to single actions by armies or even individual soldiers as reasons why battles and wars were won or lost. So it was in almost every individual battle or war.

The mental state of commanders in every one of these wars, both real and imagined, had substantial impact as well. The difference in philosophy between James Longstreet and Robert E. Lee was a classic example. It appears that, during the war, Longstreet was devoted to Lee. But he still appeared to disagree with his commander over the method of combat. If we look back to Shakespeare, characters such as Macbeth, Othello, and Henry V were affected by their mental state, which affected their decision making.

It was said of Lee at Gettysburg that his "blood was up." The intensity of his desire to defeat the Federal Army at Gettysburg and end the war may have overtaken his logic and decision making. After the failure of Pickett's Charge, Lee took responsibility and submitted his resignation, which was rejected by President Jefferson Davis.

But his mistakes in judgment on the third day of the battle were certainly not the only ones made, on either side. The inability to read the minds of the people involved makes it difficult to know why the battle went the way it did. More than fifty thousand soldiers lost their lives during the three days of fighting. The arrival of Paul Diamond, his men and weapons would add a fourth day and additional deaths. The mistakes that were made had made that number higher than it should have been. Many of the names have been forgotten, except by historians. Some bear review and remembrance.

CHAPTER 23

General Lee had a very specific battle plan for the second day of the battle. His planning always seemed to be very personal. Besides talking to his highest-level commanders, such as Longstreet or, before his death, Stonewall Jackson, he kept details to himself until it was necessary to reveal plans to his corps and brigade commanders. Lee left it to his corps commanders to implement his orders. One problem both sides had in almost every engagement was the lack of reliable maps. Not only were they unreliable, but also, trails that were supposed to run behind battle lines sometimes ran into trees that were impassable or the paths just did not exist. To depend on such maps was both dangerous and, at times, impossible. Thus, every corps had someone with certain degrees of experience in topography, and that person would be used to scout the terrain that the commander wanted to use. The maps had far too many errors to rely upon.

The battle plan for the second day, as devised by General Lee, was based upon attacks on the Federal line on both of their flanks. As General Ewell had chosen not to attack Cemetery Hill the night before, the Federals had troops working all night building fortifications to prepare to defend against an attack George Meade and Ulysses Grant knew would come the next day.

The two federal commanders had been together for only a few incredibly busy days. Grant was very sensitive not to step on Meade's toes, while Meade worked very hard to control his temper and made sure Grant spent time with each of the corps commanders. Grant made sure to give Meade his opinion on strategy only while they were alone. It was a courtesy Meade would always remember. Because working together was so new, mistakes could not be avoided.

They were so busy meeting in Meade's headquarters that Grant went outside to smoke a cigar and barely noticed that eight wooden crates had appeared out of nowhere and were stacked neatly behind the cottage. He turned around and went back inside to tell Meade the news, and Meade came rushing out to see for himself.

With Grant standing next to him, Meade pried open the top of one box. He removed the straw used to cushion the guns and took one of the BARs and whispered, "Well I'll be damned." He gave the weapon to Grant, who stood holding it with a big smile on his face.

Grant sent wires to Sherman, who had his own difficulties in Vicksburg. Sherman was preparing for a new assault on the city from the west, while avoiding the foothills on the outskirts of the city where Rebel soldiers had dug caves that were virtually impenetrable. Sherman had experienced them firsthand a few days earlier. His men suffered severe casualties in an attack.

CHAPTER 24

Lee decided to send Longstreet's corps to the left flank of the Federal position and ordered an attack on that side in the morning. Ewell would follow with an attack on the Federal right flank to take Cemetery Hill. That would begin with a prearranged signal from Longstreet's artillery commander, Porter Alexander, after Longstreet was well into his action.

But before any of this could happen, Lee had to know what, if any, Federal forces were on their left flank. He still had not heard anything from Jeb Stuart and felt as he was going into action with one arm tied behind his back. Lee was left to assign his chief topographer engineer, Captain Samuel Johnston, to reconnoiter the enemy lines and scout alternate routes and then return as soon as possible. Johnston followed a narrow trail to try and see what Federals were on the field. He was supposed to check two hills, which would be known thereafter as Little and Big Round Top. His report to General Lee would be that he saw no evidence of Federal activity on either of the hills. That would encourage General Lee to order Longstreet to prepare and go around the Confederate right flank and begin the attack as soon as he could.

This information proved wrong and was a serious mistake. Either Johnston had found the wrong hills or had simply lied about what he had seen. Or perhaps he'd arrived too early—before any Union troops began to occupy the two small hills on Seminary Ridge.

Leading the Rebel column was Brigadier General Lafayette McLaws. Suddenly, without warning, the column ground to a halt. Longstreet was farther back in the column and saw his men begin backing up on each other. He was confused by what was happening.

In another minute, McLaws came rumbling back on his horse with an angry look on his face. He pulled up next to Longstreet and immediately started yelling that, had they gone any farther around the curve in the trail, his men would be in full view of Federal troops who were scrambling over the two round hills. Artillery was being dragged up trails to get to the top of the first smaller hill. Posted there was a Federal officer using a hand telescope and a few soldiers with signal flags swinging and moving them furiously as directed by the officer.

That was General Gouverneur Warren of New York. He had no formal responsibility to be where he was but was watching from farther east on the ridge and raced over to try and get as many men as possible on those empty hills. Warren's apparent goal was to mask the lack of Union troops on the hill, while misleading the Confederate force.

McLaws asked his commander to ride with him to the front of the column so he could see for himself, and Longstreet was shocked when he got there. If they proceeded, they would be in full view of the Federals on the hills with signal flags. McLaws was furious with Johnston for the misinformation, and now the entire column had to turn back on itself and swing around to find a place to cross that would keep them out of sight of the Federals filling in on the two stony hills.

The countermarch was confusing and long and delayed the start of any attack even longer. Now there were lines of Federal soldiers where Johnston reported there were none. General Hood's brigade was put in the position of having to drive this advanced Federal line and then attack the two hills.

His men also faced a slew of large boulders that had to be passed. That was the infamous Devil's Den. There were Federals there, along with artillery. Sam Hood complained to Longstreet that there was a way to the right of the hills that was wide open, and the Union looked to be "in the air." If he could swing around the left flank of the Federal line, there would be nothing to stop him from "rolling up the Federal line."

Longstreet denied Hood's request and responded that General Lee wanted it this way. He also claimed to have argued against it. Hood announced he was doing this under protest.

Within the hour General Hood would be wounded and have an arm amputated.

While Hood led his men to try and take the hill after driving the Federals from the Devil's Den, General Warren tried to move as many men as possible to fill in the gaps on the Federal Line on Seminary Ridge.

CHAPTER 25

In addition to General Warren, there were three other Federal officers who made substantial contributions to the defense of the Round Tops on the second day of the battle.

The best known of the three was Colonel Joshua Lawrence Chamberlain who led the 20th Maine in defense of the extreme left flank of the Federal line. They were placed there by Colonel Strong Vincent shortly before the attacks on the Big Round Top that started to the right of the end of the Union line. The Rebels came in waves at the beleaguered Federal troops who were falling in their defense. If they broke, the Confederates could roll up the line, as they did at Chancellorsville.

Vincent was found by one of General Warren's aides as they were all making a desperate attempt to find men to defend the ridge. Vincent was in the 3rd Corps of General Sickles, who had disobeyed his orders and extended the position of his corps out from the rest of the line. That famous move left undefended part of the Union line that included the two Round Top hills.

General Warren saw the tactical importance of the hills and scrambled to find men to cover the hole in the line. Warren found Colonel Paddy O'Rork and his men and commanded him to get all his troops to cover the gap in the line. O'Rork replied he was following General Weed, but Warren assured him he would take responsibility for the action. O'Rork raced with his men and immediately attacked the Confederates rushing up the slope of the hill, beginning to drive them back. To exhort his men, C'Rork jumped on a large rock and began yelling to push the enemy all the way down to the bottom of the hill, but he was shot in the neck and died instantly. Many Civil War observers considered his performance at Little Round Top to be one of the most momentous of the war.

Meanwhile, one of Warren's officers found Strong Vincent and his brigade and asked him to fill in farther down the undefended bridge. Vincent immediately complied with these orders and assigned Colonel Chamberlain the task of holding the extreme left flank of the Federal line. Vincent said the position must not be given up; otherwise, the Rebels could roll up the line toward Cemetery Hill, and it would be disaster. Vincent went back to his men.

They, like Chamberlain soon would be, were attacked in waves. Like the young colonel had done a few minutes earlier Colonel Vincent jumped on a large boulder to show his men he was with them and was soon wounded twice. He had to be taken to a field hospital, where he died five days later.

Chamberlain formed his line and withstood attack after attack from Confederate soldiers coming up the hill to the position of the 20th Maine. Their ammunition was running out, and his men were reduced to rifling their dead comrades for powder and bullets.

Finally, after realizing that his men were without ammunition and knowing he could not retreat, Chamberlain came to his only alternative. He called his remaining officers and men together and instructed them they would form a new flanking line on the extreme left. Then his men would fix bayonets and sweep down the hill.

The troops were stunned, but they understood that, without ammunition, they could no longer defend against Rebel attacks. They could not give up their position at the end of the line.

After a moment of silence as the men of the 20th Maine realized the implications of a bayonet charge, they gathered themselves. The colonel called for them to insert their bayonets in their muskets and get in position to charge down the hill as the Rebels approached to attack one more time. Chamberlain set up the flanking maneuver on their extreme left. As the Confederates called to charge, the Federals men gave their own version of the Rebel yell, and off they went.

It appeared that the Rebels had their own problems with ammunition as well. As the Maine men attacked and began spearing Rebels, shockingly, many of the Rebel soldiers threw down their muskets in surrender. Within a few minutes, it was over. The Union troops followed the surrendering Rebels down the hill and collected as many prisoners as they could, while others kept going in search of more Rebels. Many observers believed Chamberlain's action to be the most extraordinary decision made by an officer at Gettysburg.

The Union left flank, and the Round Tops, were held. If not for the actions of General Warren, Colonel O'Rork, Colonel Strong, and Colonel Chamberlain, it never would have happened. The names of these four men would never be forgotten.

There was a great deal of fighting going on on both sides of the Federal line. Sickles's monstrous error of moving his corps out from the Federal line cost many men their lives. And Ewell finally tried to take Cemetery Hill, but the fighting there went on and on until after the sun went down. The Rebels did take some of the ground, but it was not enough. Between Longstreet delaying his attack on their right and Ewell waiting, the attacks were not coordinated and did not begin until late afternoon. The heat was unbearable, and men began to fall from exhaustion. Firing was heard until after ten o'clock.

The results of the fighting on the second day were "erratic." On one section of the line, thanks to the General Sickles debacle, the Rebel soldiers broke through and killed or wounded hundreds of Union men, until they were finally forced to retreat. General Hancock stripped his II Corps bare while sending brigades to plug holes from the Round Tops to Cemetery Hill.

The fighting went on into the night, and the Federals somehow held Cemetery Hill, with the Confederates knocking at the door for hours. If not for the mess with the Round Tops and the erstwhile engineer Captain Johnston, this second day would have turned very differently; Lee's men would have broken through and would possibly be on their way to Washington. But "Marse" Robert was convinced that one more day could give the South the breakthrough and make it the last day for the Army of the Potomac. Some of his officers kept repeating over and over that General Lee's "blood was up."

CHAPTER 26

Lee brought Longstreet with him to view the field in the early morning of the third day. The commander's plan was for Longstreet and Pickett's previously unused division to lead an attack of some thirteen thousand to fifteen thousand soldiers straight at the center of the Union line. They had attacked the right and left sides of the Union line of the first two days, and the commander of the Army of Northern Virginia believed the Federals were weak in the center. He believed a concentrated attack that would start with several long lines of troops of those fifteen thousand men, preceded by an unprecedented artillery bombardment, directed by Colonel Porter Alexander would take advantage of that weakness. The Confederate line would be marching across a field and several rows of fences and would then converge at the center of the Union line that surrounded a clump of trees.

Longstreet hesitated and suggested General Hill lead the attack, since most of the men would be from his corps. Lee immediately declined the offer and decided he wanted "his old war horse" to lead the attack.

Due to the massive artillery bombardment, Longstreet delayed giving Pickett the order to charge until Alexander made sure he would have enough ammunition to support the men in their charge. Finally, Alexander sent a message to Longstreet that, if he did not send out Pickett on his attack, he could not guarantee artillery support. General Longstreet did not believe the attack would be successful but finally relented, and Pickett finally began his move toward the ridge.

The Federals on the hill were in awe of the quality of the formation coming toward them. While the attack began—and the Federals held off their own artillery barrage until the Rebels came closer—there was hurried activity in two big tents hidden behind Meade's headquarters filled with wooden crates. Diamond, Barlow, and Butler worked inside the tent with a group of Stanton's soldiers.

The exact same thing was being repeated outside of Vicksburg in tents outside General Sherman's headquarters. Sherman watched Shanahan and Lt. O'Malley carefully take the BARs out of the boxes, while two of his men loaded the bullets into each carousel. Sherman sent scouts out to mark the spots where the holes were to be dug for the shooters. They were going to have to be within fifty yards of the Confederate troops that were protecting Vicksburg and would have to dig the gun emplacements and position the men in those rifle pits before dawn, so they would not be seen. Sherman decided to use six guns and place them in a semicircle around the road going into the city. There were about five thousand soldiers protecting the entrance into the city, and they were running out of ammunition and food.

It would be a very different situation in Gettysburg.

CHAPTER 27

R obert E. Lee believed that the Federal Army was ripe to be beaten on the third day. When Lee met with Longstreet early in the morning of the third day, Longstreet disagreed. He told his commander that the Northern soldiers had the high ground, as the Confederates had the high ground at Fredericksburg and were entrenched on the ridge. The Confederate force, although outnumbering their adversary in the center of the line was going to have to march in the severe heat on open ground and climb over rows of fences before coming close to the Union entrenchments and artillery. Pickett had to bring his division to the launch point, and Johnson Pettigrew of North Carolina brought his men from A. P. Hill's corps along with Isaac Trimble to give Longstreet some fifteen thousand men.

Finally, the artillery barrage began. It seemed to take the Army of the Potomac by surprise. That was true for the men on the ground. Grant and Meade knew it was coming and from where. Meade cautioned the commanders of the brigades behind the low stone wall to have their troops keep as close to the ground as possible. While the artillery onslaught went on, there were men working feverishly in the two large white tents fifty yards beyond Meade's headquarters. General Grant used a tent right behind the cottage where Meade was housed. The Confederates sometime overshot their artillery shells, but the tents were beyond their range.

The night before, Grant and Meade reviewed with Paul Diamond their plans for placing the guns. Diamond thought it important not to do anything to interfere with the Confederate attack the next day. He was not happy with that decision because of the casualties that would be inflicted on both sides, but he was concerned about the effect on the new time line that was being created. Any changes could have an unforeseen impact on their own attack on the retreating Army of Northern Virginia.

Meade wanted to place the BARs in a semicircle, like Sherman chose to do, some seventy-five to a hundred yards from the path of the Rebel retreat. After the crushing failure of Pickett's Charge, Lee and Longstreet believed Meade would look to attack on the fourth, but his exhausted troops and heavy rains would give Meade justification for not making another try. Lee was prevented from beginning his withdrawal from Gettysburg because of the rain, and he posted skirmishers to be on the lookout for Federal troops.

Lee then changed his mind and decided to begin the withdrawal of the Army of Northern Virginia as soon as possible. These soldiers were not posted until the morning of the fourth before the retreat began, giving Grant and Meade time to send men out to start digging the holes for the emplacement of the guns. The holes would have to be deep and long enough for the shooter and one other man, who would be responsible for changing the bullet carousel and replacing the mortar shells.

Meade and Grant called in the officers who would lead the defense on Seminary Ridge but had to be careful about how much to tell them. Meade asked General Grant to explain that there would be the possibility of an attack on their positions the next day and arranged for extra ammunition to be brought up and to pick out eight groups of their best to do the digging for the guns. Grant did not say anything more than each hole would be six feet long by four feet wide. Each spot would be marked with a stick near the edge of the woods past the Emmetsburg Road. The men would have to perform their task in silence. That was of paramount importance.

Meade and Grant met with General Hunt, who oversaw artillery, to use a telescope to scope out placements for the sticks. Eight men would be sent out the night after the charge to place them. They did not fully realize that the field would be littered with the bodies of Confederate dead and wounded. Meade sent doctors and hospital wagons to collect the wounded and get as many as he could from the open field so that the Union soldiers would have a clear line of site going down the hill. The placement of the firing positions was on the extreme Union flank and a section toward the center and was aimed to hit the Rebel right and their center behind the trees. There were thousands of Confederates there. It was a mathematical equation and the placement of the guns were designed to have the maximum coverage on the enemy. The guns should be placed to kill as many Rebels as possible. There was no other way to explain it. If the plan worked it would be a devastating amount of carnage.

The planning was done. All that was left to do was to wait for the attack the morning of the third day. Diamond, Butler, and Barlow waited in the gun tents and tried to sleep. But Paul Diamond warned his men to stay out of sight and check the guns again. He knew they were out of range of the Confederate guns, but he wanted to make sure that no Union soldier stumbled inside either of the tents. He walked over to the other tent and told Stanton's men the same thing.

One of Diamond's favorite generals was in the meeting of officers. Winfield Scott Hancock was wounded the afternoon of Pickett's Charge on this third day. For his efforts at Gettysburg, he would be dubbed "Hancock the Superb." His use of the 2nd Corps on day two was remarkable, filling in holes in the Union line to cover for Sickles's mistakes and to help on Cemetery Hill. Diamond slipped out of his tent during the night to at least get a look at Hancock. He dared not get too close to him or any of the other commanders. He did not trust himself not to say the wrong thing, like, "Be careful tomorrow afternoon," or, "Stay off your horse during the artillery and musket fire."

As much as he and his men wanted to see the Confederate formation in the afternoon, it would be too dangerous. Artillery shells and bullets would have the same effect on them as they would on any of the Union soldiers. Dead is still dead, regardless of the element of time. They heard the Rebel bombardment begin, and some shells felt like they were too close. But they weren't; what they felt was the percussion of the explosives. A few musket balls from rifles seemed to land even closer. There was a constant yelling of the Federal officers for their men to stay down and hide behind the stone wall on the Ridge. Paul peeked through the tent covers and could see some of the troopers spread out on the ground to keep from being hit.

Suddenly, they could hear the command, "Stand and prepare to fire."

Seconds later, the firing of the Federal troopers began as the remaining Confederate soldiers reached the last fences. For many, it was as if they were shooting at ducks in a pond. The moment the Rebels climbed over the last fence, many were immediately shot. To come all the way across that field and climb over the fences to get to the last one and then be shot to death was a horrible way to die. Some remained and staggered forward to the Federal line, where they were met by artillery fire and blown away or stabbed by bayonets and shot by musket balls. More Union troops were plugged in to fill gaps in the line.

What remained was a melee of soldiers of both sides at the stone wall that included fistfights, bayonet stabbing, and finally the Confederates trying to run back toward their own lines or surrendering by falling to the ground in exhaustion. Many fell on the dead or wounded of their comrades. Finally, the Confederate battle flags fell or were taken by Union soldiers.

George Pickett was devastated by the carnage suffered by his men. General Lee rode around apologizing to his retreating men. He whispered, "It was my all my fault." He'd expected too much of his men and the cause. Longstreet was proven right about the wisdom of making the attack.

They would now have to face, not a Federal counterattack, but an attack Lee could never have foreseen.

The battlefield was littered with bodies and streams of blood. The moaning and screaming of wounded soldiers echoed all over the field. As the Rebel division slowly withdrew into the woods from where they started the charge, the Federals sent doctors and medical wagons to collect as many of the wounded as could be saved.

Longstreet sent skirmishers out in case there would be a follow-up attack by Meade. He still did not know his old friend from the Mexican War, Sam Grant, was even there.

After another few hours, the doctors had finished their messy and depressing work. Meade pulled his remaining men back.

CHAPTER 28

Meade saw the withdrawal of the Confederates and talked to Grant about confirming when to send out the men who would dig the trenches for the shooters. Grant agreed and then pulled out a map Paul Diamond had given him. With the use of field glasses and a telescope, he showed each of them where to plant their markers. The line started from the extreme left flank and circled around to the center of the field. There would be six markers. The men who would do the digging would go out after 10:00 p.m. There would be two men per hole, and they had their instructions directly from General Grant. He emphasized the need to be as quiet as possible and to insert the markers when they were done.

Grant and Meade had a meeting with the shooters after the first group came back from inserting the marking sticks. The men had difficulty finding their way around the dead bodies of the Confederate soldiers and cautioned the shooters to watch their step. The skies cleared, and the moon would provide some illumination. The shooters delayed leaving the Federal line until after 2:30 in the morning. That would give them time to set up the guns before there was any movement in the enemy camp. The Confederates would be preparing to begin their retreat to beat the Federals to the Potomac and safely return to Virginia. Federal pickets reported movement on the other side as early as 2:00 a.m.

Grant asked Meade to talk to the shooters while he sat in a chair next to him. General Meade simply said to the men grouped in front of him that this mission was as important as any the Army of the Potomac had attempted. As important as their victory at Gettysburg was, this final attack could be a hammer blow that could break the Confederate Army. "All our hopes and prayers go with you," said Meade.

Hancock would lead them past the stone wall and point them to their spots. They had fashioned a kind of knapsack to carry each gun. Another would be used to hold the shell carousels and extra mortars. They waited in the tents until 2:30 and listened to Jackson Barlow and Steven Butler give them last-minute instructions on the weapon and remind them to adjust their aim after their first few shots. Most importantly, the shooters should expect return fire. And when their ammunition ran out, they were to get the hell out of there and get back up the hill to the Federal line. Barlow and Butler told the men not to stop firing and to hit as many Rebels as they could and keep shooting at anything that moved.

At 2:30 a.m., the men who'd dug the firing pits returned and reported that they had been shot at by skirmishers. One of their men had been hit in the arm. He was immediately attended to by a doctor and nurse. The firing pit diggers were all taken back to the tents to brief the shooters on what they had accomplished.

Grant told Meade he would instruct General Webb to have 1,500 men ready and armed to go down the slope toward the tree line in support of the shooters should the Confederates decide to attack them. Webb had to be told what was going on, and he was happy to comply. Since Meade did not go after Lee after the Charge of Pickett, this was the next best thing to him.

At 3:00 a.m., the tent flaps were thrown open. In walked Hancock the Superb He had a scare during the fighting during Pickett's Charge. While riding along the Federal line, Hancock had been shot in his abdomen. He'd immediately been taken to a doctor, and the bullet had been removed. The medics had managed to stop the bleeding and wrapped him in a tourniquet. The general was in pain and would not be able to return to active duty until he healed.

Diamond immediately went over to introduce himself, and Hancock invited him to watch the attack with him on the ridge. Hancock was the one General Diamond wanted to meet besides Grant, Sherman, and

Meade. He was grateful to have shaken his hand. The general did not know all the details of the attack, and Paul knew he would not be able to give them to him.

Hancock addressed the soldiers who were sitting with their bags next to them. "Men, it is time for you to go. I will walk you out beyond the stone wall, and you will go directly to your assigned positions. Give them hell and do not stop firing. Good luck and Godspeed."

They all stood and picked up their bags. Jackson grabbed Steven and walked over to Hancock and shook his hand. Barlow said to him, "We came a long way for this sir, we will do our job."

Hancock looked confused but then remembered hearing rumors about these men. "Thank you, son. Good luck," was all he could say.

Before an orderly opened the tent flaps for General Hancock and the men who followed him out single file the skies opened, and rain began to fall in torrents. Before he led them out Hancock looked back at General Grant who had stepped into the tent and nodded his head to proceed. Hancock led the men out past the wall and had them split up on the side where each team would be going. Butler and Barlow would be on different sides of the field and hugged each other before they got in line, Steven to the right and Jackson to the left. Steven Butler was with an Irishman named McMahon and Barlow had a Wisconsin soldier named Lafollette.

Hancock said one last thing in a whisper, "Get down there as fast as you can and watch out for bodies on the way." He turned to salute the men, who were ready to go down the hill to their positions.

Hancock looked back beyond the stone wall where Meade, Grant, and Webb were standing. Grant nodded his head and Hancock whispered, "Go."

The men started down the hill, while he was taken by a nurse to a hospital tent to rest and have the wound he had suffered attended to.

CHAPTER 29

Two of the men slipped on pools of blood and the bodies the pools had apparently come from. They got back on their feet and caught up to their partners. Within a few minutes, all had safely made it to their assigned pits. Each team quickly took their guns and inserted the first carousel, which was preloaded with a hundred shells. The guns were in perfect working condition.

Steven and Jackson each gave a prearranged whistle that everything was good. Soon enough, all teams were ready to begin. Grant had a sharpshooter ready to fire one shot as a signal to start firing.

Jackson had field glasses, as did every team. He was about a hundred yards away from the tree line and another fifteen to the Confederate men, who were beginning to stir as they got ready to pack the supply wagons for their retreat to the Potomac and Virginia. They were moving quickly, as if they were still concerned about the Federal Army coming down the hill. There was heavy rain that had begun to fall as the shooters had come down the hill a few minutes s earlier, and the Confederate wagons would have trouble with the mud, causing the retreat to be difficult and draining.

It was Justin's partner who had been one of the two who tripped, and Jackson asked if he was all right.

"At least he was an officer," he replied as he wiped some of the blood from his pants.

Jackson smiled in response and turned to get his line of sight right on his BAR. He said to Private LaFollette, "Remember this, son. For as long as you live, you can tell no one about this. I was never here, and this never happened."

The private immediately said, "Yes, sir."

The young private would keep his word until the day he died sixty years later.

Steven said the same thing to McMahon and received the same response. Butler told him, "We should get the signal in about a minute."

Steven was already prepared to start firing. He had a group of Confederates in his sights and did not have the same concern as Jackson about the firing distance.

McMahon said in his heavy Irish accent, "Are you ready, sir?"

Butler answered, "I have been waiting for this my entire life, Private." Then he smiled.

Thirty seconds later, a single rifle shot came from behind the Federal lines. It broke the silence of the early morning, and the men would count to ten, with Jackson the first to start firing. He counted to eight and put his finger on the trigger. When he hit ten, he began to fire right where he aimed.

There was a group of Rebels packing and loading boxes into a wagon. They turned together when the single shot was fired and turned back when they heard the deafening roar of Barlow's gun. They all dropped when the bullets hit their target.

Jackson did not react to his success. He just re-aimed, this time firing on the next group behind the first.

By then, all the BARs had begun to fire, and screaming could be heard down the Confederate line. Their men were dropping as soon as they were hit.

Meade and Grant were watching, along with all their men on the ridge. General Meade immediately sent a wire to President Lincoln. who was with Secretary Stanton at the War Department telegraph office.

When Lincoln read Meade's message that the attack had begun, the president lowered his head in what seemed liked sadness that the attack had begun. Many young men would lose their lives this day. Stanton took the message from the president and stared it as he shook his head in wonder.

At about the same time, Paul Diamond walked away and sent his own message to the 21st century that the attack on General Lee's army had just begun.

Grant and Meade watched with their field glasses. They were in shock at the impact of the weapons. It looked like hundreds of Rebel soldiers had fallen in the first two to three minutes. The firing was loud and relentless.

McMahon watched Butler do his business and murmured, "Oh shite, this is a beautiful thing for these eyes to see."

Butler did not react. He was focused on killing as many men as he could as quickly as possible.

There was some return fire from the trees, but the Rebels could not see where the strange guns were firing from. The shooters fired back from their position. The enemy was within range. In another minute, after one carousel was empty, another was inserted. The gunners adjusted their fire to mow down the Confederate line as far as they could. The murderous shells were finding their targets, and as the sky grew lighter, Steven could adjust his aim toward the end of the Confederate line.

The Rebels made it easier for him. As they saw their comrades fall, hundreds more moved in with guns to fill in. As soon as that happened, they were well within the range of the BARs, and the gunners continued firing and killing whoever was in their sight line.

As Diamond watched from the tent, he sent a second message home: "Attack underway."

Grant told General Webb to get his men ready to move, in case his men began to falter or ran out of ammunition. The sound of firing echoed for five miles, and after Pickett's Charge, this was now even more of a killing field.

Steven Butler told McMahon to take the field glasses and look to see if there were Confederates to the right of his position.

He did and said, "There are only a few behind those trees. All the rest are down. Glory be."

All McMahon could do was stare at Butler, who said, "Now look as far as you can see further to their left and see if there were any left standing."

"They are all down, sir—all of them."

Butler looked down at his gun and then took the glasses back to see for himself. It was true. As far as he could see, there were dead men. He was concerned about the ones they had missed and may have been hiding behind the dead soldiers.

The Federal shooters shot the mortars every few minutes. They could see the bodies of Confederates flying after the shattered bodies landed among their dead compatriots. Barlow and Butler began to arm and toss the claymores in a long looping arc, and they landed in the first line of Rebel soldiers. More dead bodies were sent flying from the explosions.

The sound of a bugle came from the Rebel line to their right, and what appeared to be at least 150 men began riding out toward the shooters' position. But the Federals switched their fire to the cavalrymen and began picking them off one at a time. Four shooters were firing at the same time, and they killed at least 75 in two minutes. The remaining riders immediately turned their horses and rode back to the tree line.

One of those who fell was General Jeb Stuart, who had finally returned to the army after his seemingly endless ride that had left the Rebel Army blind to the Federals whereabouts. What the Federals did not know was that Richard Ewell, A. P. Hill, and George Pickett were also dead—killed by the automatic rifles of the shooters in the rifle pits.

Longstreet was meeting with General Lee to discuss what they should do. They had lost two of their three corps commanders and the commander of their cavalry who had caused the Northern forces so much trouble since the war began. They had lost what appeared to be at least five thousand men in thirty minutes. General Lee wanted to try and break out from this massive attack, while Longstreet could not see how it was possible.

On Seminary Ridge, Grant was talking with Meade about sending in Webb and his men. But they did not know how many men were still on the Confederate line. They could not know how destructive the attack had been and how many Rebels had been killed. Meade suggested waiting to see how Lee would react to what had happened so far. Grant agreed.

A shot was fired in the air from the Federal line. It was a signal to the shooters to hold their fire and maintain their positions. Another shot would be the signal to withdraw.

CHAPTER 30

A few interminably long minutes after the shooters stopped firing, a solitary Confederate officer carrying a white flag rode out from between the trees toward the Union lines. This brought an enormous roar from the Federal soldiers. Meade exploded and told his officers around him to have them stop.

General Grant told General Alexander Webb to ride out and greet the Confederate. Webb quickly got a horse. He rode out from behind the rock wall and the edge of the field and down the slope to meet the man carrying the white flag of truce.

Webb saluted, and the salute was returned in kind. The rider introduced himself as Colonel Walter Taylor who acted as General Lee's chief of staff. He handed General Webb an envelope addressed to George Meade, saluted, and turned to ride back to his line.

For a moment, Webb stared at the envelope. Carrying it in his left hand, he rode quickly back to his own lines and went directly to see Meade and Grant.

Meade waved at Webb to join them. Webb had become aware of the details of the attack and had contact with the shooters. General Webb handed Meade the envelope. When asked if he had read the contents, Webb immediately replied, "No, sir."

A crowd began to surround the commanders, and Grant thought it best to go back to Meade's headquarters to read the note. Amidst a crowd of officers and enlisted men they made their way to the white cottage and went inside. Meade had four soldiers at the door standing guard.

They sat at the round dining room table. Meade passed the envelope to Grant, who immediately passed it back to Meade and replied, "It is addressed to you. I have a feeling our friend General Lee does not know I am here." He smiled.

Meade took the envelope, slowly opened it, and read out loud:

Dear General Meade,

Due to the results of your attack on our lines this morning, I have concluded that it would be prudent on my part to meet with you to discuss the terms of our surrender.

I am prepared to meet with you this afternoon at your convenience. I also request the ceasing of any activities by either of our armies until the conclusion of our meeting.

Please respond and advise.

Robert E. Lee
Commander, Army of Northern Virginia

After a moment of complete silence, Webb began to whoop. But Grant immediately said, "No." That silenced the younger general.

Meade looked at Grant and said, "I will be damned. It worked."

Grant answered, "There was a moment when I thought we should send Webb and his men down the hill. Tell the sharpshooter to take the third shot and get those men out of those holes. Send some troopers down to help carry everything back quickly and make certain the guns are covered. Then send a wire to President Lincoln and let him know what is happening. But don't tell him too much. I don't want him to be disappointed if this meeting does not go well. I will wire Sherman. He should be ready for his action at Vicksburg."

Meade waved for a messenger to have that third shot fired for the withdrawal of the shooters. Within thirty seconds, they heard the shot fired.

Down the hill, the shooters hugged their partners in excitement. Turning, they saw twenty teamsters come down the hill to help bring them back. Barlow made his way to Butler and they stared solemnly at each other and then warmly hugged each other. Butler whispered in Barlow's ear, "Thank you." Jackson Barlow answered, as hugged his teammate back, "My friend you are welcome, and I thank you. I understand how hard this must have been for you. The other shooters came out of their holes and were shaking hands with each other and smiling.

Meade sent another message to the president and the secretary of war that stated that the firing had ceased after a Confederate soldier had ridden out under a flag of truce with a letter from General Lee requesting terms.

The president stood and shook Stanton's hand.

"Congratulations Mr. President," said Stanton with an unusual smile.

The President answered, "They haven't surrendered yet, but this is a very good sign."

Grant instructed cavalry to ride out and find a suitable house in which to meet General Lee as quickly as possible. Grant walked to the telegraph officer and dictated a message to General Sherman, bringing him up to date on the news from Gettysburg.

CHAPTER 31

Lincoln sent messengers to find Secretary of State Seward and the rest of the cabinet requesting they report to the telegraph office at the War Department immediately. After a half hour, they all came rushing in asking questions that Lincoln did not have the answers to yet. He preached patience until he heard more from Meade and Grant. The president sat in the chair he always used in the telegraph Office and took out his copy of *Hamlet* that he sometimes carried with him and silently began to read. The members of the cabinet sat quietly and watched.

At about the same time, the cavalry returned to report to General Grant that they'd found a small isolated house belonging to Joseph Robinson, who was willing to donate it for the meeting. It was only one and a half miles from the Federal lines and had not been badly damaged by the fighting over the past three days.

Grant and Meade responded to General Lee with the location of the Robinson house and asked the meeting take place at half past two and for confirmation by return message.

Webb delivered the message to Colonel Taylor, who asked Webb to wait for a response, which came rather quickly. Taylor brought the response back to Meade and Grant. Lee had agreed to meet at 2:30 and had asked for a guide to bring him and his men to the Robinson house.

Paul Diamond decided not to bother Hancock, who was resting. Paul had paced throughout the attack. When it had ended and knew his own men were safe, he began walking down the slope to their position to congratulate them.

Butler and Barlow ran up to greet him. They stopped and saluted. Diamond walked over to hug both and then shook the hands of all the men who had been part of the team of shooters. The teamsters quickly covered and carried carried the guns, mortars, and bullets back to the tent they had been using. When Diamond and his men returned to the tent, they immediately began repacking the guns and other supplies into the wooden boxes from where they had been taken the night before. Diamond decided to wait to send the signal to transfer them back to 2022 until after the meeting between Grant, Meade, and Lee.

The commanders came into the tent to congratulate Diamond and his men.

Meade said quietly, "I am sorry I doubted you, Mr. Diamond."

Paul smiled and answered, "Please do not let it bother you, General. I would have reacted the same way. You know this is considered top secret, and you can never speak of this business to anyone."

Grant said, "It will never come from us."

"Thank you, Sir," answered Diamond.

All Commanders of the Army of the Potomac were instructed to hold their positions until told otherwise and to instruct their troops not to fire any weapons. The Rebels had done the same.

Grant and Meade sat in the cottage and were reviewing a message from President Lincoln. He had requested that the Rebels be "let up easy." Lincoln strongly believed that states who had seceded be allowed to regain their standing in the Union. It was the President's opinion that those states had never left the Union. They did not have the constitutional right to leave the United States of America.

George Meade sent a return message to Washington that said, "We understand."

Grant sent General George Custer to be the guide for General Lee and his staffers. Knowing Custer's personality, he was very specific in his instructions that General Lee and his staff should be treated with the utmost respect.

Custer rode down slowly and waited at the edge of the field in front of the trees. Six additional Union cavalrymen who were acting as escorts stayed ten yards behind Custer. The young general could see the dead Confederate soldiers piled on top of each other. Custer was considered a man full of himself, with a certain amount of arrogance. But this sight shook him. He turned his horse away and waited for General Lee.

Within a few minutes, three horses came out of the tree. Robert E. Lee was first and was dressed in a full dress uniform. He was followed by Colonel Taylor and his secretary Colonel Charles Marshall.

Custer saluted Lee, who responded. The commander looked sad and withdrawn. Custer introduced himself and said he would be leading them to the Robinson house, which was a short distance away. Custer said, "Please follow me, sir."

The confederates began their sad ride to surrender.

Five minutes later they arrived and there were five horses in front of the house. Generals Meade and Grant came out to meet them and escort General Lee inside. They saluted the Confederate commander and his men, and Meade asked them to follow him. There were six chairs surrounding a round table. Lt. Ely Parker was there as Grant's military secretary to take notes. Custer, General Webb, and John Rawlins stood against a wall behind their superiors.

CHAPTER 32

General Grant asked Lee and his men to sit at the table, while Meade took a seat next to Grant. Lee waited for them to sit and adjusted his sword before taking his own seat next to Colonel Marshall, who would be taking notes on his behalf.

Grant began by mentioning that he and Lee had met while they both served in the Mexican War. Lee responded that he did not recall their meeting at that time. He then asked what Grant was prepared to offer for the surrender of the Army of Northern Virginia. He made it clear that he was not speaking for the Confederacy but only the army he commanded. Meade could see that Lee was anxious to come to some sort of agreement and leave. Lee did ask Grant about the weapons that had been used that morning. All Grant said was that they were new to the Federal Army, and he hoped never to have to use them again. He went on to say that he had communicated with President Lincoln and they agreed on having the Confederate soldiers lay down their weapons, pledge a loyalty oath to the United States, and peacefully return to their homes. Lee mentioned that many of his men owned their horses and asked that whomever that applied to be allowed to take them home, as many were farmers and needed their horses to work their fields. Grant thought for a moment and looked at Meade, who nodded his agreement. Grant agreed to Lee's request. Lee expressed these terms would go a long way toward beginning an era of peace between the two sections of the country.

Grant then requested that their secretaries write what they had just agreed to. Parker and Marshall sat together to write up the agreement their commanders had negotiated.

General Grant said to Lee that he imagined that the Confederate soldiers may be hungry. He offered to supply them with twenty-five thousand rations and then requested the Army of Northern Virginia lay down their weapons at 10:00 a.m. the next morning. General Lee agreed and commented that supplying the rations would also help to foster peace between the men of each army. He then asked Grant if their business was concluded, to which Grant responded, "Yes, General. And thank you." They each signed a copy of the handwritten terms and took a copy for their governments.

Lee and Grant stood, with Lee bowing slightly. He turned to leave, but Grant said, "General, I would like to send a few brigades to you to help with the disposing of your soldiers who have fallen."

Lee looked down and answered, "Thank you, General Grant. That is most kind."

Grant and Meade then walked to accompany him to his horse.

Lee got on his favorite horse named Traveler and turned to Grant and Meade. Both Union Generals gave the former Confederate a final salute that he returned. Lee looked balefully at the Robinson house and then turned around to return to his men.

The two generals stood together and watched their former adversary ride off and then turned to each other and shook hands with a smile.

Meade leaned over to Grant and said, "Thank you, Sam."

Grant responded, "You're welcome. And thank you for accepting me to work with you."

Grant called Parker over and instructed him to send the following message to the President:

Dear Mr. President,

We are pleased to advise you that, at 2:45 p.m. today, Robert E. Lee surrendered the Army of Northern Virginia to General

Meade and myself. We will accept their guns and battle flags tomorrow morning at 10:00 a.m. The terms are being sent in the next few minutes. As their soldiers, have not eaten well, I am delivering 25,000 rations to General Lee. We offered to send a few brigades to help with the burial of their fallen men.

Your most humble servants,
Ulysses Grant and George Meade

Meade directed John Rawlins to arrange to send the rations to the Confederates as quickly as possible. Once that was done and after giving them time to eat, he ordered Webb to have two unarmed brigades go with shovels and wheelbarrows to walk down and help the Confederates bury their dead on the field.

The Federals rode quietly together to their lines. Generals Custer and Webb asked if they could go ahead of the others to spread the word of the surrender.

Meade said, "Yes but this is not to be a party. Tell the men to celebrate quietly." He then looked at Grant, who nodded his head in agreement.

Grant said to Webb, "Have General Greene and Colonel Chamberlain of the 20th Maine report to our headquarters. I have a job for them."

Meade instinctively knew what it was and smiled.

By the time Generals Grant and Meade returned to their lines, word of the surrender had spread throughout the army. They were welcomed by thousands of men, who clapped their hands as they passed by on their way to Meade's cottage behind Seminary Ridge. They dismounted to greet General Pap Greene and Colonel Joshua Lawrence Chamberlain. Greene had led the defense of Cemetery Hill with a limited number of men, and Chamberlain had done the same at Little Round Top. Both fights had taken place on the second day of the battle and were extremely important to the Federal's cause. They both saluted as the commanders approached, and Meade asked the commanders to join them inside.

Grant asked Greene and Chamberlain to sit with them for a few minutes and then told them, "We have been told about your excellent work in the field. As you may have heard, we accepted the surrender of the Army of Northern Virginia. We would like you both to represent our army tomorrow morning in formally accepting their laying down of their guns and battle flags. Rawlins will give you details, and we thank you."

Greene and Chamberlain looked at each other and smiled. They stood and saluted. "Thank you, sir," both said.

Greene and Chamberlain returned to their men and told them the good news after talking with John Rawlins. They told them it was a substantial honor and explained they would be required to salute every Confederate officer who escorted his men to lay their arms down. Their men were very excited. They knew what their officers had accomplished in defending their positions and how important an honor it was. If the Confederates had taken Cemetery Hill, they would have taken the high ground. And Little Round Top was the end of the Federal line, which represented an enormous opportunity to sweep the Federal Line all the way back to Cemetery Hill and destroy the Army of the Potomac. The surrender that took place could have been reversed.

Meade welcomed a steady stream of officers who came to offer congratulations. They all seemed to be astounded at the shocking turn of events.

Paul Diamond and his men supervised the packing up of the guns and ammunition. When the boxes were nailed shut, he sent a message by Morse code from the device in his leg to transfer these guns back. As they finished, the two commanding generals walked into the tent with big smiles on their faces.

Grant said, "Sherman has just taken Vicksburg."

It seems that word of Lee's surrender had reached General John Pemberton in Vicksburg by telegraph. He commanded the Rebel forces defending the city during the siege. Shanahan and O'Malley had been in position to begin the attack when a rider had come out from the Rebel lines carrying a white flag and holding a letter addressed to General Sherman requesting a meeting to discuss their surrender. Captain Shanahan had walked out to meet the officer and accepted the letter. He'd waved back at his lines. And Sherman, in his excitement, had ridden out by himself to take and read the letter. He immediately agreed to meet Pemberton in one hour on the field where they were standing. It was unconventional, but so was Sherman.

He had orderlies brought out six chairs and a table for his and Pemberton's staff. By the time the meeting was concluded, the surrender was complete. Sherman offered identical terms to Pemberton as Grant had to Lee. The surrender ceremony would take place the next morning. The soldiers defending Vicksburg and the civilian population had been living on hardtack and dead rats for the last few weeks. Sherman offered to send as many rations as he could. Within an hour, fifteen wagons carrying twenty thousand rations rumbled to the Confederate lines. The drivers and accompanying guards were told in no uncertain terms to treat these people with respect. "They are no longer our enemies. They are our countrymen."

Sherman sent a messenger to have as many more rations as possible delivered to the city of Vicksburg.

Sherman wired Grant the good news and then sent the following to President Lincoln:

Mr. President

I am pleased, and proud to present to you the city of Vicksburg, which surrendered to our Army this afternoon. We sent rations for their people and will help them any way we can. The terms are identical to those offered by General Grant.

Congratulations, President Lincoln, and Happy July Fourth.

William Tecumseh Sherman

Pemberton told Sherman he had received a wire from Lee. Lee had advised him of the attack that morning, saying the Rebels were still counting dead bodies from the effect of the new weapons the Army of the Potomac had used. He'd advised Sherman to make his own decision about continuing to fight on.

At the telegraph office in Washington after Stanton read Sherman's letter out loud, there was whooping and hollering and hugging and shaking hands. The president sat in his chair and reread all the wires over and over. He then took his large hands and covered his face as tears of joy fell from his eyes. As he had for three years, Secretary of State William

Seward stood next to Lincoln with his hand on the president's shoulder. The room immediately grew quiet as the cabinet began to appreciate how the president felt.

President Lincoln was crying from relief and joy over the news from Gettysburg and Vicksburg. But that was not the only reason for the tears that fell down his cheeks. He was crying for an unknown future, one that was unknown because of the decisions he'd made to order the attack on the Confederates at Gettysburg and Vicksburg.

He slowly stood and looked at the members of his Cabinet that stood around him with a surprisingly sad look on his face, and said, "Gentlemen, I cry for the news we have received that this nightmare is over. I cry for the men who have fallen, those who wore blue and grey. In the four days of fighting at Gettysburg, I have been told that more than fifty thousand men from both sides have been killed. And I cry for them, as well as the hundreds of thousands who have given their lives in the last two years. I cry for the mistakes we have made that have cost men their lives because of those mistakes. But I do not cry only for them. I cry for the unknown future that time has in store for the United States in the years to come because of what happened in Gettysburg and Vicksburg. I ask, no, I beg you to stand with me as we begin the struggle to rebuild our nation in peace and harmony. We have a difficult job ahead. But if we stand united, it can be accomplished."

He then walked to each of the cabinet members and shook each one of their hands.

Stanton turned to the men and said, "Now our work really begins."

CHAPTER 33

Ulysses Grant and George Meade stood among a group of generals and watched ten supply wagons carrying rations to the Confederate lines. They were accompanied by fifty teamsters who were sent to help distribute them to the Rebel soldiers. Grant could see his old friend Longstreet walk out through the trees. As he looked toward the Federal line, Longstreet saluted his old friend. Grant took off his cap and waved back in recognition. They would meet and spend an hour walking the field reminiscing and smoking cigars later that evening.

Once the wagons stopped, the Union men jumped off, opened the flaps of the wagon and made ready to begin. Longstreet waved to his men to start coming out. The Confederate soldiers were a sorry sight. Most had no shoes. They looked ragged, dirty, and hungry. Meade had requested their supply depot twenty miles away to deliver another twenty-five thousand rations, along with as many shoes as they could spare as soon as possible. Quartermaster General Meigs had done his job well, making sure enough provisions were nearby for both sides.

In the end, the Union had more men to fight, as well as better weapons and supplies. The ultimate result was simply a mathematical equation. With all of Lee's brilliance, he almost led his army to win this fight. If not for the guns sent from the future, the war would have gone on until the

Union Armies wore down the Southern forces. But here they were. The matter was decided, saving untold hundreds of thousands of lives, as well those yet unborn—the children of the men who survived this nightmare.

Many soldiers, on both sides, wrote of their experiences after the war. Most accounts were chilling to read. Some were not able to write about it. It was a horror for them to even think about what they experienced. Many were tortured by their dreams of the war for the rest of their lives. They could not forget the sight of heads being blown off bodies, limbs being ripped off, and rivers of blood. They were tortured by the sounds of screaming soldiers, lying on a field or being bounced around in a medical wagon for miles until they could be tended to. So many lost arms and legs. For these men, that was their reward for fighting. Surprisingly, only a few mentioned anything about the devastating attack on July Fourth. Not one disclosed what they did or did not know about it.

In the twentieth and twenty-first centuries, there was a resurgence of interest in the Civil War from both the North and South. For many, it became romantic to imagine the fighting. Thousands of people became reenactors. They replayed battles and bought replica uniforms and grew beards to match the soldiers who did fight. But they could never recreate the pain and wounds suffered by those men. We should honor all of them, while remembering the price they paid.

Diamond walked over to Meade and Grant to watch the food distribution. It appeared to be going quietly, without incident. Meade deployed a third brigade to help collect and then bury the bodies. General Alexander Hays would lead those men. This would be difficult and terrible work, but it needed to be done. And the Federals had to help their beaten former enemy. Both Meade and Grant realized that, considering how it had ended and why.

One of the wagon drivers walked over after unloading his rations. He came right over to Meade and said, "Sir, I have been in this army for more than two years. I have never seen a sight like the one I have just seen. The bodies are piled ten deep as far as you can see. God have mercy on them, sir."

All Meade could do was shake his head and say, "Thank you, Private."

Paul and his team had successfully completed their mission. They kept to themselves in their tent while they waited for the two commanders to make their farewells and arrange for their return trip to Washington.

The initial distribution of the rations was completed, and more were needed. Three more brigades would follow a few hours later because of the sheer numbers of bodies that required burial. Meade allowed groups of his men to go down and bring additional supplies to their defeated enemy.

Although the formal surrender would not take place until the next morning, both sides were so used up that all they wanted to do was finally go home. Many of the Confederates were shoeless and had not had a good meal in a very long time. Soldiers on the two sides had been fighting each other for more than two years, and they had developed a strange respect for each other. During breaks in the fighting, they were so physically close pickets and skirmishers would have conversations with each other and trade different things. They would call each other "Billy Yank" and "Johnny Reb." When their officers told them to stop, they would separate and restart their shooting and killing each other. Many would scratch their names and hometown with a pencil nub and pin the paper to their uniform, so they could be identified if they were wounded or killed. Both sides believed it would never end.

Paul Diamond and his men could not help but think of the names of places where battles were fought in their time line—such as the Wilderness, Cold Harbor, and Petersburg—that would now never be remembered because they would never be fought, and the carnage avoided.

Grant and Meade were watching the mass burials taking place on the field. One officer came back and told them that, along with the thousands of Rebels killed from the charge, just as many, if not more, were lying behind the trees on the Confederate line. The men from the Army of the Potomac were shocked at the death that the shooters had inflicted. Anyone who saw it would never forget. Those few who did write about their experiences would say it was unspeakable what happened that morning. Thousands of men from each side gathered and combined to dig and carry each body and place each body in the graves. Chaplains from each side said prayers for as many of them as they could. This dirty work would continue for almost three days before all the dead were properly buried.

Grant and Meade walked back to the tent of their visitors from the future. General Grant carried a piece of paper that he handed to Paul

Diamond. It was a wire from President Lincoln that asked Grant to thank their guests on his behalf and asked them to come to the White House upon their return to Washington.

Paul smiled as he read it and gave it to his team members to read. He thanked the generals for coming and reiterated the importance of maintaining secrecy about what had happened. He knew it would be difficult, but he felt comfortable about Grant and Meade not telling anyone. However, he was concerned about the cabinet members in Washington. Diamond could, nonetheless, do nothing more than reiterate how important their silence was upon his return to the White House.

The team from 2022 had done its job. The war was as good as over. Northern soldiers would still have to take Richmond. Grant would leave that to the Western armies and General Sherman. His army left Vicksburg after releasing the soldiers of Pemberton's army and leaving as many rations as they could spare.

The citizens of Vicksburg had very little food. Sherman did what he could to help them. He was preparing to go north because Grant asked him to as soon as General Haupt arranged transportation. Grant asked Sherman if he thought he could get to Richmond and clean up any resistance on the way. Word of Lee's surrender and the fall of Vicksburg were spreading across the country, but it was still possible for some Confederate soldiers not to have been informed or wanted to fight on.

General Herman Haupt now had more work to do. Paul talked to Meade about arranging for transportation back to Washington. Meade wired Haupt to see if he could arrange for a train to leave from York, which was easier now that Lee had surrendered. Haupt started immediately. He ordered a one-car train to arrive at 11:30 a.m. the next morning and take Stanton's men and Diamond and his team back to Washington and Abraham Lincoln. General Haupt's next task, and it was a big one, was to begin planning to bring Sherman's Army of Tennessee to Richmond.

Grant told Paul he did not know what to expect. They had to finish burying all the bodies at Gettysburg and give the army a few days to rest and recover before they went to York. From there, they would travel to Virginia should Sherman need help.

Jackson, Steven, and Gene were visited by two troopers from the quartermaster, who brought officer's coats of different sizes for them to try on to take home with them. Paul smiled and agreed. The men had been instructed by General Grant to give the four anything they wanted. All they knew was that the four men had been of immense help to the army and had a long trip home.

Paul asked for an officer's wide-brimmed hat and a long lightweight coat that would fit in his saddlebag. One of the men ran out and came back in ten minutes with one of each that fit perfectly. The boys were very happy with their jackets, except Steven, who had to wait twenty minutes until the quartermaster's men found one that would fit over his broad shoulders. When he finally put it on, Butler had a huge smile on his face as well.

Paul's team asked him, since they were not leaving Gettysburg until the morning, if they could take O'Malley and take a walk around the camp. Diamond agreed but warned them not to talk to anyone and, if need be, let O'Malley speak. They all liked the brash Irishman, who would have fit in well with their officers back home.

O'Malley said, "Sure, boyo. I'm getting stir-crazy in here!"

His men knew better than to ask to come along. They realized how much O'Malley had put into this mission and that he needed some time alone.

Later in the day, he asked Paul if the other men under his command could watch a few minutes of the formal surrender in the morning.

The four men spent an hour walking around the camp and seeing how happy and relieved all the men were. The surrender was beginning to sink in, and they understood this living nightmare was coming to an end. Every brigade commanding officer had read to the men of his command two messages. One was from the president thanking them for their service and praising their sacrifice and promising that he would not forget all they had endured.

The second message was from Ulysses Grant and George Meade. That one was similar in tone and expressing their gratitude. But it stated they had one more goal to reach—the occupation of Richmond. Once that was completed, they would all return to Washington for a Grand Review. Then most of the men could finally return to their homes. It appeared that the hard fighting was finished, and there were rumors that Jefferson Davis and his government had left or were about to leave Richmond in search of a haven. *Lincoln told Seward he hoped they would leave the country, rather than putting him in the position of needing to hunt them down and prosecute them for war crimes.*

Diamond was excited about spending more time with the president and Robert Lincoln. Meade had two wagons ready to take everyone to York the next morning. They made their final goodbyes to the generals.

Meade's demeanor had radically changed. Being thrust into his position as commander of the Army of the Potomac had increased his levels of anxiety, which had been there before his appointment. Since the final attack had begun, he was much calmer and had no problem in deferring to Ulysses Grant.

Grant seemed a bit more relaxed but as taciturn as ever. He continued to direct Meade and his chief of staff, John Rawlins, and now was preparing to have the army move south to Richmond with the help of Herman Haupt. Sherman had begun to mobilize the army of Tennessee to leave Vicksburg and move north as soon as he could. There was still the formal surrender the next morning in both Vicksburg and Gettysburg.

CHAPTER 34

Washington City, July 5, 1863

While this was happening in Gettysburg, word of Lee's surrender had spread all over Washington City the day before. Fireworks were set off that night and every night thereafter for the next week. Alcohol was consumed in enormous levels, even if some of the whiskey was not as good as advertised. The streets were full of parades of people waving American flags and burning the flag of the Confederate States of America. They looked for people they believed were Southern sympathizers and tried to hang them in the street before they could be stopped by soldiers and police officers.

The President was very clear that he wanted none of these people touched. He planned to address the crowd that would mass in front of the White House, as it had the night before.

Lincoln wanted to include how he felt about the Reconstruction plan that was beginning to crystalize in his mind. But Secretary of State Seward tried to have him take the tone of gratitude to the armies and the people for maintaining their support of him and his administration despite any mistakes they had made. Lincoln finally agreed and confined his brief remarks to those obvious topics.

Seward was relieved. The secretary of state, the president's closest advisor in the cabinet, believed there would be plenty of time for Lincoln to spread the word of reconciliation and the forgive ness he wanted to extend to the states who had been in rebellion. So much anger remained in the citizens of the North. They remembered all too well the daily lists of casualties that had been printed in the newspapers. They'd read them with dread as they searched for the names of husbands, brothers, and sons. There was a palpable sense of hatred that remained and that would take time to dissipate. For many, on both sides, it would take years.

Lincoln would take the approach of offering forgiveness to the Southern soldiers but would take a harder line with those of the planter class who had pushed for war and the firebrand politicians of the Confederacy who'd pushed and prodded for war in the name of states' rights and their inherent right to own slaves.

The Northern abolitionists had begun their fight on a smaller level forty years before. They never gave up the fight. Now in 1863, it finally appeared to be over.

The President had decided that keeping the border states as part of the Union was of paramount importance, while the Abolitionists and Radical Republicans had wanted to free the slaves over a year earlier. Lincoln had said that was all very good, but if he took such action, he would lose the border states, which would never sit still for that and would jump to the Confederacy. And the North would likely lose the war.

Nonetheless, it was now done—with the help of four men from the future. And hopefully, only a few in 1863 would ever know they existed.

Gettysburg July 5, 1863

The formal surrender would take place at 10:00 a.m. General "Pap" Greene and Colonel Joshua Lawrence Chamberlain rode down the slope with some of their men toward the former Confederate lines a few minutes ahead of time. The ceremony would be simple and dignified. The Army of Northern Virginia would surrender its battle flags and muskets one brigade at a time. The commander or highest-ranking officer still alive of each brigade would ride out and salute the Union officers. The union men would follow. And the Rebels would lay their guns and battle flags on the ground.

Diamond and his men watched men of both armies form in the field through the open flaps, while Stanton's men would watch from the outside, as the latter had their uniforms on and would not be noticed. It was incredibly moving. Paul and his team were quite affected, knowing what their part in all this had been.

At 11:15, the wagons pulled up to begin the ride to York. Stanton's men brought carbines along, just in case there were Rebel soldiers making mischief on the Emmetsburg Road. Before he pulled himself up into the wagon, Paul Diamond saw Meade and Grant watching them prepare to leave the battlefield. Paul saluted, and the two Commanders returned the salute with serious looks on their faces. Paul Diamond would never see them again.

The wagon ride to York took almost ninety minutes, and they had a cavalry escort of twelve men from General Custer's Michigan Wolverines. They were battle-hardened veterans and were there just in case there was any difficulty. The wagon drivers and cavalrymen were cordial and did not ask any questions.

When they arrived at the train station in York, the train was waiting for them and ready to go. Just before they arrived, Jackson asked O'Malley for a carbine to take with him on the ride to Washington.

"Do you think there will be any trouble?" asked the Irish Lieutenant.

Jackson responded, "No, but I am a little concerned about Washington."

O'Malley said he would take one from his men and give it to him on the train on the ride back to Washington. Jackson asked O'Malley to keep it between them.

The group leaving said thank you and goodbye to the drivers and cavalrymen, who saluted as they allowed their horses water and forage before they began the return trip to Gettysburg.

The train engineer said to Paul, "You must be pretty important to get your own train car. They told me to get you back to Washington City as soon as I could."

"Thank you. We really appreciate it."

Paul had not said anything to his men, but his internal clock was running down, and he had only one pill remaining that would get him to the next afternoon. His team members were younger and stronger and could squeeze out an extra day without taking any more medication. The three weeks that Paul could remain in 1863 ended the next day. They had to get back to Washington, report to President Lincoln, and check to make sure the one gun in the naval yard had gone back to the future.

After an uneventful trip they arrived at the Washington City train station and there were two buggies ready to bring them directly to the White House. Gene, Steven, and Jackson were still wearing their Army of the Potomac coats, although it was quite warm. Paul led the way, and the guards at the White House were ready for them. Paul and his men passed right through, and John Nicolay was there to usher them in to see the President, who was meeting with Secretary Seward. They stood up to greet Paul and his men with broad smiles on their faces. The President shook each of their hands with both of his, and Seward did the same.

Paul noticed that Lincoln looked ten years younger. After they had talked for fifteen to twenty minutes, Lincoln asked if he could have a few minutes alone with Paul.

Jackson said to Paul, "We have to go back to our rooms and pack for the return trip tomorrow."

They said their last goodbyes to President Lincoln, who spoke to each of them individually but gave Steven a little more time. President Lincoln said quietly to him, "I pray that true equality between our races will take less time than I believe. I promise I will do all I can to make it so."

Steven felt a tear trickle down his cheek while he said, "Thank you, Mr. President."

Jackson put an arm on Steven's shoulder as they saluted the president, and then Nicolay walked them out. As they made their way out, Paul got up and told his men that he wanted to go over to the Naval Yard and check on the crate.

Gene replied, "We will go with you."

Paul said, "If you like, but I should be fine. Meet me in the lobby of the Willard in about an hour."

Now the President and Paul were alone. There would be a final goodbye the next morning, but this was more of a business meeting. Lincoln intently listened while Paul described how the attack was planned and the degree to which Grant and Meade had been involved. The Army of the Potomac did not have a good record insofar as the chain of command and orders reaching the right brigades. Over the last few years, orders would get waylaid and never reach the intended officers. Due to the secrecy of the mission, Meade had circumvented that line of communication. He'd gone directly to Webb and Hancock for their orders, rather than go through his own chief of staff.

When Paul began discussing the attack itself, Lincoln was visibly affected by the carnage it had inflicted on Lee's army. He whispered, "I had no choice."

Paul placed one hand on the president's hand and quietly answered, "Mr. President, if you had not ordered this action, it is likely both sides would have lost more men in the next few months, and the war would have continued for a few more years. That I promise you, sir."

The president looked balefully at Diamond and said, "Is there anything more you can tell me?"

Paul looked out the window behind the president's desk and watched the warm sun come through it. Then he turned his head back to the president and answered, "Unfortunately, I cannot. Everything is different now. We have drastically altered the time line and will not know how much until I return home. I wish I could say more. I only ask that Robert be with you when I come back tomorrow to say goodbye. I must speak with him."

With a quizzical look, Lincoln said, "Of course."

"Thank you, sir," Paul answered and stood to say goodbye.

CHAPTER 35

Steven, Gene, and Jackson went to the boarding houses and packed the few things they'd brought with them on their trip. They made sure to put all their belongings in their saddlebags, but Gene noticed it looked like his bag had been opened while they were in Gettysburg. Before he had a chance to say anything to his friend, Jackson said, "Someone has been in here and opened my bag."

Immediately they went flying downstairs to talk to the older woman who managed the rooming house. Jackson asked, "Excuse us, ma'am, has anyone been in and asked for us while we were gone?"

She thought and answered, "Wait, why yes. A few days ago, a man did come in. He was well dressed and wanted to leave you a letter from Mr. Blair but had to give it to you personally. He asked if he could leave it in your room, and I said I didn't think it was wrong, since I don't get around as well as I used to. He brought me back the key and said thank you as he left."

Gene said, "Thank you, ma'am. We must go meet our friend. And we have to leave for home tomorrow."

She replied, "You have been very nice to have as guests. Since you prepaid, you don't owe me anything else."

They bade her farewell and walked out to the street to wait for Steven.

They turned and saw him walking toward them. Before Gene and Jackson had a chance to talk about what they had seen in their room, Gene asked, "Did it look as if anyone had been in your room?"

"I don't think so, Why?"

"Because someone came around looking for us with a letter, supposedly from Mr. Blair. And for some reason, the lady who owns this place gave him the key to our room! He said he worked for Mr. Blair. And our bags were opened. Luckily, we had nothing in our bags that could hurt us."

The three stared at each other in front of the house. And Steven, who had an angry look on his face, said, "It was Martin Duffy."

"Yeah, I think so," said Gene.

"We better find Paul," Gene said.

The three walked rapidly towards the White House. They'd gotten two blocks closer to Pennsylvania Avenue when a rider came toward them very quickly. The man glanced at them and spurred his horse to go even faster as he passed them.

Steven exclaimed, "That was Duffy!"

Jackson said hurriedly to Shanahan, "You are the fastest. Follow him and, if you can, see where he goes. Stick this in your jacket." He handed over the carbine O'Malley had given him on the train. "Meet us at the White House. If Paul isn't there, go to the Willard and wait in the lobby. We'll go find Paul."

"Got it." Gene slid the gun in the sleeve of his jacket, turned, and began running in the direction Duffy had gone. He had to run four blocks. There he found Duffy's horse tied up in front of a well-appointed three-story house. As he passed the house, Gene took a quick glance in the front bay window and could make out the face of Martin Duffy talking to a slightly older man, who was pointing and looked like he was very excited.

Gene kept walking and did not look back. He did notice a small wooden sign with the name F. Wood carved into the sign. He thought the name looked familiar but could not be sure.

Gene realized he had to get back to the others and talk to Paul. He would recognize the name. Gene crossed the street, went one block toward the Potomac River, and circled around the Wood house. He could not take the chance of passing the house again and Duffy seeing him. He had not met Blair's man, but he may have somehow seen Gene.

He got back to the beginning of Pennsylvania Avenue and ran the two blocks to the White House. Now he was concerned that the guards would recognize him and let him go upstairs.

Something was bothering him as he got closer to the gate. It was the fact that Paul wanted to go back to the naval yard to see if the first box sent had been transferred home to NASA. He would have to find Jackson and Steven and then somehow find Paul before he went. It might not be safe.

He made it to the guards at the doorway to what would eventually be known as the West Wing, and one of the guards looked familiar. Shanahan took a deep breath, "Hi," he said. "I was supposed to meet my friends here. Have you seen them?"

The guard answered, "The tall guy left about twenty minutes ago, and the other two came and left when I told them he was gone. I think they were going back to the Willard."

Gene thanked him and started running to the hotel. It was only a short run to the main entrance and the steps that led to the lobby.

The first thing he always noticed was the cigar smoke. It was heavy and thick. Somehow, he saw through the clouds of smoke and spotted Jackson and Steven sitting in chairs opposite each other on the far side of the large lobby. He walked quickly to them and Steven asked, "How did it go?"

Gene took a deep breath and said, "We may have a problem. Where's Paul?"

Jackson replied, "He's changing and then coming down. What problem?"

Gene quietly told them about following Duffy to a house and seeing him talking to a man. He mentioned the sign in front of the house that read, "F. Wood." And he explained that he'd doubled back and, after going to the White House, had ran here to the Willard, in hopes of finding them.

Jackson said, "Paul should know when he comes back down. He wants to go look for the gun box. He will know who this guy is and what it means. I think he is beginning to wear down," he added.

Two minutes later. Paul Diamond slowly walked down the steps after washing up and changing clothes. The three went to meet him and asked how he was, to which he answered, "My time here is beginning to run out. I think I can make it to tomorrow afternoon. I must talk to Robert

Lincoln in the morning." He sensed something was wrong and asked them what it was.

The trio caught Paul up on what had happened. When Gene mentioned the name "F. Wood" Paul looked stunned and said, "Let's finish this conversation in the alley. I do not want anyone to hear what I have to tell you."

They followed Paul to the corner of the Willard and walked around the corner to the alley from which they would be transported home the next day. He looked worn out and tired. The amount of time they had spent in 1863 was beginning to wear on him. The men were all concerned and would do whatever they could to help him. For now, though, what they were about to hear would answer many questions about Martin Duffy.

Paul stopped and turned to his three younger friends. He began to quietly talk, "This is something I did not count on. Sometimes there is something that we find when we go back and are surprised or hurt by something we did not anticipate. Martin Duffy is the glitch on this mission. Okay, here it is. Fernando Wood is a Democratic Congressman from New York City. He was the two-time mayor of the city and was the champion of those who wanted New York to secede from the Union and make it an open city, allowing Confederate ships to deliver their cotton and sell it there. Had he succeeded, it would have become an economic bonanza for New York, as well as the Confederacy. He could not find the support he needed. But there is more to his story.

"Here in Washington, he was closely allied to the 'Copperheads' and Clement Vallandingham and the "Knights of the Golden Circle." They wanted the war ended and a peace treaty signed, to allow slavery where it existed and return things to where they were before the War began. Wood was a threatening presence in the House and, in our time line, led the opposition to the passage of the 13th Amendment, abolishing slavery in 1865. Now, with the time line changed and Lee having surrendered, the passage of the amendment could happen sooner and with less opposition. Abraham Lincoln's reelection in 1864 would likely come with a bigger Republican majority. The congressmen who would be against the 13th Amendment believed that Negroes were inferior and did not deserve or were not entitled to be on an equal legal footing with the white race.

All Steven could say was, "Bastard."

All Gene said was, "Damn him."

Jackson could not say anything right away but finally exclaimed, "So our friend is an agent for Wood and these people and tells them everything he hears from the Blair family and has been watching us since we got here."

Paul answered, "I am going to go the Navy Yard—"

Before he had a chance to finish the sentence, Jackson interrupted him. "We are going with you, and I am bringing a present from O'Malley, just in case we have some company." He pulled the carbine from his jacket that Gene Shanahan had given back to him. Paul smiled.

Gene said, "I'm going to go back to the White House and see if I can get Nicolay or Hay to get us a ride there."

Steven replied, "Good idea. Have them pick us up on this corner—fewer people to see us."

Paul's mood changed because of this information about Duffy. Shanahan asked him, "Brother, are you okay?"

Steven stared across the street and said., "I want that son of a bitch."

Gene answered, "I have a feeling you just might get your chance Steven."

Gene took off and ran over to the White House. The same two guards were still there. He told them he needed to see Nicolay or Hay, and they let him go up. It seemed like the same crowd was there as the day before.

Hay was surrounded by half a dozen people, all of whom were talking at the same time. Gene was six feet tall, which was taller than most people of 1863. He waved, and Hay recognized him and pushed through the people surrounding him to get to Gene.

"Thanks for saving me from those people. They all want jobs!"

Gene said, "We need some help. Is there any way we can get two carriages to ride to the naval yard? There may be a problem."

Hay stared at Shanahan and asked what was wrong.

Gene answered quietly, "I am not sure, but we have to check on the first crate. And we believe someone may have been spying on us. It is important, and we have to check it out before we leave tomorrow."

Hay asked where the others were. Shanahan told him they were in the alley just past the entrance to the Willard. The young Hay told Gene to go back there, and he would have the carriages there in less than ten minutes.

Gene thanked him. He made his way back down the stairs, left the White House, and headed toward the Willard.

When he made it back, he told Paul and the others to get ready. Five minutes later, two carriages pulled up, a waving John Hay in the first one.

Jackson walked over and said, "I don't know if it is a good idea for you to come with us. I have no idea what's waiting there."

Hay thought for a moment and said, "Sir, the President of the United States has directed me to accompany you and made me promise to be safe and stay out of your way. In addition, he has ordered Secretary Stanton to send some of his friends, some of whom you know, to be nearby in case they are needed. I cannot disobey my orders from the finest man I have ever known."

Jackson smiled and answered, "I guess that settles it. But if one of us tells you to do something, you do it."

"Yes, sir," Hay answered with a grin.

Paul and his men piled into the two carriages, and they started off on their ride to the Naval Yard. On the way, they talked about how they should handle the possible approach should someone else be there. Jackson believed, since they felt Duffy had been trailing them, they should be ready if he was there waiting.

CHAPTER 36

Steven believed that, if the gun had not yet been retrieved, that would be Duffy's target. And Duffy would have no compunction about killing any of them for it. When they arrived at the yard, there was one guard, who they had seen when they were there with the president for the gun demonstration. Gene and Steven got to him first.

Before they had a chance to say anything, the guard said, "Your friend got here a few minutes ago, with a letter from Mr. Blair authorizing him to meet you inside."

"Unbelievable," Gene said.

How long has he been inside?" Steven asked.

"Only a few minutes," the guard answered.

Gene shook his head and asked, "Do you have the letter?"

Yes, right here." The guard pulled it from his jacket pocket.

Gene waved for Hay to come over and said to the guard, "This is John Hay, secretary to President Lincoln. Please give him the letter."

"Yes, sir." The guard handed the letter to Hay, who shook his head while he read it and put it in his jacket pocket.

Gene finished by telling the guard that the man who'd given him the letter was a dangerous man and represented a threat to the President.

The guard's face flushed, and he said, "I am sorry. I had no idea."

Gene said, "You could not have known. But you can make up for it now."

The door most used to enter the building was the main entrance where the guard was posted. When the demonstration of the weapon had taken place, mattresses had covered the walls to protect the President and those viewing the demonstration. Jackson hoped they had been taken down and they no longer covered the walls of the room and the rear entrance. He went to the left side of the building down a walkway. He called the guard to come with him. The two made it to the end of the wall and found a small locked door. The guard confirmed this door led to the back room where the gun was tested for the President. If Duffy was inside, they might be able to surprise him. He had the guard quietly unlock the door and went back to the others.

Paul deferred to his men the decision on how best to get inside as quietly as possible. They agreed to use that rear side entrance. Steven would take the lead, and Paul would follow, with Gene and Jackson behind. They hoped that Steven could slip around to the rear of the room and Gene and Jackson would follow. Gene would stay hidden but close enough to Paul to shield him if there was any trouble.

The guard had already unlocked the door. Steven opened it as quietly as possible and kept as low as he could. He saw right away that the box was still there, and there didn't seem to be anyone in the room. Paul walked in behind the two others, who crawled in behind him. Steven kept down and managed to slip around the room, hugging the wall as he made it around to the back without making a sound. Gene stayed near Paul and hid behind a box, while Jackson slipped the carbine from his jacket and was ready to use it if Duffy should be there.

Paul stepped to the crate and opened it to see the BAR inside. *Why did they not transfer it home?* he wondered. *Could they have just forgotten?*

At that moment, Steven heard footsteps. His body tensed as he prepared himself for any eventuality.

The footsteps stopped and they all heard Duffy sarcastically speak. "Hello, Mr. Diamond. So nice to see you again. You did not believe you could just come in here and take that gun?" He pointed his gun at Diamond's head.

Gene jumped to get in front of Paul.

At the same time, Jackson slowly stood and pointed his carbine at Duffy, who seemed to be thrown into confusion. He must have believed Paul would come alone. As he looked around, he kept the gun pointed at Gene and Paul. He didn't hear Steven Butler come out of hiding and put his massive arms around his neck. As he squeezed, Duffy began to flail around and started to have trouble breathing, the headlock was so tight.

Duffy managed to get one shot off that missed Diamond by a few feet.

Steven coldly whispered in his ear, "Now you are *my* nigger!"

Jackson took aim and purposely shot Duffy in the thigh.

He screamed and began to fall to the floor, but Butler kept him up.

Jackson called out, "Steven, no! we need him alive!"

Butler looked back at his friend with a steely eyed look, took a deep breath, and let the spy drop to the floor.

Just as that was taking place, the main door flew open. Lieutenant Will O'Malley, together with fifteen of his men, came running in with carbines and muskets and surrounded Duffy. John Hay followed. He told Shanahan he'd heard the shot and told O'Malley to get inside.

Jackson thanked him and told him everything was now under control. He said, "You may want to keep this piece of garbage and arrest him as a spy."

Paul was a little shaken but came over to Hay and said, "Please tell the president what happened here. Ask him to have Mr. Blair at the White House at 10:30 tomorrow morning. He should hear about this from me."

Hay said, "Yes, sir."

"One other thing. I think it would be a good idea for Stanton and Seward to have a conversation with Fernando Wood. He had a role in Duffy's spying."

The soldiers put a tourniquet over Duffy's thigh and covered his head with a pillowcase so he could not see where they were going to take him.

O'Malley said to Shanahan, "Good job, boyo."

Gene answered, "This is what we do," and laughed.

After Hay and the soldiers left with their precious cargo, Jackson sent a message in Morse code to bring the crate home as soon as possible.

Gene decided he would wait until the transfer was made. As soon as he said it, the blue orb appeared and encircled the crate. Three seconds later, the crate disappeared.

The four men from the future stood quietly for a moment. Then Jackson said with a big smile, "We really did it."

That smile spread to the others, and they instinctively began to hug each other.

When Steven came to Paul and put his arms around him, Paul placed his hands on his shoulder and whispered in his ear, "Thank you, Steven. I am so proud of you."

With tears running down his cheeks, this proud man said, "Thank you for convincing me to come, sir. I will never forget it."

Paul smiled and commented, "I think we have enough money for a big celebration at the Willard!"

He said he needed to rest a little while, and they should meet in the lobby at 5:30. Jackson asked if he wanted someone to stay with him, and Paul assured him he was fine.

They went outside. The carriages were still there to bring them back to the White House, where they separated.

It was almost 3:00 p.m., and Jackson asked the driver of Paul's buggy to take him to the Willard. He mildly protested and finally agreed.

CHAPTER 37

Steven, Jackson, and Gene agreed to meet at the "whites only" boarding house and walked together to the Willard. They quickly walked to the hotel, where Paul was waiting for them. He had made a reservation for them, and they had a nice table by a large window, where they sat down and ordered a bottle of wine and large amounts of meat, potatoes, and string beans. The men toasted Paul Diamond, who was slightly embarrassed. He made a toast and told his men there was no one else he would have gone on this mission with.

There was some business to discuss. Paul explained that he had to go to the White House in the morning to see Francis Blair, the president, and Robert. There was one last task he had to complete. He told the men they should prepare to leave the next day before twelve and that he would follow shortly thereafter.

The three looked at each other.

Then Gene said, "We should wait and go home together, sir."

"No. The crisis has passed. I will be fine. I can always get someone to walk with me to the alley."

Steven squeezed Jackson's knee under the table and looked back at his friend and smiled.

They had to agree that the meal was delicious. Paul ate as much steak as he ever had in his life.

While they enjoyed their dinner, a dozen of Stanton's armed men, led by Lieutenant O'Malley, went to Congressman Wood's home and kindly asked if he would accompany them to appear before Secretaries Stanton and Seward.

CHAPTER 38

Paul arrived at the White House at 10:00 a.m. the next morning. He fought through the crowded steps and looked for Nicolay or Hay. He towered over all the people standing around, hoping for an audience with the President. He suddenly felt a tap on his arm and looked down to see Nicolay smiling up at him.

Paul said, "Thank you, John. I will never forget how crowded it is up here!"

The first secretary to the president said, "Follow me, sir," and led him to the president's office door. After knocking twice, he walked Paul inside, where he saw Francis Blair sitting with President Lincoln.

The president immediately stood. He put his hand on Paul's shoulder and exclaimed, "It is good to see you well, my friend.

"There are things for us to talk about, but I know you want a few minutes with Mr. Blair. So I will sit at my desk and pretend to do some work, and the two of you can talk."

"Thank you, Mr. President." Paul greeted Blair Sr. warmly.

The latter stood carefully and said, "I am so happy to congratulate you on the wonderful success you had in Gettysburg."

Paul answered, "It would not have happened if you had not believed in our story."

"You must admit; it was hard to believe," Blair answered with a smile. He went on to say that he had an idea of what Paul wanted to tell him. Martin Duffy had disappeared, and Mr. Blair's daughter had gone through his things and found a letter from Congressman Wood written a week before that was most disturbing.

Paul took a breath and said, "I should not tell you much, but I can say you will need a new body man, and Mr. Duffy is in the custody of the secretary of war. Of course, we know that you had no thought anyone in your household had anything to do with all this."

"This is very shocking to our family. I blame myself for not seeing any clues to his treason."

The President, who had heard every word, stood and walked to Blair. "Do not blame yourself, Blair," he said. "It seems that Mr. Duffy was very good at what he did. Now, I must ask that you excuse yourself. My friend Diamond has a long trip ahead of him."

Blair shook the president's hand and clasped Paul's hand and smiled goodbye.

The president asked Paul to sit with him and tell him what he could about the events of the day before.

Paul thought for a few moments and then answered, "I will tell you that there was an incident at the Naval Yard. It was clear that Duffy wanted the weapon, as well as to murder me. That did not happen, and he is in your custody. I think it would be better that you get the rest of the story from Secretary Stanton. Please be sure he tells you the whole story. Oh and watch out for Fernando Wood. He was an associate of Duffy's."

The President shook Paul's head and thanked him. "I think some of our military people began a conversation with Congressman Wood last night."

The President went to his office door and asked Hay to get his son Robert.

Paul and the President could not help but look at each other with sad expressions. It was time to say goodbye. In three short weeks, they had developed a bond Paul would carry for the rest of his life.

The President had asked him a few days earlier to call him Abe or just Lincoln.

Paul had answered, "In my time, someone has written, 'You may not respect the man, but you must respect the office.'"

Lincoln had laughed and said, "Well then, that must be why so many people call me by my last name."

Now, the President said softly, in a lower pitch than his normal higher tone, "You'd better get a move on; you have a train to catch."

"Mr. President, may I ask a favor?"

"Whatever I can do, Paul."

"Could I please have a memento of our time together?"

With a laugh, Lincoln looked at Robert, who had just come in the office, and said, "I think I have something you would like. Bob, pass me those books on that table."

Robert quickly grabbed three small books and gave them to his father.

The president took the middle of the three and said, "This one should do the trick. It is a little dog-eared, but I don't think you will mind. Now let me write something for you."

Holding his quill pen, he sat down behind his desk. He carefully wrote a few lines, blew on the ink to dry it quickly, and stood and handed it to Paul.

"Thank you, sir. You don't know how much this means to me."

The president answered solemnly, "Friend, I think I am beginning to do just that."

"Sir, I need to speak to Robert, please."

"Would you like to be alone?"

"No, sir. I think you should hear this."

Robert walked over to stand in front of Paul as the older man put his hands on the younger's shoulders. He said, with a tear in his eye, "Bob, you will never see me again. But there is something very important I must tell you. You will live a long, successful, and happy life. Twenty-six years from now, someone you may remember will come to see you. That person will have a message from me. You will open the envelope and read it. Please do exactly as I ask. It is extremely important. Then please write me back because I would love to hear from you. And don't worry. I should still be alive. Time passes differently in my world. Now, promise me you will do it."

Bob looked overcome with emotion as he nodded and whispered, "I promise, sir."

Then they hugged.

President Lincoln walked over to hug Paul and said, "Thank you, Mr. Diamond."

"Sir, it is I who thank you both. It has been my honor. I will never forget having spent this time with you, sir."

Then feeling as though he were about to break down crying, he took his book and placed it carefully in his saddlebag. He turned and looked back one last time at Abraham Lincoln, who gave him a sad smile. He smiled at Robert and left through the side door.

On the other side of the door he wiped the tears from his eye, took a deep breath, and walked down the back stairs of the White House to Pennsylvania Avenue and the Willard Hotel.

The president turned to his son and said, "Bob, I want you to take Johnny and Lamon and follow Paul to his ride. After the last few days, I think we should do whatever we can to make sure Paul gets to where he needs to."

"Yes, sir," Bob answered. He rushed out the door, grabbed John Hay, and called to Ward Lamon. "Come with me. Paul Diamond just left, and the president wants us to make sure he gets to the Willard without any problem."

John said he could finish the letter he was working on when they got back. And Lamon was always ready to do something for Mr. Lincoln and was always armed. The two men grabbed their hats and ran down the main stairway, rushing through the always-crowded lobby and out the door.

The President watched through his window as his son ran down Pennsylvania Avenue toward the Willard.

At that moment, the main door to his office flung open. In rushed an agitated Thaddeus Stevens, who exclaimed, "I don't see anyone here, Nicolay!"

"I assure you, Congressman, there was someone here with the president!"

"It is all right, John," said the president. "Please calm down, Stevens, before your head flies off your shoulders."

"Don't give me any of your folksy down-home stories, Lincoln. Where is he?"

"Where is who?" the president replied.

All that did was get the congressman even more frustrated. "You know damn well who I mean—your friend Diamond. We have questions to ask him. Sumner is waiting in my carriage outside."

"Oh, Paul Diamond. You just missed him. He was with me not five minutes ago. We were saying our goodbyes. I am afraid he is preparing to go home. I don't think we will be seeing him again."

"What!" Stevens said in a low roar. "Which way did he go? He has been staying at the Willard. Did he go there?"

With one of his sly smiles, the president said, "I am the President of the United States. And as such, I am a busy man. I don't make it my business to ask where people will go once they leave my office, Congressman."

"Lincoln, do you expect me to believe that hogwash? I know what I have to do!" He stormed out of the office just as he had come in.

The president waited for a moment and then looked at his first secretary and said, "Go with them. They are going to ride to the Willard."

Nicolay nodded and sped out to catch Stevens and Sumner. He made it to the carriage just as Senator Sumner was about to pull away. He jumped into the back seat and said, "Good afternoon, Senator. President Lincoln thought I could be of assistance."

"Shut up, Nicolay,' Stevens said. 'If I was a few years younger, I would throw you to the street. Hurry, Sumner, or we will lose him."

Paul Diamond was exhausted. He had run out of his cell reconstruction pills the day before, and he was feeling the effect. Combined with having to say goodbye to Lincoln and his son and the end of the mission, all he could think about was making it back to the chair. Just behind him, he heard the voice of John Hay.

"It is a fine day for a walk, isn't it, Mr. Diamond. I was asked to accompany you to make sure you arrive safely. Paul saw Bob Lincoln and John Hay smile and Ward Lamon with his perpetual stone face and one hand on a waist revolver. Paul had to admit he appreciated the escort and silently thanked President Lincoln.

Soon, they reached the corner of the hotel. All he had to do was to get around the next corner to his chair and portal to home. Suddenly, from behind them, Paul heard yelling and a commotion. He turned and saw John Nicolay yelling at Thaddeus Stevens and Charles Sumner in a buggy. Ward Lamon immediately ran back toward them, waving John Hay and Bob Lincoln to keep going with Paul to the corner.

Time was running out. Paul felt the one-minute warning beep go off from the implant in his leg. He was growing more tired. And he was beginning to worry about whether he would even make it to the chair.

He whispered to Bob, "Help me ... Tired ... No time."

Bob called to Johnny Hay for help, and they each took an arm and began to drag him closer. They walked past a stack of crates. Suddenly, Jackson, Steven, and Gene stepped out from behind them. The trio grabbed Paul and ran with him to the wooden chair.

Paul felt the thirty-second beeper go off as he got closer to the chair. He had to whisper, "Please, carry me."

Steven whispered in return, "We got you, sir."

As Steven gently lowered him into the chair, Paul removed the book Lincoln had given him and held it in his hand. It was *Hamlet*.

Robert Lincoln and John Hay stood and watched in wonder as the men placed Paul Diamond in the chair and quickly stepped away.

Sumner's buggy came flying down the alley toward them.

Paul held on to the saddlebag and the book as he slumped down on the chair. A brilliant circular blue orb surrounded Paul and the chair, but the edge of his right foot was sticking out slightly as what looked like electric thunderbolts were going off inside the circle. Paul Diamond was on his way home.

Then, one at a time, the three men looked at Robert and John Hay, smiled, and sat down and waited for the orb to take them back to 2022.

Jackson Barlow was the last and said to the two younger men, "Never forget what happened here."

The witnesses were dumbstruck at what they were watching and could never say a word of what they saw. Even Thaddeus Stevens kept his word after a private meeting with the President Lincoln. For the rest of their lives, they all shared the bond of silence about what they saw. Not for fifty years did Robert Lincoln speak or write about all he knew.

PART THREE

CHAPTER 39

Goddard Space Flight Center, July 6, 2022

It is said that the passage of time varies for beings in different realities—especially for those who are put in an induced coma. Paul Diamond suffered severe burns on his right foot and toes because of the foot sticking out slightly from the protection of the orb. Upon his return, he was screaming from the terrible pain—although he was truly not aware of the injury having happened. Nor would he ever remember it. He was immediately rushed to a surgical theater to be examined by a team of trauma physicians and burn specialists, who were immediately called for.

Jim Conklin was terribly upset. And Paul's team was waiting for his return from his first surgery. They were told to go back to their recovery rooms, but speaking on behalf of his two teammates, Jackson said, "With all due respect, sir, we will wait here. He is our older brother and leader."

Dr. Conklin smiled and said, "Very well. Just stay out of the way. It's going to be busy here."

Gene answered, "Thank you sir."

For the next eleven days, Paul was in an induced coma and underwent three skin grafts. All the while, there was always one of his men sitting outside his room. They had been released after four days of their own recovery, but they were there in full uniform, maintaining their watch.

On day twelve, Paul heard someone talking and felt pain in his foot. He grimaced and moaned. Butler, who was at his post outside the room, heard Paul. He rushed to get a nurse and told another to get Jim Conklin. Paul was whispering for water and Butler moved a nurse to give it to him to sip through a straw.

Conklin was upstairs in less than two minutes and rushed to the bedside of his old friend. He whispered, "Paul, you made it back. Thank God." He put his hand on one of Paul's, and Paul squeezed him back.

Conklin said, "Your men never left your side."

In response, Paul raised his hand as he saw Steven Butler and then Gene Shanahan standing erect, Tears ran down their cheeks.

Conklin then said, "Paul, there is one thing I have to do for you. I will be back as soon as I get it done."

Paul nodded his head affirmatively as Conklin shook hands with the three officers who had been there waiting on Paul. He knew they would be right there when he got back.

He ran down to his office and said to his assistant, "Margaret, please get me the number of the Lincoln Museum in Springfield, Illinois. I need to have an important conversation with the Director."

Within two minutes, Jim Conklin was talking to the office of the Director of the museum. He introduced himself as a representative of NASA, who needed to speak to the Director on a matter of utmost importance.

He was put right through and heard a very pleasant voice say, "Hello, this is Dr. Lincoln. May I help you?"

Conklin could not speak for a moment. The rational side of his mind knew that he could not possibly be talking to a natural descendent of Abraham Lincoln. But that rational world no longer existed. He coughed slightly and said, "Excuse me. I am Dr. James Conklin, and I run a department at NASA that is involved in the researching of artifacts. We have found something that I think would be most interesting to you."

"I had no idea NASA was involved in that area," she replied.

He answered, "Yes, most people think that. But before I go any further may I give you our number and ask you to call me right back? It helps with due diligence that you believe I am who I say."

"That would be fine."

Conklin gave her the main number for the Goddard Space Flight Center and said, "Please ask for me and you will be put through to my office."

"Thanks. I will call you right back," she said.

Within a minute, Margaret came running into his office to tell him there was a Dr. Lincoln on the phone. "Please put her through, Margaret."

"Jim Conklin," he answered. "This is Nancy Lincoln. Thank you for giving me your number. It does take away some questions, and I must admit you have me intrigued."

He thought with a smile, *Just wait till you hear the rest of the story!*

"I do get that every so often. I get some crazy things coming through my office because of our research." Dr. Lincoln said, "You have my attention."

"Unfortunately, I must limit myself on the telephone as to what I can tell you. But before I tell you what I can, there is something I need to confirm. Forgive me for being blunt. Are you a natural descendant of Abraham Lincoln?"

Nancy Lincoln was confused and getting a little annoyed. "Yes, I am," she said. "Now tell me, where this is going, Dr. Conklin?"

He took a deep breath and said, "As a scientist I had to ask and hear you confirm it. Forgive me if I offended you. We have discovered an artifact that we have authenticated that came from President Lincoln's desk in the White House with an inscription in his hand from July 1863."

Now it was Dr. Lincoln's turn to be speechless. When she gathered herself, all she could say was, "How is this possible?"

Jim Conklin explained that, although this was a secure line, one could never be sure of crossed wires and recordings. He did say he would be happy to send a NASA jet to pick her up in Springfield and bring her to Goddard the next day to examine the artifact and meet the man who had discovered it, along with hearing the astounding story of how it had been brought to NASA.

She was speechless and thought, *This is impossible. Could the family or his staff have missed anything when the office was packed up after he left office? Could someone have stolen it and it has reappeared after all these years?*

Conklin said it was unfortunate he could not reveal more. But in order to see the artifact, she would have to come to "the mountain."

She finally said, "Of course I want to see it, not that I believe it is genuine. You know, we get a few of these claims every year."

Conklin answered, "I understand your position and opinion. But I assure you; you have never seen anything like this."

She checked her calendar and said she would be free two days later. Conklin said Margaret would be in touch with her office about the details, but he was sure he could have a plane waiting for her at the Springfield airport the day after tomorrow.

She interrupted him to ask, "You can do that without checking with a general or someone?"

He laughed and said, "You would be surprised at what we can do here. Thank you very much, Dr. Lincoln. I look forward to meeting you."

She replied, "Same here," and hung up and just shook her head.

Nancy Lincoln had, over the years, gone on some wild goose chases for Abraham and Robert memorabilia, as well as Mary Todd Lincoln dresses. Some of the episodes were hysterical, but this felt different. If this wasn't real, the worst that could happen was her getting a flight in a NASA jet.

Conklin went running out of his office back to Paul Diamond's room. All three members of the team were standing right where Jim had left them, and they all had big smiles on their faces. Jim went right into the middle of them and said, "You are not going to believe who I just spoke to."

"We don't do well with guessing games, sir," answered Barlow.

"Sorry," Jim said. "Nancy Lincoln."

Steven Butler laughed and said, "Well, I'll be damned." He then quickly said, "Excuse me, sir."

Gene said, "Is she definitely coming? We have a lot of work going on."

Conklin nodded and said, "And the work we started after you got back, we redouble our efforts. Gene, get the research team back together and check the time lines for any aberrations. Right away."

Once the team was released from quarantine Gene Shanahan led a handpicked group of researchers to check for changes in the time line.

The first thing he looked for was President Lincoln. The new line showed President Lincoln was alive until the early 1870's. He stopped in the middle of his own search and ran to find Steven, Jackson, and Jim Conklin to give them the good news. In Conklin's mind President Lincoln had never been assassinated. The three Captains fist bumped and hugged each other over the news.

Conklin stared at their reaction then said, "Jackson, make sure that a jet is available for early morning the day after tomorrow. You will pick up Nancy Lincoln at the Springfield airport at 10:00 a.m. Get the flight plan filed as soon as you can. I want Steven to go with you while Gene keeps working here. And I have never been so excited about a case in all the years we have been doing this. How is our patient?"

Jackson answered, "He is slowly coming back. He asked for his saddlebag. He's holding the book and refuses to wash his right hand. He doesn't realize they had to do it for the surgeries."

Gene asked when Conklin was going to tell him about Lincoln.

"I am going to wait until tomorrow, let him get a little stronger first."

Within an hour, Gene Shanahan had a team of a dozen researchers back working on comparing the two time lines. Before every mission, historical data on the original time line was saved to CD-ROM for comparison to changes that were made by any mission, whether intended or not. For example, if Gene Shanahan had caught the eye of a young wench at the Willard and they had ended up in his bed at the rooming house he was staying in and nine months later a bouncing baby boy slipped into the world, there would be an entire new line to contend with. And what if Gene Jr. was mad he didn't have a father and decided to rob banks and kill innocent people who would otherwise have happy productive lives—people who would now no longer bear children of their own because they were killed by the young Gene.

But there was another side. What if Gene Jr., because he had no father, was determined to prove his worth to the world and developed a cure for a killing disease, saving thousands of lives.

The vagaries of changes in the time line were incredibly difficult to prove, let alone find. But if something was changed and was found, what should be done about it?

All the obvious leads were checked first, but Shanahan had them go down three more levels. Meanwhile, Diamond grew stronger but would be unable to walk for a month and would depend on a wheelchair until he was able.

Conklin told the boys he was going to wait until the morning of Dr. Lincoln's visit to tell his friend about her arrival. Paul began to read *Hamlet* aloud to himself and still refused to wash his right hand.

The morning came to bring Nancy Lincoln to meet Paul Diamond. Barlow and Butler took off in their jet at 7:30 in the morning. Dr. Lincoln was met at her home by two marines, who would escort her to the plane that had landed thirty minutes earlier. When she arrived at the airport Dr. Lincoln asked the marines if they knew anything about her trip.

The taller of the two simply said, "No, ma'am. But your pilots are coming now."

They seemed to be in their late twenties. Each was carrying a thermal container for liquids and was in a full flight suit.

The marines briskly saluted. One pilot said, "Thank you men. We will take it from here." He turned to Dr. Lincoln and introduced himself as Captain Butler and then introduced her to Captain Barlow. "We will be your pilots to NASA."

All Dr. Lincoln could say was, "Oh my."

The plane was pure white, sleek, and long and had the NASA insignia on its side and tail and looked incredibly fast.

Captain Barlow said, "There are a bunch of people looking forward to meeting you, so we should get a move on." He started to laugh and apologized by saying, "Forgive me, ma'am. Someone said that to me just the other day."

Butler took her arm and helped her up the outside steps to the plane and Barlow escorted her to her seat and strapped her in as he explained, 'This bird goes pretty quickly, so it's not a good idea to get up and walk around. If you need to use the ladies' room, Lieutenant Carlson will help you."

A smiling woman in an air force uniform came over to shake her hand.

Dr. Lincoln raised her hand to ask a question, and Butler said, "Yes, Ma'am?"

"Do either of you know anything about why I am getting this treatment? And can you talk about it?"

The two pilots smiled at each other and her, and Butler said, "Yes ma'am. And not yet. And you never asked that question."

What was normally a four-hour flight on a commercial flight took three and was smooth as silk. They landed on what seemed to be a special runway at Goddard. There were only three people there to greet her. Dr. Conklin introduced himself and his assistant, Margaret, along with Gene Shanahan, who was wearing his Marine Special Forces uniform. He had a big smile on his face when he shook Dr. Lincoln's hand.

Conklin said, "We are so glad you are here. We have much to discuss, and there is someone very anxious to meet you. After we talk alone, I am sure you will feel the same way."

There were two large NASA vans waiting to drive them to the office complex, but first Dr. Lincoln had to get IDs and fingerprinted.

When they finally arrived at their operations center Conklin told the men, "I will bring Dr. Lincoln to my office and then meet you downstairs later."

They each said, "Yes, sir."

On the way upstairs, he asked her if she was hungry or thirsty.

"I could use a good cup of coffee; it has already been a long morning, and I have a long list of questions."

He answered, "Coffee I have, and I promise all your questions will be answered."

Margaret said, "I will bring the coffee to your office, sir."

CHAPTER 40

D r. Lincoln and Dr. Conklin settled in front of his desk and Margaret brought the coffee, which, for a government installation, was surprisingly good.

Conklin began telling Dr. Lincoln that what she was about to hear was on a top secret level and, if she repeated anything she was told in this facility, it would be considered an act of treason. "I want to make sure you understand what I just said," he concluded. "Please say I understand."

After saying she understood, her first thought was he kidding and then realized from the look on his face that he was stone-cold serious. "Am I in trouble?" she nervously asked.

Conklin laughed and answered, "No, you, Dr. Lincoln, are the second most important person in this facility. Now I will tell you why. And for the next hour, he told her everything.

His assistant stepped out and closed the door behind her. About ten minutes later, she could not help but hear Dr. Lincoln yell out, "That is impossible and against the laws of science!"

Inside the room, Jim Conklin smiled and said, "Why don't you look at what is in this envelope? But please put the plastic gloves on first."

She put the gloves on and gently opened the envelope. Out slipped a dog-eared copy of *Hamlet*. She went to the publishing date; it was 1855 from a London publisher. Then she went back to the front page and read the inscription:

Dear Paul,

Please accept this as a token of my thanks for your help, friendship, and support.

A. Lincoln

Suddenly, Nancy Lincoln's head snapped up. She studied Jim Conklin and said in a very serious voice, "Do you know who Paul is?"

Conklin answered quickly, "Yes, I do. He was our team leader, Paul Diamond. The president gave it to him just before he came home. Why do you ask?" Nancy Hanks Lincoln sat speechless in her chair. Then she whispered, "This is not possible, unbelievable."

Conklin asked her, "What is it? Is there something wrong?"

"Wrong." She laughed. "This book may have answered one of the great mysteries of my family history. Just before he died, the President wrote a note in an envelope to a Paul Diamond and gave it to his son Robert. It was never opened, and just before he died, Robert did the same thing and gave both envelopes to his son Senator Jack Lincoln. They are in a lockbox in my office in Springfield. We have spent years trying to find out who this man Diamond was. There is one mention of a "P. D." meeting with the President in July 1863 in John Nicolay's logbook. But he never shows up again. He was a ghost."

"Well, Dr. Lincoln, Paul Diamond is in a hospital bed two floors below us and is very anxious to meet you."

"The feeling is mutual," she said.

"There is something else I must tell you," said Jim. "In the time line that existed before our team went back to 1863, Robert Lincoln accepted the appointment of ambassador to Great Britain. While he was in London, his son, Jack, died."

Nancy whispered, "That never happened."

Jim went on and said, "Just before the team returned, Paul went to the

White House to see the president, Francis Blair, and Robert Lincoln. Blair left, and Paul was alone with the father and son. Two things happened before he left. The first was he asked the president for a memento to bring home. He was given Mr. Lincoln's copy of *Hamlet*, which he inscribed. You have that in front of you. The second thing was that Paul told Robert he would get a visit from someone he would recognize who would give him a letter from Paul with a request. That request would be that he decline the ambassadorship. Thus, your grandfather would live, become an outstanding United States senator, and represent the state of Illinois—and would have made his own grandfather and father very proud. Oh, and one more thing happened that I was not aware of until our conversation on the telephone; you were born and are sitting and talking with me right now."

Nancy Lincoln was stunned.

Dr. Conklin said with a smile. "Shall we go? We can pick up on the rest of the story later."

"Yes please. Oh my. I cannot believe this is happening."

When they got out of the elevator, Jim stopped and told her that Paul was as naturally smart a man as he had ever known and that he'd learned much from him over the twenty years of their friendship. But he felt badly that he had taken advantage of their relationship by sending him on four trips; he was afraid those journeys had taken its toll on him.

"How old is he?" Nancy asked.

Jim smiled and answered, "Forty-seven, and physically he is in good shape, outwardly. But this science is still so new that I worry about the long-range effects on him, or anyone else who makes the trip. By the way, he did not even know of your existence until this morning. I wanted to make sure he was strong enough to handle meeting you. But I was wrong about that. He started to crawl out of his bed as soon as I told him you were on your way. He gave me the book to show you right away. He hadn't let go of it since he woke up." He laughed. "One last thing—I just want to remind you again about what we talked about upstairs. The book can never be shown at the museum or to anyone. Technically, it belongs to Paul anyway."

An air force nurse came over to lead them to Paul's room, and Jim asked Nancy, "Are you ready?"

She said, "I have never been more nervous in my life!"

The nurse smiled and opened the door. Paul was lying on the bed with his bad foot elevated, and he was brushing his hair with one hand as he said, "Sorry, I wanted to be presentable."

Jim said, "Dr. Diamond, allow me to introduce Dr. Nancy Hanks Lincoln."

Paul stared at her and immediately said, "Oh my, you have his eyes." He was immediately struck by her eyes as well as her height. She was at least six feet tall and was lovely. She appeared to be in her late thirties.

With a tear in her eyes, Nancy said, "I wanted to meet the man who gave me my life." She walked over and sat in the chair next to his bed and took Paul's hands in her own.

They both began to cry.

Jim Conklin was overcome and slipped out of the room to allow them some privacy.

Gene Shanahan was waiting in his dress uniform and asked, "Well?"

Conklin answered, "They will be just fine. When you talk to her mention, that she has the president's eye color."

Gene smiled and nodded. The others came over and Jackson said everything was ready for what they'd planned.

Conklin then said,

"Why don't we give them fifteen minutes? I think they both have months of questions to ask each other."

Nancy and Paul sat and held hands for most of their initial meeting—until she asked Paul one question with tears in her eyes, "Was he a good man?"

Paul considered the question, looked into her hazel eyes, and answered, "The finest I have ever met."

She started to cry again.

Just then, Jim knocked on the door and came back into the room. "May I come in?"

Paul nodded.

The director went on to say, "The medical team wants you to start getting out of that bed, Lieutenant, come in, please." The nurse came in with a wheelchair and helped Paul leave his bed and sit and get comfortable. She carefully guided his left foot up and locked it in place, and the four slowly left the room.

Waiting for them in their full dress uniforms was Paul's team of Captains—Barlow, Butler, and Shanahan.

Barlow said, "Ten-hut."

The three saluted and gathered around Nancy Lincoln to say hello again and what an honor it was to meet her.

Dr. Conklin said, "would you please follow me?"

The nurse began to push the wheelchair. Nancy came over and said to her, "May I?"

"Of course," she said.

They came into a long hallway that was made up of rooms for the military personnel of the unit. Standing in front of each door was the occupant of each in their full dress uniforms. Men and women from a mixture of skin colors and services were represented.

Paul's three men walked in ahead of them in formation, and Barlow called out, "At ease."

The others responded crisply and immediately.

Dr. Conklin stepped out and began to speak. "We are honored and very proud today, honored by the visit of the great-great-great-granddaughter of the sixteenth president of the United States, Abraham Lincoln. We are proud of our team—all of whom have returned safely from their successful mission that has saved over 125,000 lives, plus the ones who lived because of those who were saved. I am personally honored to recognize the leadership of my close friend, who, as of today, will be addressed as Colonel Paul Diamond with all of the accompanying benefits and honors the title brings with it."

Everyone applauded furiously as Jim shook his friend's hand.

Steven Butler stepped out and called out, "Ten-hut. There is an officer on the floor and a direct descendant of a president of the United States."

Every soldier smartly saluted and could not help but smile as Nancy Lincoln wheeled Colonel Diamond down the hallway to a door that was opened for them to go outside and sit in the sun.

She bent over and softly asked, "How do you feel?"

He smiled and said, "Never better. But I would like my hat back."

Nancy laughed and said, "By the way, I have some mail for you."

Paul turned and said, "How can you have mail for me?"

She patted him on the shoulder and said, "It's a surprise. And if you want to read them, when you are up to it, you must come pay me a visit in Springfield."

Paul said softly, "I was there a few times, but you weren't. I think I would like that very much."

CHAPTER 41

Six weeks later, Colonel Diamond was sitting in Nancy Lincoln's office with a lockbox sitting on her desk. He'd made a good recovery from his burns and had flown to Springfield along with a naval nurse to watch over him.

After he greeted Nancy Lincoln, he simply said, "Where is my mail?"

She laughed and said, "Calm down. Let me bring you inside my office."

There was a knock on the door, and two curators came in the room holding white plastic gloves.

Nancy said, "Paul let me introduce Amy Bluestein and Suzanne Kamen, our senior curators. Ladies, we will now be opening this box. But before we do, I should tell you what is in this box is considered top secret. Any disclosure of the contents will be considered an act of treason. Are we clear?"

They both nervously nodded their heads.

"It would be better if you both acknowledged this by saying I understand."

In tandem, they both did.

Dr. Lincoln took a deep breath and, with the key in her right hand, put it in the lock and slowly turned the key. She lifted the top of the box that revealed three envelopes, each addressed to Paul Diamond. She said with surprise, "I thought there would be only two."

She stepped away from the desk allowing the curators, now wearing their gloves, to gently remove each envelope and lay the three on the desk. They examined each for any other information and, seeing none were sealed, delicately removed the papers from each of the three envelopes and laid them on the table.

Dr. Lincoln said, "Thank you, ladies. Please leave us gloves, and we'll take it from here."

They nodded and left her office.

The doctor asked Paul, "Are you all right?"

He answered, "I don't know what to say."

"Nancy, I may be more nervous than I was when I first met the President," he added. "I think it would be easier if you read it out loud. His handwriting appears to be not as clear as it was when he was younger."

April 10, 1876
Springfield, Illinois

My dear friend,

I have no idea if you will ever read this, but I feel I must try to communicate with you. Upon my death, Bob will take possession of this letter and hopefully add his own and give it to one of his children before his time comes. Hopefully it can make it all the way to you.

My health has begun to fail, and I wanted to make sure you heard from me in my own words.

Before I go any further, I should tell you, although I suspect that you already know, Martin Duffy was hung as a spy. And Fernando Wood was convicted for conspiracy and served eighteen months in federal prison. I commuted his sentence after nine months and had him brought to the White House. I explained that I had done it to put that business behind us, but if I heard or read one thing that he had spoken against the federal government, he would be back in jail as fast as a squirrel could climb a tree. I assured Mr. Wood that my successor would be told the story and be ready to act in my place about his status. He proved to be quite cooperative.

I assume you know that I was invited to make a "few appropriate remarks" at the dedication of the Gettysburg Cemetery in the fall of 1863. The primary address was made by the master orator Edward Everett, He spoke impressively about the battle and touched on the last counterattack made by the Union Army on the 4th of July. I could not duplicate that and chose to offer a few hundred words about honoring the men who had fallen and the debt we owed them for their sacrifice.

During my preparation, I read various articles about how both sides proclaimed that God was on their side. I wondered, How can this be? Could God be both for and against the same cause? I wrote about it but chose not to use it in my speech. You have my remarks, and I felt that it would not be appropriate.

I have been thinking lately about our conversation in my office about the "hypo.", I wish to remind you about my request of treating me with fairness and a certain degree of grace regarding my condition. Feel free to use my thoughts about God and his position in the conflict. It is something I have wrestled with for several years and may explain my confusion about his role in the human condition, Paul.

I must confess, we had problems with the initial Reconstruction of the Union. My friends in the Radical Republicans wing of our party were adamant about punishing the seceded states of the South. Many wanted to confiscate the planter properties like General Sherman wanted.

We managed to find a compromise. Any plantations that the owners had walked away from would be used for the purpose of being carved up and distributed to former slaves to build homes and work the land. And as Southerners voted to return to the United States, the percentage of voters willing to rejoin our Union was increased to 15 percent, rather than my 10 percent. I could not fight too hard over that. Those plantations were cut up to give Negroes "40 acres and a mule." At least it *gave them something to call their own, and they could provide for their families.*

Elections were held, and there was rampant racism. I wanted the first election after the war ended to be pushed through quickly, but it may have been too soon. Going through the war as we did—the horror of it, all the dead and wounded— was unforgettable. I still have nightmares of it. We could not expect many Southerners to forgive and forget so easily.

The ending of the war eased my path to a second term, but it was not all dessert. The party had substantial majorities in Congress, but it was a constant struggle to fight the Jacobins.

After the 1868 election, President Grant was more than gracious in allowing Mary, Tad, and I the time to prepare to move back to Springfield. As you may remember, Mrs. Lincoln was not the easiest person to get along with. I was concerned about her relationship with Mrs. Grant, with whom she had very little contact until after the war ended, Mary did have a proprietary feeling about the White House, and part of her felt we should be allowed to stay as long as we wanted to, I had to sit her down and explain we did not own the White House and the new president and Mrs. Grant would now live there. She was not entirely pleased but finally relented and realized we had to move on.

President Grant did ask that I stay on for a few weeks to help with the ongoing plans for Reconstruction, so Mary and Tad started the trip back to Springfield while I stayed on in the White House. Sam Grant and I continued our good working relationship, and I gave him my views. I thought we should let them up easy and do what we could to bring the states that seceded back into the Union smoothly. The problem was the views of the Radicals like Stevens, Sumner, and Henry Wade—who led a group that wanted to make the punishment severe. I am sure you know the details of how difficult it was.

I was disappointed in some of Grant's choices for his cabinet, but he did get Seward and Stanton to stay on.

After those three weeks, I began the trip home. It was an emotional parting for me, Nicolay and Hay had left after the 1868 election, and Stoddard was the last remaining secretary from the early years, The government gave me a three-car train to bring me home, along with a group of friendly reporters and Ward Lamon and a group of my guards who had been with me for a few years. I was hoping not to make many speeches. But there were a few I could not avoid.

You know, Paul, there was a part of me that never believed I would see Springfield again. We finally made it back and received a home that gave me room for my papers and an office I could use to do some writing that I wanted to do. But once we got settled, it was time for us to do the traveling we always wanted.

Before I left Washington, I asked the ambassadors from Great Britain and France if they could help us out with planning. And in no time at all, they took care of everything. You know, Paul, I was never considered wealthy, so we could never have made the trip without the help of these two governments. I felt a little like I was taking advantage of the situation. But I was assured by President Grant that I was not.

We spent five weeks in Europe. I cannot begin to tell you how kind everyone was and how well we were treated by the regular people, as well as those in the two governments. I never ate so much in my life! Mrs. Lincoln and Tad had a wonderful time seeing museums, and I must admit she did some shopping too. I had no idea how I was going to pay for it all!

We finally returned to New York and received a wonderful welcome. After a few days of seeing the sights, we got on a train that would bring us back to Springfield and home.

There was one more trip I wanted to make, and that was to see California and the Pacific Ocean. Tad was a little under the weather, and Mary did not want to leave him, Se said I should go alone. I did not mind, so I wired the president to let him know I was going and did the same to Governor Low in California.

The next thing I knew, I received travel orders from General Sherman for my journey whenever I wanted. I went to San Francisco and spent two weeks out there, and it was wonderful. I saw some incredible things and met so many interesting people. I ate like a cow grazing at a field. I had not felt so relaxed in years, I returned to Springfield so refreshed and happy to see Mary and Tad and even had some presents sent.

The years passed with ongoing trouble in the South. Negroes were given the right to vote and some were elected to Congress, to my delight. But there were ongoing troubles there. Former Southern representatives were sent back to the House and Senate, and although the war was over, it was not forgotten. We had fought a violent and bloody war with these people. We could not expect the animosity and hatred for one another to pass away like the sun at the end of the day and wake up to a new day with it all forgotten, Human beings are incapable of living that way.

After my return to Springfield, I restarted my law practice and confined my activities to smaller cases between people, as opposed to larger corporate cases. They came banging down my door. Tad and I spent time together working in my office. He was a help with paperwork once he figured things out.

Robert and the family came to visit every other month, and that was a joy, He convinced us to spend some time in Chicago, so we spent almost all of 1870 there. I went into his law office almost every day. I could see the business was becoming more formal, but I handled some cases in court and was proud to have won my share of them. He seemed so happy that we were doing it together as equal partners. Of course, he was more organized than I and even made me buy a case to hold my papers when I went to court rather than put them in my hat!

I began to miss the quiet of Springfield and our friends and chose to move back in early 1871. It was good for all of us, except for Mary missing the fancy parties. I went along if I didn't have to wear those silly white gloves. As President I had to, but Abe Lincoln could go without them. I seemed to always forget to put them on.

We were having a good and happy life until the bad times hit us. I learned as president to take each day as the creator gives it to us. We lost Tad suddenly in 1871. He was such a sweet boy and dealt with his physical problems as best as he could. He was never that close with Bob. My dear Molly was crushed at Tad's death and died within a year. She just lost any desire and hope for living. Bob had drifted away from her because of his own family and her emotional problems.

He wanted me to move back to Chicago and live next door to his family, but I decided that Springfield was where I belonged. Now Beth is pregnant again, and I pray I will be here to see the baby born.

Paul, I do believe that I had lived in "the inferno" for three plus years, and with the help of you and your men, I was released from it. I still have dreams of all the soldiers I ordered to their deaths, but the purpose was still not enough for it. I only hope that history will be kind to my actions, as well as the mothers and fathers who lost loved ones and those who were maimed from their service to the Union.

I am growing very tired, and I want to wire Bob and ask if he could find a way to come for a visit. He is busy with his work and family these days. His wife, Beth, is a bit sickly and it is a strain on him. I pray for her health.

Tell Captain Butler that I did my best for his people. Paul, know that a day has not passed that I have not thought about the effects of what we all did will have on your future.

I hope that you find the happiness that you have earned and deserved,

Your friend,
A. Lincoln

Abraham Lincoln died three days later in Springfield, Illinois. His son Robert did not arrive until the next day.

CHAPTER 42

Paul broke down a few times during Nancy's reading and she had to stop a few times. He said, "I can still feel his arms hugging me goodbye."

When Paul collected himself, Nancy said, "I think Robert is next. Are you ready?"

Paul answered, "He was just a young man, I can still see him standing outside the orb as I left."

July 3, 1926
Chicago, Illinois

Dear Mr. Diamond,

It is a bit odd addressing you in the same way I did over sixty years ago. But I still feel that age difference when I was twenty-two years old. Although the differences in how time passes in our two worlds are substantial, I still feel the need to address you as sir even though I am 83 years old!

I am following my father's wishes before he died, and I am looking at the letter he wrote you. It is unsealed, and I have a suspicion he wanted me to read it, but I have chosen not to. What he wanted to tell you is between the two of you. I do not wish to insert myself in your communication.

Please know this: During my final conversation with him two weeks before he passed, he mentioned his affection and gratitude for you and a relationship that lasted three short weeks but became a lifelong friendship that lasted almost 160 years! Please know that I share his feelings for you regardless of your motives, which I know were pure. Your actions saved our country and not a day passes without my thinking of all the lives those actions saved.

I followed your instructions and declined the appointment to London. My intuition and intelligence have told me that going there would have meant something would happen to me or to a member of my family. Ironically, my beloved Beth took ill during that time we remained home. She still lives today. My son, Jack, is coming for a visit tomorrow. I will give him my letter, as well as that of my father. I will have to explain something to him and will try to come up with something believable.

Before I forget, when your letter was delivered to me by Jackson Barlow, I was as giddy as a schoolboy. We hugged, laughed, and talked. He waited until I wrote my response that I hope you receive. There was a meeting going on in my office, and I think the people there were quite sure I had taken leave of my senses.

Paul, you were right, I have led a long full life that could have turned very differently if not for your intervention. Thank you for everything.

I remain your most humble servant.

Robert T. Lincoln

Paul became weepy again, and it was clear to Nancy that he had true fondness for the President's son.

The third letter was from Robert's son, Jack. For some reason Nancy did not expect to see this one. But based on what Robert had written, it made sense. She read the letter from her grandfather:

April 14, 1949
Springfield, Illinois

Dear Mr. Diamond,

Before my father died, he handed me two envelopes and asked me to write a letter to you at the end of my life. Although we never met, the strange circumstances surrounding this request became clearer once he told me the story before he passed. It is an astounding, unbelievable tale that I had a hard time accepting at the time. I attributed it to his memory lapses and illness.

But there was one thing his mind was always crystal clear about. That was his father and my grandfather and namesake. Despite their differences while he was growing up and reconciling the President's appearance and demeanor to his friends from Harvard and the upper crust, my father idolized him as he grew older. My grandfather began to rely on him more during the second term, and they both mellowed to each other. My grandfather began to respect his opinion on many things. Hay and Nicolay had moved on and Stoddard was the last of the "old guard" who had worked through the war, so it became easier, and the president become more approachable to him.

So he told me the story of you and your three friends who suddenly appeared bearing gifts that ended the war within one month. All he would tell me is that you were there to combat an unknown adversary who had tried to intercede in the conflict the year before and failed. You were from a future alternate time, it seems, and he left it at that.

I have no idea how long the war would have continued, and it was clear that we had driven the Rebels back. But what if they came back? Mr. Diamond, I have seen two world wars in less than thirty years, with the loss of untold millions of people. Being able to save one single life is miraculous to me, and in my political career, I have made that plain. Frankly, I think humanity drips with madness when it comes to this. Now that we have weapons capable of killing eighty thousand people in seconds, maybe that is enough to act as a deterrent. It is possible, but I am afraid it is not. What you and your compatriots did was save thousands of lives. I vote for that!

From my weakness in mathematics, it seems that we are getting closer to your being able to read these. What is interesting is that both letters are unsealed. But I will not read them. My affection for my father and grandfather knows no limits. So I will not take advantage of what appears to be an offer. I will give these three letters with specific instructions.

I have not told anyone, nor will, of my conversation with my father. Based upon all my father told me, I regret not having the chance to meet you. I will give these envelopes to my son John with specific instructions that they not be read by anyone. There are rumors of a Lincoln Museum opening. I will have to see if I can trust these people to keep them safe, but I think it will be best to keep these in the hands of the family. They are too dangerous to be available to the public.

I must confess that there were many people who urged me to run for the presidency. But I truly believed I could achieve more good for this country. as a United States Senator and was concerned about comparisons to my grandfather and being found wanting.

Please accept, on behalf of my entire family, our respect and thanks for all you have done.

With my warmest regards,
Abraham Lincoln II

After they had recovered from the emotional gut wrenching of reading the letters, Nancy and Paul sat wiping their eyes and holding hands. They had different reasons, of course. Paul had met and spent time with Abraham Lincoln and his oldest son Robert. He changed their lives and hundreds of thousands of others, but their relationship was natural and real. How could he forget smiling back at Robert as he was in pain under the orb just before he jumped back to his own time? John Hay had his arm around Bob's shoulders as Paul vanished into the ether. For Nancy, this was her family and a life she never would have had if Paul had not told her great-grandfather not to accept the appointment as minister to England from President Harrison. She truly owed her life to Paul Diamond, and that was not the only reason she was feeling so comfortable with him.

She said quietly, "My great grandfather never told my grandfather the entire story."

Paul answered, "I was concerned but not worried. Maybe on his deathbed he wanted to cleanse his soul, but I really did not think he would burden his own son with such information. What he did reveal was enough. But Jack never said a word to anyone—not that we know of, not even his wife or kids. Did your father ever allude to anything about the war?"

"My father was not as smart as his father but still went to college for agriculture. My mother's family owned a small farm that he enjoyed working, and when my grandfather died, he took it over and did a very good job. Don't get me wrong. He was very proud of who he was and where he came from. He just didn't have interest in talking about it all the time. When he died, he told me that there was not a prouder Lincoln than he." She sniffled.

Paul smiled and said, "I think we have a lot of work to do, Ms. Lincoln."

"Well, old man, we better get a move on." She laughed.

To this he replied, "I am only eight years older than you!"

They laughed and smiled together and got ready to work.

CHAPTER 43

Washington DC, Three weeks later

For the past four years, Jackson, Steven, and Gene would meet one night per week at a bar called Semper Fi. They had been so busy with debriefing and filing their reports on the mission that this was the first chance they had to get out. The bar was frequented exclusively by men and women of the Special Forces of every branch of the service. It was in the District near Foggy Bottom. Non-military personnel were discouraged from coming in, especially any college students from any of the many colleges and universities in the neighborhood. Single women were politely escorted out. The patrons were men and women who worked under enormous pressure and had to be ready at a moment's notice to answer the call to fly halfway around the world to help Americans in need or citizens of allies who were threatened by terrorists. Semper Fi was a refuge where they could be together and enjoy time with their brothers and sisters in arms without fear of anything said being repeated and recrimination.

This night, there were about twenty customers in the bar. They were all dressed in fatigues and looked as strong as martial arts fighters. And they wolfed down enormous amounts of meat. Although Semper Fi came from Semper Fidelis, which was the motto of the Marine Corps, they were all family and would lay down their lives for another without a second thought. That possibility was never more than a few minutes away from happening.

Most of the soldiers noticed two men in fatigues slip inside the front door. A female army ranger had noticed one of the two because he was smaller than any of the other soldiers in the room. She elbowed an enormous Navy SEAL who was sitting with her as he finished his meal and drank a very tall beer. He nodded his head and looked toward the bar where Jackson, Steven, and Gene were laughing with each other.

Joe Cortese was the owner and a retired marine sergeant who had taken over the bar ten years earlier from a fellow marine who had moved to North Carolina. He came over and started clearing away the plates of the three. As he did so, he saw one of the two strangers come over and noticed the fatigues he was wearing were clearly not genuine. Cortese whispered, ' Behind you."

Shanahan had the best peripheral vision of the three and was sitting to the right of Butler. He could see the man reach into his pants and pull out a .357-caliber magnum and quietly say, "Steven Butler, I have a message for you from my ancestor, Martin Duffy."

The three froze for a split second. Shanahan turned instantaneously to his right. Butler turned around to face the voice. And Barlow made ready to launch himself at this piece of trash who was pointing the weapon at Butler's head. Shanahan jumped and knocked the .357 down as it was fired, steering the shots to Butler's chest as Barlow grabbed his neck and put him into a headlock and threw him down. Butler moaned as he slumped off his stool to the floor. Shanahan knew they were required to wear heavy-duty bulletproof vests by Director Conklin before they could be out in public again.

Five other officers ran over immediately to help. The female officer had the second perpetrator in an arm bar as the one on the floor whispered, "You're too late. You can't stop it. We have been planning for thirty years for this day. It is happening right now, you fools." He crunched down on a tooth and instantly fell dead.

Jackson screamed out to the woman, "He has a pill!"

The larger SEAL hauled off and sledgehammered the second man's face with his massive right fist, and a pill flew out of his mouth. The female officer opened his mouth while he was semiconscious to make sure there was no backup and, when satisfied there was nothing else there, slapped him hard across the face and yelled into his eyes, "Give me a name, you piece of crap. Who sent you?!"

"They will kill me; they have my wife."

"She may already be dead, you idiot. Give me a name and tell me where they are, or I will kill you right here!" She was one of the best interrogators the Rangers had, and she was totally serious.

The prisoner whispered, "Colonel Uriah Stephens; he's in Nashville."

"You just saved your life and, I hope, your wife's too," she said. "I got a name," she yelled at Jackson, who had just said to Gene. "This is really bad. Where is Paul?"

Shanahan thought he was still in Springfield with Nancy Lincoln. He said to Barlow, "You'd better call this in."

Simultaneously, wireless phones went off on every soldier's belt. Steven was bruised but not seriously hurt. He whispered, "Turn on the TV."

Joe jumped and put on CNN. A female reporter was talking to a voice in her ear and the audience at the same time. Behind her was a camera shot from a helicopter of what looked like a school. There were dead bodies littered around a schoolyard. She explained that details were very sketchy, but they were looking at a high school outside of Dallas, Texas, and there were reports of at least three other incidents in Mississippi, Georgia, and Alabama. Each school's student body was predominantly made up of minorities. The attacks had come from outside the school and were directed at students and teachers who were on a break from class at what appeared to be the very same time. There was no way now to have any total of the dead and wounded, and the White House announced that President Warren would be speaking to the nation in fifteen minutes. Each site that was attacked looked like a battlefield except the victims were not soldiers but children and their teacher's.

Before Jackson could call anyone, his phone rang.

He answered, "Barlow."

Jim Conklin was calling. He had been told of what had happened at Semper Fi and was checking on his men. Barlow told him everything quietly, including what the two assailants had said.

Conklin immediately mentioned Paul Diamond and Nancy Lincoln in Springfield. He asked Jackson, "Can Steven travel?"

"If we're going to help Paul, he can. But he has to have his ribs taped," Jackson replied.

Conklin said, "There are cars on the way for the suspect. The others will stay with him. EMTs will be there in two minutes to look at Steven. If he's all right to move, the three of you will be taken to our base and a jet will be waiting for you to fly to Springfield. In the meanwhile, the police chief is on his way to the museum with a load of state troopers, and we have another fifty Special Forces on route that are about an hour away. Dammit, this all comes from Martin Duffy getting hung after he was convicted for treason and sedition." He paused, "I have to ask you, do you want to go out in the field or go to Springfield and take care of our friends?"

Jackson paused and then answered, "We are going to Springfield, sir."

Conklin said quietly, "We are going to take care of our friend."

"Yes, sir. You can count on it. I will see you at Goddard."

Conklin said, "We don't know what we are dealing with there yet. Thank you and Godspeed."

"Thank you, sir."

By the time he hung up with Jim Conklin, EMT's were taping Butler's ribs. He was in some pain, but he was good to go as soon as he heard their orders from Conklin.

Gene said to his friend Steven, "You do not have to do this."

"Are you kidding, I would take a bullet for Paul Diamond, and Miss Lincoln too. Help me get off this damn gurney." With a grimace, he got up.

Gene Shanahan helped him get his vest and shirt back on.

Barlow was talking with a colonel who had shown up with another ten men. Captain Barlow saluted and nodded at his partners, who walked toward him. He said, "The ambulance will take us right to the airfield. The jet is almost ready. Some other things have come up. I'll tell you once we suit up."

The others nodded and understood. The colonel had known who they were, and they were given the highest possible clearance on the latest news. They would be able to hear the President in the ambulance on their way to the airstrip.

"Boys," said the driver, "I have been instructed to get you out to Goddard the fastest way possible. We will have an escort on the way. I suggest you buckle up."

Three army sedans pulled in alongside and behind the ambulance, and they took off with sirens blasting. The cars and ambulance were already speeding away from the bar before Shanahan could put the seatbelt on Steven, and he almost slid off the seat.

In two minutes, the driver turned on the radio, and a voice said, "And now the President of the United States."

Her voice was firm, cold, and angry. "Good afternoon my fellow Americans. Today has seen the United States victimized by four major attacks and a fifth on members of our Special Forces. We have limited information, and I will be back later this evening to tell you whatever we learn. What I can tell you is that we have, within the last forty-five minutes, received communication from a group that claims responsibility. All indications are that these attacks were internal and do not involve groups from any other countries or terrorist organizations. I can tell you is that these four major attacks were on schools in the southern part of our nation and that the student fatalities were, in the main, made up of minority children. I want to reemphasize that. They killed our children. This act is an abomination and will not be accepted by the government of this nation. We will have retribution, but I demand our citizens not take the law into their own hands. As of this minute, our forces are pursuing every possible lead wherever it takes them. And we will have justice. I can promise you that. You will forgive me if I cannot take any questions now, but I will later today. I have issued a series of executive orders that will be in effect during this crisis. The secretary of Homeland Security will discuss those with you. Allow me to say to anyone listening to my voice who is a part of these attacks: Be very ready because we are coming for you.

"God bless America and the families of those poor children, who were taken from them today without reason or cause."

There was dead silence in the pressroom, as well as in the ambulance carrying Butler, Barlow, and Shanahan.

After a few seconds, all Barlow could say was, "Get us to that damn plane."

In what would normally have taken twenty minutes, the driver was pulling into the Goddard airfield in less than half that time. The army cars accompanying the ambulance pulled to a screeching stop a hundred feet from the jet sitting on the tarmac. There were a few hundred soldiers surrounding the plane. Many were from the unit of the three passengers inside the ambulance. His two teammates gently helped Butler from the ambulance and walked him to the steps to the plane.

Jim Conklin was there waiting for them and gave them each a hug while an honor guard saluted. As he held Captain Butler carefully, he whispered, "Bring my friend home."

All the wounded Butler could do was nod and whisper back, "Yes, sir."

Except for Steven Butler, who walked carefully, they rushed up the steps into the jet where Captain Charlie Yeager was waiting, along with his copilot Lieutenant Larry Klein. They saluted, and the captain pointed to the flight suits that were waiting for them. They suited up and then helped Steven finish getting dressed.

Yeager said, "I know you guys are certified for this bird, but Conklin thought it might be better if you guys tried to relax for a few hours. Besides, I have over four hundred hours on this beauty."

Jackson nodded and answered, "No problem. We have to talk and figure out if there is anything waiting for us in Springfield beside a nice sleepy city."

Yeager nodded back and said, "Let's buckle up, Captain, and get the hell out of here."

CHAPTER 44

As part of her executive orders, the President had ordered every plane that was on route to a destination to get there, land, and remain. No new takeoffs were allowed, except military surveillance transports and jets. They would have a clear trip from Washington to Springfield.

Two minutes later, the men were in the air and on their way. The pain pills Steven had taken were beginning to kick in. His two broken ribs, together with the brace he was fitted with, restricted his movement. Gene and Jackson were talking about what happened at the bar. Steven remained silent. They all knew that his capturing Martin Duffy in 1863 had led to today's events and the slaughter of all those men, women, and children, coupled with any more that may yet come. Jackson had a hunch these maniacs were going to try and find Paul Diamond. He was the man behind Duffy's ultimate death, but at least the Special Forces and military had a name—Uriah Stephens in Nashville. He knew there would be planes already in the air and troops in motion to find and terminate him and whatever men he had under his command. But if this Stephens had any military sense, he would already have left Tennessee. The three were all drained. Using their field training, they closed their eyes to sleep if they could. They would need it. The fact that Stephens knew Paul Diamond was responsible for the death of Martin Duffy and his men were on the ground in Washington in 1863. What they did not know was how but they did not care how they were able to be there.

Forty-five minutes into the flight, alarms went off in the cockpit, and Gene Shanahan moved with a start. He would have jumped if he weren't buckled in his seat.

"Sorry, boys. We seem to have something on our tail a few miles back." Yeager's voice was in total control. "Lieutenant, what do you see?"

"Sir, I am tracking what looks like a shoulder rocket heading straight at us, but …"

"Say it, son."

"It has the signature of a missle that is at least fifteen years old! It could never catch us."

"Well, boys," he said in his Texas drawl, "I am not a man who likes surprises. I'm of the feeling we should double back and put that thing out of its misery. This is your show, men. What do you think?"

Butler answered coldly for the three of them, "Take the mother out."

Yeager answered, "I am right with you. Hold on."

The captain took the jet on a wide angle to get back behind the missile, which appeared incapable of compensating for his actions. "Lieutenant, as soon as possible give me a firing solution and turn on rockets A and B."

"Yes, sir. You are armed and ready."

Yeager called out, "Three, two, one," and fired.

With that, the attacking missile disintegrated on contact.

Yeager asked Klein if there were any other hostiles in range.

Klein answered, "Not within twenty-five miles, Sir."

Shanahan wondered, *Why would they send a fifteen-year-old rocket that could not possibly catch what it was aimed at? Were they sending a message that they know we're here and where we're going?*

"Okay, boys," Yeager said. "Let's get to Springfield."

None of the three could get back to sleep now. Within another hour, they were safely on the ground surrounded by police and Marine personnel.

The mayor was on hand to greet them as they came down the steps. Before they did, they made sure to thank Captain Yeager and Lieutenant Klein, who said, "You get those animals."

Jackson thanked him for the ride and said with a steely look on his face, "Count on it."

Springfield Mayor Leonard Trumbull was there to meet them, along with local police and state troopers. Otherwise, the airfield was deserted. The mayor approached Gene cautiously and asked, "Excuse me, son. We don't know much. But the people in our town are concerned about being in danger. We have nothing here except the museum and library, and we're a little concerned."

Gene took his arm and said, "Mr. Mayor, I really don't know much more than what the President said. I hope to know more when our men arrive in a few minutes."

Within two minutes, six vans pulled up and an army ranger, Colonel Jerome Williams, jumped out and went right to Gene and his partners. He pulled them aside and said, "The President received a letter from this Uriah Stephens. There were specific threats against four other schools and three presidential libraries. One of them is President Lincoln's. We don't expect school attacks today because there is no one there—unless they plan on blowing the buildings. I have seventy-five Special Forces and weapons for the three of you. I suggest we clear the streets and work out a signal with the town if anyone sees anything we should be ready for. Captain, I am committed to my last man to defend the President's papers and books."

"Colonel, because of our connection with Colonel Diamond, we have a strong affection for Abraham Lincoln. Our friend is in the office with Nancy Lincoln. I don't know if they have any idea what is happening. In addition, an old shoulder missile took a shot at us in the air on the way here."

"I heard," said the colonel. "We should get moving. Let the locals lead the way. I have no idea how to get there."

Gene called his partners over and filled them in on the letter and the plan to get over to the museum. He told the mayor, who instructed the local police and state troopers. The caravan then pulled away. If they were trying to stay hidden and quiet, they did not do a very good job.

Jackson Barlow figured they were being watched. The hunch he'd had on the jet was right. It was going to be a busy day in Springfield.

At that moment, all he could think of was seeing that Paul and Dr. Lincoln were all right. As it was all over the country on this day, a twenty-minute ride took less than ten minutes.

When they pulled up outside the museum, Jackson said to Gene and Steven, "I think we are going to have a busy day here, boys. Buckle up."

The others nodded. They ran over to the arms van to collect the gear they would need.

The colonel said, "They told us your sizes, and I think we got it close. Take whatever you think you might need. Listen, I want you to know how proud we are of what you have done." The colonel had been secretly briefed on certain details of the team's trip to the past but was not told of their impact at the battle at Gettysburg. But Gene realized that the old time line no longer existed.

"It's our job, Colonel," Steven answered.

When they turned around, a sergeant called out, "Ten hut." Seventy-five Special Forces operatives stood in salute for three very brave men.

Gene would say later that was the moment more than any other when he almost started crying. But the trio nodded, saluted back. and ran up the steps to the library.

Gene grabbed Butler and said, "You stay back. Work with Colonel Williams. Paul would never expect you to go in with your injuries. Make sure he knows what we are doing and beep us twice if there is something we need to do. You have a direct line to us."

Captain Butler did not look happy but understood his restrictions.

Before they made it halfway up the steps, Colonel Williams told them to wait. He came running up the steps and whispered to Jackson and Gene, "We just got a report from our recon planes. There are an estimated 750 hostiles coming this way, and they are circling Springfield. We also picked up two traces of isolated chemicals in two boxes in the basement and the first floor. How are you two with disarming bombs? Should I send in my specialist?"

Shanahan looked at Barlow and said, "We got it. Five years training at Goddard."

"Okay," said the colonel. "But if you need us, we will be inside in thirty seconds. Good luck."

Barlow whispered to Shanahan, "This keeps getting better and better."

They were met at the front door by twelve Springfield patrolmen in SWAT gear. A Lieutenant said, "Where do you want us Sir??"

Barlow said, "We just found out there may be two bombs hidden in the building, one in the basement and one on this floor. Do any of your men have experience with disarming?"

One immediately stepped forward and said, "I do, sir—three tours in Afghanistan."

Barlow answered, "Good. You're with me."

Shanahan said, "I'm fine. You could use him more."

"Okay," answered Barlow. "You have more experience in Iraq."

Barlow turned to the rest of the men and said, "Split up and search every inch of the two floors. If you see anything that looks like it's even close to not belonging there, you get on the radio. And touch nothing until we get there. Also, I need four of you to clear out the building as quickly as you can. Bring everyone to our men outside. They will find a safe place for them. My partner and I have a special affection for President Lincoln, so let's get this done, fast and hard, men."

The patrolman immediately saluted and said as one, "Yes, sir."

Gene Shanahan continued, "Now, someone has to take us to Dr. Lincoln's office right away."

The lieutenant answered, "Follow me, Captain. Men, you know what to do. Get moving."

They immediately split up and began to follow their orders. Shanahan and Barlow followed the officer to Nancy Lincoln's office and pounded on the door.

They heard a distraught Nancy Lincoln answer, "Who's there?"

Barlow answered, "Ma'am, it's Jackson Barlow and Gene Shanahan. It is safe to open the door."

The door opened slowly, and Nancy stuck her head out to make sure it was really them.

Jackson smiled to relax both her and Paul Diamond and said, "Are you two all right?"

Diamond answered, "As well as we can be with all those sirens and soldiers outside. What the hell is going on?"

Shanahan answered, "We have a dangerous situation here, Paul. We need you to open the door and get you two out."

Inside the office, Nancy and Paul talked quietly. "I can't leave, Paul—especially, after we read those letters."

Paul slowly stood up and walked over to Nancy. He took her in his arms and whispered, "We can put them back in the box and take them with us. I have trusted my men with my life. I don't think there is anything they can't handle. But if you really want to stay, we will stay."

All Nancy could say was, "Oh, Paul. I don't think I could live with myself if anything happened to anything in here." As she finished, she could hear footsteps of people leaving the building. "I'll stay. You go," she said.

Paul laughed and answered, "It has taken a lifetime for me to find you. I'm not leaving your side."

Paul put the letters back in the envelopes and then the lockbox. He turned the key to lock the box and gave it to Nancy. She nodded to Paul, who took the box and slowly opened the door to see his two men waiting.

He hugged each of them and said, "We have decided to stay here. Nancy just cannot leave the museum, and I will not leave her alone."

Shanahan was about to protest but Barlow put his hand on his friend's shoulder and said, "We understand, Paul. Do you want us to take the box?"

"Yes, please. There are very important letters inside that were written to me by the President Lincoln, his son, and grandson. They are irreplaceable. If anything happened inside the museum, Nancy would be devastated. She has the key. Please get them out to Steven. Where is he? Is he all right?"

Barlow answered, "He got nicked up in DC, he's okay, thanks to his bulletproof vest. He is outside."

Paul asked, "If you could keep a few men here to guard the door I would appreciate it."

Shanahan then explained the situation they were facing and instructed three of the SWAT team to stay and guard the door. He told them to let no one other than the two of them inside.

Shanahan and Barlow stood at attention and saluted. Barlow said, "Colonel, with your permission, we will do our jobs here."

Paul smiled and returned the salute. "You are dismissed," he said.

Paul closed and locked the door while the three officers arranged themselves outside the door.

Meanwhile, in front of the museum, fifteen soldiers were herding the museum employees to the Springfield High School gym and locking them inside while trying to keep them calm. Only a few seemed genuinely upset, but they all found some chairs and were given water to wait out whatever would come next.

It would only take another ten minutes before two mortars were launched at the museum that landed about twenty feet short of its target. But the explosion did shake the walls of the building, and inside, Nancy rushed into Paul's arms. There was damage to windows and bearing walls on the other side of the structure where Dr. Lincoln's office was.

Another two minutes later, twelve Humvees filled with National Guard troops arrived. The guardsmen jumped out, waiting for their instruction.

Colonel Williams gathered his troops and decided not to wait any longer. He told his remaining Special Forces troops to gear up and get ready to attack. He had a good idea where Stephens's men were. The trajectory of the mortar led him to believe they were in a semicircle around the museum about 250 yards away. Williams decided to send a small group of twenty-five skirmishers straight at the hostiles and flank them on each side with his remaining men, reinforced by the guardsmen. He knew he had five hundred army soldiers on their way, but he could not afford to let these maniacs get closer to the museum and library.

He called the two Special Forces captains over. "Men, on my mark, you move in. You take out anything that is in front of you holding a weapon. If they drop it, take and hold them. The mayor has texted everyone in this area to clear out or get in their basements. You leave no one standing. Am I clear?"

Both captains said as one, "Yes, sir."

The officers gave their men and women instructions and then spoke to the guardsmen. They were very specific in their instructions. They did not want them going off half-cocked and shooting at trees. Within a minute, everyone was in formation and ready to move. Williams gave the order to move on the radio. The Special Forces soldiers' men and woman in the center led the maneuver and, within another minute, were met by enemy fire. They responded with grenades and their own AR-15 fire. Although there were only numbered twenty-five, they pushed the enemy to their left and right directly into the path of the two wings on their flanks.

As the soldiers in the center maintained their movement forward, the two groups on the flank moved toward the center until they saw the enemy force waiting to respond. There were at least five hundred men across a line with their rifles up. They were dressed in Confederate-style butternut-colored uniforms and hats of half a dozen styles.

As soon as they saw the soldiers in full battle gear, someone called out, 'Ready, aim, and fire!"

They hit a few of the Special Forces soldiers, but most were protected against the rifle fire by their bulletproof vests. Fifteen of the enemy went down and crawled behind the cover of a large tree.

What the hostiles did not see was the guardsman approaching on their extreme right, which was "in the air" and unprotected. The lieutenant in charge steered his men closer to a position where there was an opening in the trees and gave the signal to fire as soon as the hostiles had stopped firing at the Special Forces men, who had taken out a group of the enemy. The guardsmen were preparing to fire at the unsuspecting enemy as the lieutenant gave his signal.

CHAPTER 45

After the police lieutenant suggested they stay away from the windows, Paul followed Nancy into her office and locked the door behind them. Nancy made sure the windows were locked and the blinds drawn, while Paul put two chairs in the center of the room. After all he had been through on his jumps back in time, Paul still felt a certain amount of fear, even though he felt optimistic about their safety. He could not help worrying how Nancy was feeling. She sat down in one chair and smiled, patting the other and motioning to Paul to sit next to her. He grinned back and walked toward her and sat.

Putting her hand in his, Nancy leaned over, kissed him on the cheek, and said, "This situation we are in reminds me of a story about a farmer in Salem who wanted to sell five of his pigs."

Paul realized she was trying to make him feel better by telling one of President Lincoln's favorite stories and he laughed. Nothing had changed in terms of where they were and why, but he felt her concern for him. He remembered President Lincoln sitting across from him in the White House and telling a few stories while they waited for Stanton to arrive for a meeting, now Paul could sense the same delight in Nancy that he'd felt in her famous ancestor at being able to put the listener at ease and make him or her laugh, regardless of the situation and Paul could sense the same in Nancy that he'd by her famous ancestor feel the pleasure the President felt in making someone laugh. Seeing Nancy do the same thing led his mind to a subject that he wanted to bring up; but he didn't want to make her uncomfortable. He did feel Nancy was intellectually able to handle the subject matter, but it could cause self-questioning and confusion for her.

Paul decided that, since they were alone and would not be disturbed, this would be as good a time as any and delicately plunged in.

***

Shortly before Paul and Nancy went inside her office, FBI interrogators at Fort Meade in Washington completed their interview of the man who had been captured at Semper Fi. His name was Lyndon Teague. Once he started talking, he could not stop. All he cared about was the safety of his wife and children. A squad of FBI agents arrived in Nashville to guard his family. As soon as he spoke with his wife, he began to talk, telling the FBI all they wanted to know about Uriah Stephens.

It seemed that one of Stephens's ancestors had been a lieutenant in the Confederate Army and had served under General Nathan Bedford Forrest, who proved to be a massive thorn in the side of the Union Army. Stephens was approximately fifty years old. Ever since he was a young man, his father had drummed in his head a hatred for all things Yankee and love for the cause of the Confederacy. He joined groups that promoted "whites only" and, in one of these, met a fellow traveler who was a descendant of Martin Duffy.

The two were kindred spirits and began to make plans for a series of attacks on a grand scale against the federal government, African Americans, and Jews. Over a period of ten plus years, they recruited members for this new organization and were very careful who they told what their plans were. The two men fueled each other's hatred. Their plans included killing as many people as they could. They counted over 1,000 active members committed to joining them in their plans.

As soon as he was informed of the results of the interrogation, Jim Conklin called Paul to pass on the report. They discussed it at length. Conklin said to Paul, "This fills in the holes."

"It sure does," Paul responded. "This is the time pushback, and it also tells us this Stephens led a full life." He told Jim he would call back when he heard news from the outside.

Paul turned back to Nancy. Before he could say anything, Nancy asked who had called. Paul explained that it was Jim and slowly told her what he'd said.

After explaining, he asked, "You remember I told you I had been here three or four times doing research in my time line, and you were, of course, not here."

Quietly, Nancy answered, "I have no memory of ever meeting you."

"You couldn't have. I am not a physicist or mathematician, and there are things I do not have knowledge of. But if we follow the logic, it seems we were on two parallel time lines traveling on top of or next to each that merged because of what we did in 1863. Because Lee and, ultimately, the Confederacy surrendered, the 13th Amendment abolishing slavery was passed earlier and without the complication of the Peace Democrats. The group was fighting passage because they believed the rumors that Jefferson Davis had sent peace commissioners to negotiate a peace between the two countries—something that President Lincoln would never have agreed to, as well as the abolition of slavery. Because of what we did, that never happened. And because of your grandfather living, so have you." Paul looked and hesitantly asked, "Can you tell me what you remember of your childhood?"

Nancy closed her eyes for a moment and looked back at Paul and quietly said, "I remember my father driving me on our tractor in the wheat and cornfields, playing on swings he built, and my Mom tucking me in at night. I was born after my grandfather died, so I never met him. There were cousins who we did see, but they were much older. Why do you ask?"

Paul thought for a moment and then said, "I just wanted to understand that your memories are of your entire life and they did not begin when this timeline did. If that is true, then Uriah Stephens lived his own full life and had all that time to plan this abominable attack that killed all those people. This is the definition of time pushing back at the changes that were made."

He looked toward the locked office door and said, "Everything I have done, all the jumps I've made, meeting the president and fulfilling my dream of spending time with him, and knowing that we saved hundreds of thousands of lives and seeing thousands die now has led me to you. And

I have never been happier. But there is a cost. And I have to find a way to understand and learn to live with it."

He wanly smiled and said, "If that's the trade, I must agree to have you in my life. It is one I agree to."

Nancy shed a tear. She took Paul's hand in hers and softly kissed it and whispered, "You are the most thoughtful and kindest man I have ever known."

Paul's face flushed in embarrassment as he shifted his gaze to the black-and-white photographs of the "Lincoln men" that hung on the wall opposite Nancy's desk. On the top row was an Alexander Gardner close-up that was taken in early 1863 after Willie Lincoln, the president's third son, died. Below that was Robert Lincoln. It was taken when Robert was in his thirties. The next one was of Jack, taken after he was elected to the Senate for his first term. Next to him was a solemn picture of Nancy's father John, who, it is said, looked remarkably like the president's father.

During Paul's time in 1863, the President never mentioned his father. Diamond understood the two were not close, and the father was a cold man who was not successful and expected his son to be more of a help to him in working their small farms.

Nancy interrupted his reverie and asked, "Paul, there's something I would like to ask you about your trip."

"Of course, if I can remember." He smiled.

Nancy smiled back and asked, "Did the president ever discuss his problems with the "hypo?"

The question caught Paul off guard, and he shifted his gaze away from Nancy back toward the president's photograph on the wall. It was not the one that was his favorite. The other was taken by Alexander Gardner in his studio shortly before the assassination in the other time line. Paul quickly decided that Nancy was entitled to hear about the conversation he'd had about Lincoln's bout with depression. But he did gently say, "Why do you ask?"

She answered, "He left very little in the way of journals or notes. There's a mention here and there about it in some letters people kept. I know it was important and affected him, but I have always been unable to find very much about it. Given how well you two got along, I thought he may have …" Her voice trailed off.

Paul could tell that this subject was important to Nancy and decided to tell her everything he'd discussed with the President.

He began, "Yes, Nancy. We did talk about it, and it took me by surprise. He knew I studied his life, although it was hard for him to understand why. There had been books written about him suffering from it. But outside of Seward, Nicolay, and Hay, he never mentioned it to anyone after he was inaugurated. His former law partner Herndon in Springfield was aware of his malady. But there is some question as to how much Lincoln told him."

Paul explained things that Nancy already knew—about the deaths in the President's family and then the loss of two sons Eddie and Willie. The attacks seemed to come and go. With the personal losses, combined with the indescribable burden of the war and all the deaths that had taken place, it seemed the hypo had taken over his head, heart, and soul. Paul explained to Nancy that he was touched by Lincoln wanting to tell him about it and thought part of the reason was that their time together was limited and Paul's twenty-first century life could offer him some respite from it.

"All I could tell him was that my own father battled depression. And all I could offer was my love and support." He went on to talk about the well-known Schuyler Colfax quote about seeing the President walking past him with his head down and how it felt that "sadness was dripping from him when he walked."

Nancy looked up at the President's photograph and then down at her clasped hands. She explained that very little written evidence had survived since the President passed. If he had written anything for posterity, it had probably been destroyed by Robert, who had burned many papers that may not have been kind to his father. All that was left was given to Nicolay and Hay, who had spent years writing an epic definitive biography on their beloved employer, who they called "the Ancient" or "the Tycoon."

Paul gently asked if there were any others in the family who had exhibited any symptoms. Nancy explained that neither Robert nor Jack had shown any symptoms. But her own father would occasionally become very quiet and sit in his favorite chair by the fireplace and read one of the volumes of the Nicolay-Hay series.

"He would never talk about it, though. As I grew older and went to school, I began to realize he may have been depressed about it all." Nancy went on, "I thought, since he was named for the president's father, who he did not like or get along with, it may have been too much of a weight for him to carry. That, along with him not following the family's political tradition, he may have thought he disappointed his ancestors or his family."

Nancy finished by saying, "I was never disappointed in him. After all, look at the ones that came before and all they accomplished."

Paul pointed out, "The only one you have not mentioned is you, Nancy."

She looked down at her hands again and said quietly, "When I was offered the position here, I was thrilled. This is my family, and I loved being in Springfield. But the legacy of the President and the rest of the family is filled with certain pressures. When I did find a new letter or other evidence, it was exciting. It still is. But when I did spend time on the president's "condition," I became sad. Carrying all this can be a burden, and I have to find a way to fight off those sad and dark thoughts he carried."

She took a deep breath and said, "I just don't want to disappoint anyone. I think what I really need is some help." He smiled and looked at Paul.

He laughed and said with a smile, "Let me know where I can get an application. It looks like I will have some free time!"

Then they heard an explosion and ran to the door.

CHAPTER 46

Inside the museum, Nancy Lincoln huddled with Paul Diamond on the floor in her office as she heard the firing. All this was beyond her understanding—that these people could kill so many innocent men, women, and children was an abomination. Paul was forced to explain the background of the attack of Martin Duffy at the naval yard in 1863 and his death by hanging after being convicted for acts of sedition and treason. NASA researchers had somehow missed the changes to the time line, which led to Uriah Stephens recruiting and planning revenge. Their fury was directed at Paul Diamond and President Lincoln, as well as African Americans and Jews. Diamond was alive, and the Lincoln Museum was all that was left for them to destroy. They had plans to do more damage, but they were getting low on weapons explosives. Nancy finally began to understand the changes in the time line that led to her being born and finding the man she already cared about so much.

One of the Springfield SWAT team members found a suspicious-looking box with wires sticking out its side in the basement near the boiler. The team notified Gene Shanahan, who got down there in less than a minute. He told the men to back off while he began to slowly and carefully examine it. He put on his goggles underneath his helmet and took out a few tools he always carried, got down on the floor, and crawled over about a foot away from the contraption. To his eyes, the wires sticking out looked like a sloppy rushed job. He could not take the chance of rushing to disarm it until he got a look inside the box. He put on his rubber gloves and slowly lifted the top of the cardboard box to look inside. The first thing he saw was enough C-4 explosive to demolish half the building. The wiring looked very simple, as if it had been put together by someone who was not experienced.

Could it be that simple? There was a timer that showed there was less than five minutes before it would detonate. There were three wires—red, green, and yellow—attached to the explosive. Shanahan closed his eyes to remember his basic training as to which of the wires would be the dummy on something so basic. He still had enough time. If he cut the wrong one, he could come back and get the right one. But if the bomb designer was trying to be cute, he could have the bomb go off if the wrong wire was cut. Shanahan took off his goggles, wiped the sweat from his forehead and eyes, followed the wires coming out of the C-4, and traced them to the timer. He found what he was looking for. The green wire hung loosely, and he could disregard that one. It was red or yellow. He remembered his instructor saying that, in more than 75 percent of homemade explosives, the red would be the one to cut. It was psychologically proven. But what if he was wrong?

The hell with it, he thought. He thought of shaking the hand of Abraham Lincoln and cut the red wire. The timer shut off.

Gene Shanahan took another look to make sure there was not a backup and then slumped against the wall. He took a deep breath and called Barlow to tell him the news. But Barlow didn't answer. He then called for the SWAT officers to take the box out to the bomb disposal truck, which was stationed outside. He called Barlow again as he made his way up to the first floor to look for him.

On the first floor, Gene would find an entirely different situation. The sergeant with Barlow found the second box in a room with copying and fax machines. The box was pushed against the wall under the fax machine. He immediately called for Barlow, who came running into the room and saw the box. He turned to the sergeant and said, "What branch did you serve in in Afghanistan, Sergeant?"

"Rangers, sir."

Barlow asked him his name. "Andersberg, sir."

"Good, Sergeant Andersberg. Come on over. Let's see what we are dealing with."

Barlow put on his gloves and goggles and took out his tools from a side pocket inside his jacket. He had no idea that the box was identical to the one Shanahan had disarmed on the floor below.

Something was bothering Shanahan as he raced up the steps to the first floor. The first bomb seemed too easy to disarm. He prayed the second would be the same. As he burst through the door, he thought he saw a very large shadow turn toward the room where Barlow and the SWAT sergeant were carefully approaching the box with the bomb inside. He stopped immediately and pulled out his Glock 47 and moved into firing position. Trained to step silently, he moved to follow.

He heard a loud strong voice with a heavy Southern accent say, "Well, hello, boys. What are you all up to?"

The sergeant whirled around to face the voice and looked up to see a massive man with a bald head and a long gray beard.

This monster of a man said to Andersberg, "I really don't care about you. It's your friend I want." He pulled out a large Colt and shot him in the face.

Andersberg fell where he stood.

"Hello, Captain Barlow," he said and shot him in the thigh. "Now I will watch you bleed out before that bomb explodes. Then I'll go upstairs and torture your friend Diamond before I kill him in front of his girlfriend. Then I'll finish her off too."

Barlow rolled over and pulled his Glock and pointed it at the man. But he saw Shanahan in the doorway signaling Jackson not to shoot. Barlow was in agony but blinked his eyes in response.

Suddenly Shanahan said, "I don't think that's going to happen, Mr. Stephens."

Stephens turned to face Shanahan. But as he did, Shanahan shot him in the head, and he fell to the floor like an oak tree, stone-cold dead.

Barlow whispered, "The bomb."

Shanahan took a quick look at his friend's leg. He took out something he could use as a tourniquet and wrapped it to stop the bleeding. Then he whipped out his radio and called Colonel Williams and said as calmly as he could, "This is Shanahan. We have disarmed one bomb in the basement. I have one SWAT man down, and Barlow is down and wounded badly. We are in the copy room on the first floor, and I am about to try and disarm the second bomb. Oh, and I don't think Uriah Stephens will be causing anyone any trouble. Steven, can you hear me?"

"I am here, Gene," Steven answered.

Shanahan responded, "Make sure the EMTs gets in here fast. I'm going to work on the bomb now." And he hung up.

Shanahan delicately moved Barlow and Andersberg as carefully as he could to the doorway and then rushed back to the box. He took two deep breaths and tried to focus on what he had to do. He was still bothered by a feeling about this bomb versus the first. It had wires sticking out like the other, and he slowly lifted the top of the box. He looked first for the timer and saw there were less than seven minutes before it detonated. If his feeling was right, he had enough time. One thing he saw right away, there was twice as much C-4 explosive in this bomb. That would be enough to blow the roof off the museum.

He slowly and calmly traced the wires and found that the red and yellow wires were reversed. He seemed to have been right. These maniacs may have been smarter than he gave them credit for. The green wire was loose here, but it looked as if the red and yellow were purposely switched. If that were true, then he would have to cut the yellow this time. As he was taking his clippers, he looked at the timer. It showed less than three minutes. The EMTs had just arrived.

Shanahan called out, "Take Barlow first. I don't think the sergeant is alive. Then take that big piece of garbage last. I need another thirty seconds here."

CHAPTER 47

Gene took his clippers and, without hesitation, put it on the yellow wire and cut it at the connection to the explosive. The timer clicked and shut off. Shanahan smiled in relief as he took a deep breath.

From his gurney, Barlow grabbed the arm of a soldier f and asked, "Did he get it?"

The soldier smiled and answered, "Yes, sir. He sure did."

Shanahan stood and walked over to the body of Uriah Stephens and whispered, "You scum," and spit on his chest.

He then went to check on his friend. After examining the wound on his thigh, he grabbed his hand and squeezed, saying, "We got them, brother."

Shanahan stepped back from the gurney carrying his friend and leaned against the wall. He was exhausted. He followed the EMTs toward the front door but stopped at the doorway of Nancy Lincoln's office.

The three Springfield SWAT officers were still standing guard and saluted Gene Shanahan as he approached.

As the gurneys carrying Barlow, Adamsberg, and Uriah Stephens were taken outside, an eerie silence passed through the crowd outside. The museum employees were walking back to the group standing in front. There would not be a total of the death toll for a few hours. But the federal soldiers had killed over four hundred and lost eleven. The bodies of the eleven were kept separate, with American flags taped to their body bags.

More than 250 of Stephens's men had thrown down their weapons. The Special Forces and guardsmen were about to shoot the rest, but Colonel Williams told them to hold their fire, as he realized it would go against everything America stands for. Shanahan watched from inside the front door before he went inside the office to tell Paul and Nancy what had transpired. Before he did, he saw Butler in the crowd and waved and pounded his chest with his fist.

He said to the leader of the SWAT soldiers guarding Nancy Lincoln's office, "Okay. I'm ready to go in."

The lieutenant said, "Of course, sir." He knocked and called out, "Captain Shanahan is here."

The door quickly opened, and Paul Diamond jumped at Captain Shanahan to hug him. Nancy stood off to the side. When the men were finished, she gave Gene her own hug. The captain had tears in his eyes and wiped them away with his glove.

His phone rang, and he excused himself to answer. "Yes, Director," he said. "Thank you very much, sir. I'm with them right now."

Conklin said, "Before I speak to them, someone here wants to speak with you."

"Captain Shanahan, this is the President."

Gene's body stiffened. "Yes, Madam President," he said.

President Franklin expressed her thanks to the team for their bravery and all they had done on behalf of the country.

Captain Shanahan responded after listening to the President's question about the losses, "Thank you very much. But we were here to help our friends, I can't answer about the casualties outside, I was in the Museum. I think we lost one local SWAT officer and he deserves whatever honors possible."

He listened for another few seconds as the President asked about the status of Uriah Stephens and where Nancy and Paul were and answered, "I can confirm Uriah Stephens is dead. Yes, they are both here. One moment, ma'am. And thank you very much."

He handed the phone to Paul Diamond smiled and said, "The President wants to speak with you."

She said, "Colonel Diamond, I have been made aware of the success of your mission and the injury you suffered. I envy you for the experiences and sacrifices you've made. Although we cannot publicly acknowledge them, you have my sincere thanks and gratitude. I hope we can find some time where we can quietly talk for a little while."

Paul responded, "It would be my honor, ma'am."

"I will put her on now." He handed the phone to Nancy.

"Yes, Madam President. Thank you, but I just sat locked in my office with Paul." Nancy smiled.

Then the President said, "I honor you and your family and especially your great-great-great-grandfather. He showed what we can be as a nation. Regardless of this horror, we have experienced all those brave men and women honor his life and family, including you, Nancy. I hope when I meet Paul you will be there, and we can get to know each other. I have many questions to ask about your family."

Nancy answered with a smile. "I look forward to it. And thank you for your kind words."

She said goodbye to President Franklin and said, "One minute, Jim. I will put him on." She had tears in her eyes as she handed the phone to Paul.

Paul took the phone and, after a minute, said, "Yes, Jim, we're all right, just shaken up. I understand. We'll be ready. First, we should show ourselves to everyone outside. I will talk to you in about half an hour."

When he hung up with Jim Conklin, Paul said to Nancy, "It looks like they want us all back at Goddard, but first I need to find Steven Butler."

He did not have to look far. Butler was allowed in by the officers and went to hug Diamond and then Nancy Lincoln. Then he took the locked box out and handed it to Nancy, who smiled and accepted the return of the box and profusely thanked Captain Butler.

The group then walked out of the office escorted by the officers. They stood on the top step to see the crowd of soldiers, medical teams, museum employees, and townspeople who had gathered.

Colonel Williams called out, "Ten-hut," and every Special Forces operative, national guardsman, and army soldier stood at attention and saluted the group. Paul pushed Shanahan out in front of the others for recognition of disarming two bombs and terminating Uriah Stephens. He saluted back and stepped back next to Butler.

Paul Diamond walked over to whisper in Nancy's ear, "We all are going back to Goddard for debriefing. I have to discuss with Jim my future with the program and its necessity. We cannot keep trying to change the past because of how strongly time pushes back. I am so grateful to have been able to know you."

Nancy smiled and said, "Whither thou goest, I will follow."

Nancy Lincoln stayed in Washington for two days while Paul continued his physical therapy. She had to get back to Springfield to make appearances for interviews. She never mentioned Paul's name or those of his team. All that was said about the bomb disposal was that it was handled by one of the SWAT teams.

Mayor Trumbull had a conversation with Jim Conklin and backed up the story that the armed forces had done an incredible job. All the prisoners that were taken vanished within twelve hours on planes that went somewhere secluded, where they would be interrogated by the same FBI agents who'd talked to Lyman Teague. They would never be seen again. For his part, Teague, along with his family, had been placed in the witness protection program.

The newspaper and television news coverage of the events of the last two days was continuous and overwhelming. The attacks at the schools cost the lives of more than 5,500 men, women, and children.

Out of guilt, Paul purposely stayed away from watching the coverage in his infirmary room at Goddard. He was readmitted to do more intensive daily therapy, rather than stay in his apartment, since he still had difficulty driving. By the second day, Paul decided he could no longer avoid watching the coverage, regardless of how responsible he felt for the tragedy happening. He could not change what he and his team had done to change the time line. It was unable to be changed back to what it was. And because of what they had done, the Civil War had ended nineteen months earlier than it would have if Paul had not sat in that wooden chair and traveled to 1863.

He reached for the remote control, took a deep breath, and turned on the television. The first channel that came up was one of the cable news channels. The anchorperson was saying they were about to switch coverage to one of the funerals in Texas. The President was there, along with groups of soldiers and politicians. The president was going to be flying to different states so she could attend as many funeral services and burials as she could get to. The cameras focused on the families and friends, and there was so much emotion coming from all these people that Paul could not stop crying from the sheer weight of his guilt.

It was later that day when Paul Diamond made the decision about his own life. He had to speak to Jim Conklin.

CHAPTER 48

Two months later Air Force One delivered the president and her husband to Springfield for a ceremony at the cemetery to honor those who had fallen and another to rededicate the reconstructed Lincoln Museum, there was a private luncheon in the museum dining room with President Franklin and her husband, James Conklin, Colonel Paul Diamond, Nancy Hanks Lincoln, Steven Butler and his wife, Gene Shanahan, and Jackson Barlow. Indeed, President Franklin had many questions for Paul and Nancy. After the three had engaged in an hour of constant conversation after lunch, a presidential aide came and whispered to the president.

She nodded and then shook her head in regret and said, "Unfortunately, we must get back to Washington. But I look forward to doing this again if it is all right with you."

Nancy smiled, "I am sure that will be fine, Madam President."

"Very good, perhaps next time I can get you to come over to our place for sandwiches."

Jim Conklin jumped in and said, "Can I can come too?"

Everyone laughed, and President Franklin stood, followed by everyone else, and they began to say their goodbyes. The President took both of

Nancy's hands in hers and whispered, "I can't tell you what a privilege it is to spend time with you."

Nancy blushed and said, "Thank you, ma'am."

Steven shook the president's hand with a warm smile and stepped back to stand next to Paul. Steven put one hand on Paul's and quietly said, "May I have you and Jim for a few minutes after they leave?"

Diamond looked back at Steven with a quizzical look. Diamond was intrigued but said, "Of course."

Barlow and Shanahan were just a few steps away, and Jackson asked, "Do you need us?"

Butler shook his head and gave him a friendly look back. Shanahan took his friend Barlow by the arm as the President walked out of the museum to wave goodbye to the cheering crowd before getting into her limousine for the five-minute ride to Air Force One.

Paul called Conklin over, and they sat down at a table with Steven Butler.

Diamond asked Steven, "Is everything all right?"

Butler paused for a moment and nodded. Then he said, "You know I'm the oldest of our group and the only one with family. Daphne and I have been talking since the attack, and we think it may be time for us to find a place and settle down. The only problem is I love you all and the work we do. I wanted to ask if we could find a way I can work on a part-time basis by training the groups that will come after us. I think I have something to offer."

Conklin smiled, as did Paul. "Well, we knew this would come sooner or later," he said. "And you are the oldest and most experienced, so logic dictates you would be the first."

Conklin thought for a moment and added, "Obviously, this is the first we are talking about this, but you should know how highly we think of you and your value to the program. I for one would want to see you continue on some basis."

Paul said, "I think your two teammates won't be so happy."

Steven answered, "Neither am I, but the kids are getting older, and there are going to be plenty of games for me to get to. Daph has done it all on her own, and I miss them so much when I am with you guys. The truth is I like it here, and we may consider finding a place somewhere in Springfield."

Paul laughed and said, "It looks like I may be a neighbor sometime soon."

Jim said, "That I expected, and you two may be fellow commuters on the NASA express if we can work it out. Paul has decided to go off active full-time duty with the program but will keep working on research and training as we review the status of the program." He added, "Steven, you and I will meet with human resources when we get home and work out details. I think it would be best if you have a conversation with Jackson and Gene."

"Yes, sir."

CHAPTER 49

It took a few months for the details to work out, but Steven went on part-time status and began his career as an operations instructor. He would spend two weeks at Goddard and fly home for two weeks and repeat the schedule indefinitely. It satisfied his need to be with his family, as well as the desire to continue working on a limited basis and help the program.

Chicago, Illinois, September 1888

Robert Lincoln was sitting in his law office with four law books spread over his desk. He was researching a maritime law case for a client in Chicago and was lost in thought when a persistent knocking on his office door broke him from his reverie.

"Come in, come in," he called.

His secretary came in and said, "Mr. Lincoln, I know you didn't want to be disturbed. But there is someone here to see you. He said he is an old friend who said he has not seen you in twenty-six years and it is important."

Lincoln's head jerked up. He had an excited feeling in his stomach. "Please bring him in," he said impatiently.

She left and escorted in a man who stood over six feet tall wearing a long brown coat and wide-brimmed brown hat and a smile that extended from one side of his face to the other. The man said, "Hello, Robert. It is so good to see you again."

Robert Lincoln stared at his guest in shock and simply said, "Oh my. Jackson, is it really you? You hardly look a few years older than the last time I saw you."

The last words Jackson Barlow had said to Robert and the two Johns, Hay and Nicolay, were, "Remember all this." He'd never forgotten any of it.

Robert jumped to his feet, came around his desk to his old friend, and threw his arms around Jackson while they both laughed in delight.

Robert asked Jackson to sit down next to him in the two seats in front of his desk. They talked for ten minutes about all that had happened more than twenty-five years before. They were quite animated as Robert then told him about his wife and three children and his work. They spoke about his father and mother and brother. Robert became emotional as he described how much closer he and the president had become before his death.

Jackson asked, "Has President Harrison been in contact with you?"

"Yes," Robert answered. "And I have a feeling that is why you are here. Paul said someone would come. I asked the President for a few weeks to come to a decision."

Jackson said, "Yes. I have a letter for you. Please read it now."

Robert took the envelope from Jackson and carefully opened it and began to read:

My dear Robert;

Please forgive me for not delivering this in person, but I suffered a small injury in my return home and it prevented me from making any more trips. It seems my traveling days are over, and I confess that my last one was the best. The memories of our time together are more than enough to satisfy me. I could not ask for anything more than to have spent time with your father and you.

When we were last together, I spoke of something important in your future that I could not tell you about.

242

By now, Jackson has probably asked you if you have heard from President Harrison. As you may have guessed, that is the reason for this letter and Jackson's visit. Both Steven and Gene wanted to make the trip, but their duties prevented it. If he has not done so yet, President Harrison will offer you the position of ambassador to Great Britain. Here is the reason you must decline it: You would be exposing your son to a fatal illness. Suffice it to say, he has many good things in store for him, and you will be very proud of what he will accomplish. You cannot discuss this with him, but those events cannot happen if he goes with you to London. You must find a graceful way of declining the president's offer.

I am aware that your wife Mary and your daughters are well and hope that continues.

Now, please write back and give the letter to Jackson to bring back to me. It will make my day.

With all my best wishes,
Paul Diamond

Robert had a tear in his eye as he began to write:

September 17, 1888

My dear friend Paul,

As I write this brief note, our mutual friend Jackson sits a few feet from me in my office in Chicago. It is difficult for me to express my joy at seeing him again. I hope you are feeling well. And please send my most sincere regards to Gene and Steven. I have such fond memories of all of you.

I received a letter from President Harrison last week offering me the position of ambassador to Great Britain. After reading it, I had a suspicion that this was what you were referring to when we talked for the last time in my father's office. I have delayed answering, as I hoped I would see a familiar face.

I thank you for not telling me any details when we were last together. I could not have borne thinking about it for the last twenty-six years.

I want to tell you one important thing that I know you will appreciate. You know my father and I were not close while I grew up and went to Harvard. But during his last years, we spent a great deal of time together, talking and working when he lived for a time in Chicago. His heart always remained in Springfield, and he moved back before he passed. Please know how often he and I talked about you. It has been an honor to know all of you.

As he said in his first inaugural address, "I am loath to close."

But Jackson keeps pointing at his watch. I believe he has a "train" to catch.

Thank you for all you have done for my family.

I remain your most humble servant,
R. Lincoln

Paul had begun winding down his full-time duties, but he made sure he was available for whatever Jim Conklin needed. He was spending more time in Springfield at the museum and library with Nancy, and there was so much work for him to do there. He and Nancy fit like a hand in a glove. There was all this new Lincoln history for him to review. He rented a small house to live in while he spent time working at the museum. Nancy insisted he accept payment of a stipend for the time he spent working there. After all, who would know more about the last few months of the war? They shared lunch or dinner while he was there, and there was never any shortage of subjects to talk about.

Three years passed, and Paul realized his feelings for Nancy were deeper than just being the best of friends. He had never married and wanted to spend as much time with Nancy as possible. Paul spent most of his time doing research in the museum, reviewing and learning about the new time line, and going through the President's papers during the years of his second term. He was planning on writing a paper on Lincoln's rationale for issuing the Emancipation Proclamation.

He came across notes that referred to John Quincy Adam's statements that justified freeing slaves for military reasons if there was a rebellion of one section against another. Paul stopped and smiled. He thought of John Quincy's father, the second president, who succeeded George Washington. The story of John and Abigail Adams was a classic love story. They were separated for many years while John was representing the new government of the United States in France, Holland, and England. They wrote each other as much as possible, and one thing was always true. They addressed each other as "my dearest friend." Paul realized that he had never felt that way about a woman until now. He was sure Nancy felt the same way. She had told him about a relationship fifteen year before that had ended because of her devotion to the history of her family and her desire to work at the Lincoln Museum.

Five years after the mission, Paul suggested, in his own shy way, that he and Nancy move in together. He was a little worried about appearances and if it would be a problem for Nancy. She punched him in the shoulder and said, "What took you so long?!"

They laughed and hugged, and Paul said, "I will take that as a yes."

Paul added, "I never thought it was possible to be this happy." There were tears in his eyes when he said it.

Jim Conklin was thrilled when Paul told him the news. Of all the things that had happened since he went to Paul Diamond's office before Paul's last time traveling mission, there was only one thing he regretted, other than the bloodshed and death in this time line. He wanted more than anything to have met Abraham Lincoln. He would sit and listen to Paul describe everything that happened on their jump but could never show his envy at not having been with Paul. Paul's face would positively glow when he was telling Jim about it.

Of course, the only person he could tell, outside of the team and a few others in the building, was Nancy. But her reaction was confusing. She understood that, if it were not for Paul going back in time, she would not have existed in this time line.

The passage of time affects every human being. Not living in England kept Jack Lincoln alive. It gave life to John Lincoln and his daughter Nancy. Not being able to meet President Lincoln was a small price to pay for Nancy, and it allowed her to meet the man who would be the love of her life. If ever there were two people perfectly suited for each other, it was Nancy and Paul.

Time seems to move faster for some than others. After he passed to semiretirement, Steven Butler felt that days were flying by. When he was home in Springfield, his life was a never-ending stream of soccer, lacrosse, basketball, and football games; track meets; and parent-teacher conferences. Daphne worked out a schedule to make sure no child was left behind, and the two of them alternated so none of the three children would feel another was favored. He could not describe how happy it made him to be there. He realized his life was now complete. He did miss his service and jumps, but the last had taken much from him, and his training duties at Goddard made up for a good amount of what he missed in his missions.

When he was in Washington, there was still time for the dinners at Semper Fi with Gene and Jackson, and they were still treated like royalty whenever they walked through the door. Steven had to admit that it seemed the other regulars were getting younger.

CHAPTER 50

Steven Butler was home on a Saturday morning getting ready to bring Eli to his soccer game. He was only a sophomore but already good enough to attract the attention of college scouts. He had his father's strength and speed. It was five years after Steven had made the break to part-time status, and it felt like only a few months had passed. Whenever Paul was in Springfield, he and Nancy never missed any of the Butler kids' games. If he was not there, Nancy went alone and sat next to Daphne.

But there was a surprise this day. As Eli was putting on his uniform in the living room and Steven was filling up water bottles and grabbing towels, there was a pounding on the front door. Steven called out, "Eli, would you get that?"

"Okay, Dad."

Steven heard Eli walking and the front door opening and then whispering. Steven's experience made him suspicious, and he called out, "Eli, who is it?"

"Dad, you better come down here."

Steven came down from the kitchen and saw his son holding the front door closed. He said, "Dad, you better be ready."

Instantly Steven's hand went to his holster that was not there. He said, "E, move away from the door."

Eli turned from his father and coughed. Steven moved slowly to the door. He turned sideways as he turned the doorknob and flung the door open and saw Jackson and Gene calling out "Surprise!"

They both jumped on him at the same time, laughing.

It took a few minutes for everyone to calm down before Steven said, "What the hell are you two doing here?"

Jackson answered, "We heard there was a big soccer game today, and we wanted to know how you felt about having new neighbors."

Steven smiled and went back to hugging his two friends. "Now let's go find Colonel Diamond," he said.

He called for Eli with a big smile on his face.

EPILOGUE

Springfield Illinois, July 4, 2051

Every year Paul and Nancy, Steven and Daphne, Jackson and Gene and their wives and children made a pilgrimage to Abraham Lincoln's burial site on the anniversary of the final attack at Gettysburg on General Lee's line. They would have a turkey dinner at one of their houses. After lunch they would walk to the president's crypt, and one of them would say a few words in honor of the occasion.

Paul Diamond was now seventy-seven years old and beginning to show his age. His body was beginning to wear down, and his wife was doing more and more to help him walk and get around. He had finished his book on President Lincoln's last years after he left the White House two years earlier, and it had received a warm reception. Many reviewers had marveled at Paul's connection to his subject, and he wrote about Lincoln as if he knew him as a friend.

In the middle of May Nancy and Paul were sitting in their living room one night. They were both reading a new book about President Lincoln and his family. Paul had a few criticism's about Jack thinking about a run for the Presidency because he knew Senator Lincoln never really considered it.

His wife laughed and said, "Sweetheart, it is time for us to have that meeting at the Museum."

Paul took off his glasses and answered, "Are you sure he is going to get the appointment?"

"Paul, I have told the Board of my plans and my recommendation of my successor and they said something the other day about scheduling a meeting next week. They interviewed two other candidates, and both graciously declined. So that leaves one left."

Paul smiled and said, "Good, then make the appointment." Two days later Springfield taxi picked up Nancy and Paul at their home and dropped them off at the Museum for their meeting with the Associate Director. Jacob Hanson rushed out to meet them and escort Nancy Lincoln and Paul Diamond to his office which was next door to Nancy's.

Once they were settled Jacob said.: I am glad to see you but I would have been happy to come to your house to talk."

His guests smiled and Nancy said, "Jacob it is time that I showed you something that I have in my office. I will be right back." Nancy walked to her office unlocked the door and went to pickup the lockbox and carried it back to Jacob's office. She placed it in front of Jacob on his desk. Then she placed a key next to box. She sat down in her chair, smiled and said, "Jacob, there is one thing you do not know, and it is in that box. Please open it with the key and put gloves on to remove what is inside"

Paul and Nancy watched with looks of bemusement as Jacob put his gloves on, unlocked the box and took out the three envelopes that were inside. Nancy came over to his side and pointed out in what order he should open and read them. Jacob stared at his guests and took the first envelope and began to read.

Halfway down the first page, he whispered, "Oh my God."

Nancy had submitted her retirement letter to be effective on New Year's Day 2052. She had been the longest serving Director in its history. Her position had allowed her to spend much time with her husband. But as he was beginning to slow down, the year before, Nancy had realized it was time to let go. She would be named Director Emeritus and went to the building two mornings a week. In looking back at the years she had spent with Paul and the others, she understood there was nothing missing in the life she had lived and was grateful for it. She had strongly recommended Jacob Hanson to succeed her and the Board of Directors approved his appointment.

As the group made their way to the Lincoln vault, Nancy let go of her husband's hand. He refused to use his cane whenever he went to visit the President, and Steven moved over to take her place in helping support Paul.

Nancy moved to face the group, smiled, and began to speak.

"My dearest friends, we gather here every year to commemorate an event that has caused us to meet and share our lives together. For me, that bloody day led to a series of events that allowed me to be born. For that, I give thanks to my ancestor Abraham Lincoln and those who followed. I especially want to thank the man I met in a hospital room at Goddard, whose actions gave me my life."

"Whatever happened to that guy?" a hoarse voice laughingly said.

Nancy paused and smiled. She looked her husband in the eye and softly said, "It was you who gave me my life and your love. But if you don't start using your cane when you are supposed to, I will have to cut off your access to the museum!"

Everyone there started to smile.

Nancy went on, "Before I go any further, I want to recognize two special guests. First is our old friend and colleague Jim Conklin from NASA, who was directly involved and managed the mission to 1863. He comes out to visit a few times a year, but this is the first time he has been here for our little ceremony. Jim, it is an honor to have you here, and I thank you so much for coming."

The now eighty-year-old retired director of the NASA Time Travel department waved to Nancy and walked to stand next to his old friend Paul and gave him a gentle hug.

Nancy continued, "Our second guest is the new Director of the Lincoln Museum and Library. I could not be happier with the board's choice, one that I heartily endorsed. Since the time of the original mission, he has grown to be an acknowledged Lincoln scholar. Without his efforts in finding a picture in a long-forgotten file, we might not be standing here today. Please welcome Jacob Hanson to our merry band."

Everyone laughed and applauded as the now middle-aged Jacob Hanson walked to Nancy Hanks Lincoln, shook her hand, and kissed her on her cheek. He then walked over to Paul Diamond and said, "Thank you, sir."

Paul answered, "Stop calling me that!"

Jacob smiled and stood behind Paul.

Nancy, now standing alone, smiled again and said, "I wanted to make this brief, and it is already longer than I had planned. It's not as if we don't see each other," and laughed. All I ask is that we hold hands for a moment of silence and think of all those who came before us. We honor them for what they have done for their families, and country. I love you all."

She walked to stand next to Paul, hugged and kissed him, and whispered, "Most of all, you."

Since Jackson and Gene moved to Springfield, they had been working, along with Steven, in managing the security detail at the Lincoln Museum. Since the attacks led by Uriah Stephens, many government facilities had camped up security at many locations and the Federal government offered to install men who would run the detail in Springfield. Nancy immediately suggested the members of Paul's team for the role. Although they were technically retired, it was not difficult for them to be reinstated to active status and be stationed at the museum and library. They made changes in protocol and had closed circuit cameras installed that covered the facility. They were thrilled with the opportunity, and to their great relief, they found their uniforms still fit.

On November 9 of that year, Paul began experiencing dizziness and pains in his chest. It was serious, and the prognosis was not good. Barlow, Shanahan, and Butler dug out the army jackets they'd brought back from Gettysburg and went to stand watch over their team leader and friend. Steven said later that the last thing Paul said to him was, "I would not have changed a thing."

Om November 13, 2052, Colonel Paul Diamond passed due to a series of blood clots in his lungs.

His last words to his wife Nancy were, "I have loved you with all my heart. Tell everyone I thank them for their love and friendship, especially my three sons, Steven, Gene, and Jackson."

He was buried in Springfield, Illinois, 150 yards from Abraham Lincoln. Three thousand citizens of Springfield and fifty from NASA were there to say goodbye.

Seven years later, Nancy Hanks Lincoln would be laid to rest next to her husband.